Tender Heart

FIRE ISLAND SERIES
BOOK ONE

ALEXANDRA BANKS

WILLOW HOUSE
Publishing

Also by Alexandra Banks

Rosewood Ranch Series

Tough Love

Heart & Hope

Saving Grace

True North

Fire Island Series

Tender Heart

For the hearts who have been through it all.

Author's Note

TW –

Vehicle accident.

Mature, explicit intimate scenes.

Coarse language.

The location and topographies of the places in this story have been fictionalized. They may not accurately represent actual location and terrain.

Tender Heart
PLAYLIST

CHASING CARS
SNOW PATROL

FIRE AWAY
CHRIS STAPLETON

WHAT I WANT
MORGAN WALLEN &
TATE MCRAE

CHANGE MY MIND
RILEY GREEN

ORDINARY
ALEX WARREN

TOO SWEET
HOZIER

TO DIE FOR
SAM SMITH

911
ELLISE

Tender Heart

One

EVIE

The air in my lungs is not my own.

The air in my lungs doesn't belong to me.

Everything is heavy. Still. Black.

I rememb—

Laughter and family and friends. Rings and words. No, not words, vows. Music and dancing. Wine and—

The rattle of tin cans.

Speeding down the highway, the night wind in my hair . . .

A blaring horn,

The semitruck.

Noise piercing my head . . .

Then, the car was too small . . .

Someone was screaming.

My world caved in. Something forces my chest down painfully. I flinch at the assault.

Air floods my mouth, throat, spewing into my lungs.

The weight on my chest sinks again. Then over and over.

I gasp, choking on something copper.

Warmth trickles from my mouth, sending heat down my jaw and neck.

"She's back," a gruff voice bites out.

Every inch of me trembles, and I fight to drag my eyes open, fingers cramping into my palms, knuckles scraping the rough surface I lie on. The sting barely registers.

Lights, amber and blue and red, flash overhead. Pain lances up my right. A man leans over me; he's kneeling.

Middle of the highway.

Stars shine straight above. Another person comes to my side and gloved hands jostle my body. A thin funnel of light shines into my left eye and I wince. It moves to the right.

"Pupils equal and reactive."

Oh . . . God . . . Paramedic.

The uniform catches my attention. Panic winds its searing heat through my limbs, one inch after another. I startle, clawing at my clothes, trying to move. To get up off the middle of the road. The . . .

I snap my gaze sideways and turn my head. Something hard and cold digs into my neck.

"Try not to move. We've braced your neck, Eve." The words are light. Kind. She knows my name.

The underside of a car blocks my view. Tin cans and rope.

Me and—

Joshua.

The car is mangled, crumpled, and smashed in. Glass is littered over the dark, shining asphalt. My heart squeezes through my ribs in ragged, bloody slices.

Joshua . . .

"Eve, can you hear me?" The words echo beside me.

Trembling, I turn toward the sound. A stranger's face is near mine. Relief straightens his features when I meet his gaze. "My name is Dave. You had a bit of a spill, hey. We're goin—"

The ground is trying to swallow me . . .

"No, stay with me honey," Dave insists.

I rally, remembering that's my car, and I was with—

"N-no." I curl upward, desperate to rise from the ground.

Hands press down on my shoulders from either side. "We need you to stay still, sweetheart. You can't get up. You're secured to the backboard."

Dave.

I search the dark sky until his face comes into view, his eyes.

"Jo—" I choke. The copper from before blooms in my mouth again.

Now, the tight eyes of a female paramedic find me. Her sad smile sets my heart on fire. Burning the last shreds of hope I had to ash.

"I'm so sorry, Eve." She shakes her head. "We're going to get you out of here, okay?"

Air strangles my lungs. I retch; bile spills over my mouth and it burns. The still-shimmering stars overhead blur. Violently, I shake, ragged sobs revolting their way up my throat.

"She needs sedation." A low voice drops the words by my side.

"Five mil," she says.

"Five mil," the low voice repeats. "We've got you, sweetheart."

"No . . . Josh." I try to reach, but my fingertips meet hard asphalt.

The board I lie on rises, taking me with it. I rock when it lands on a gurney. The night breeze plays with my hair, now slipped from its wedding updo, sending small brown waves around my shoulders. The paramedics' vehicle blocks my view of my small car, the *Just Married* sign now sagging from its ties at the trunk. My head lolls, eyes drifting downward.

The once-pristine white satin and tulle of my dress is ripped, reddened, and ruined.

"Almost away," the nice lady says with a small smile. She follows me into the back of the ambulance, talking softly. The back doors slam shut.

"Joshua?" I sob.

Kind eyes find me, a hand sweeps my hair back from my forehead.

Darkness drags me under. Down so low, numbness swallows me whole.

Five years later . . .

Icy wind bursts in squalls along the sidewalk, biting into my face. I clutch my oversized tote to my side, tucking my chin into my chest. Beanie pulled down, my long hair spills out from under it, draping over my shoulders. If only that would add a layer of warmth. A girl can dream. My small-heeled boots click along the bustling New York street in time to my frantic heartbeat. I mull over the few short words on the last unwanted letter that made its sickening entrance this morning.

A blue monarch butterfly was encased in the cream envelope, as always, accompanying the single page.

Of all the insects that might scream "stalker", a butterfly

would have been my last guess. In other circumstances, a butterfly would be sweet. Almost quaint. But after the third dead blue insect found its way into my mailbox, each with cryptic and somewhat concerning notes, they lost all appeal. That was over five years ago.

The number of butterflies that have had to die to feed his obsession . . .

I knew becoming an author would shove me into the public eye. But never in my wildest dreams did I think I, Eve Holland, would find myself on the receiving end of unsolicited, borderline terrifying letters from a fan. And, with my contract up for the second time in twelve months, I can't bring myself to mention it to my editor. Livvy has enough on her plate. My tardiness has already stretched friendships.

I push on the glass door to the publishing house. Every inch of me relaxes as the warm air mills around inside. I pull my beanie from my head, shoving it into my bag. The front desk girl has her eyes locked on me already. I'm sure they have a most-wanted list in the staff room for less-than-ideal authors. If I'm not at the top of that list, I'm betting I'm in the top three at least.

"She's waiting for you," the young girl coos with a saccharine smile.

"Thanks," I offer and make a beeline for the elevators.

As the confined ascending space slows at the fourth floor, the doors swoosh open on a ding. Hesitating, I grip the handles of my tote, willing my feet forward.

The doors start to close. I rush from the elevator and turn left. The welcoming balm of books, of print and paper pulp—despite the books not actually being produced here—makes me smile. It's almost enough to quell the anxious knot in my stomach. I sit on a brightly colored seat outside my editor's office, knowing all too well what she is about to say.

The staff of the fourth floor mill about their daily business, not paying me heed. Just as well; people have never been my strong suit. Unless they're fictional, of course. My bag—no, my phone—buzzes. I dive a hand into the tote, hunting for it. When I untangle the phone from my mess of a handbag, I flip the device over to find a text from Allie.

"Good luck this morning. Remember, you're a fantastic author! They should be grateful they still have you. Love you xx."

Typical Allie, always rooting for me, ever since we met the first day of high school. She's been my best friend for so long. I can't imagine my life without her. Yet, I still haven't found a way to tell her about the letters, either. I—

"Evie! Morning. Come on in, love." A soft, rolling accent, maybe Irish, finds me.

Livvy stands in her doorway wearing a knee-length wine-colored pencil skirt and a black top. Her short hair is neatly styled, her black-framed glasses propped on said styled hair, over a smile that's wide and genuine. She has always had a way of setting me at ease. She rounds her desk as I stand and walk into her office, and we sit. Almost a decade and a half older than me, she's been with the publishing house for twenty years.

"How have you been?" Livvy says, tapping something on her keyboard briefly before sitting back in her chair and pulling her glasses from her head to swing them around her fingers.

"Good, I've been good. Mostly."

"How's the writing coming along? Your draft was due last week." Her R's roll, and I smile.

"Yeah, I know. I'm really sorry, I've been writing . . ."

The lie that rolled off my tongue much like her R's sees my attention wane, and my gaze snags on the frames on her shelf across the room. Family photos. A few Livvy is in. Her and another woman around her age. Then one with her and a woman I assume is her mom. The last one is her and two other people. It's the same woman from the first picture, but a guy a little older than the two women stands to one side, his face half hidden. Like he wasn't totally on board with having his photo taken.

". . . have you done, exactly?"

"Huh? Sorry, what?"

"I was asking, how much have you written?"

"I—um. I've written three chapters." The words are weak.

Livvy's face falls. The pit of my stomach flips. This is bad. I know it's bad. It's the third deadline I've missed in the last eighteen months. And it's the second book in the series, so the house has already sunk money into the series, and me.

Livvy leans forward, setting her glasses on her desk. "Evie, fantasy is a hot genre, which is great. But that also means that we have hundreds of manuscripts coming in every month. Romantasy has been great for you, but it's a highly sought-after niche. We turn writers away on the daily, some with work as good as yours." She sighs. "What I mean is, your contract won't last forever. Missing one deadline is one thing; three is a problem. For both of us."

"I know, and I am trying, truly I am. I just . . . I can't concentrate. The city is too noisy. Everything seems off, and after Joshua, I—"

Livvy's face softens. "Hon, it's been five years. At some point, you need to start taking care of yourself and . . ." She shifts on her seat. "Living. You need to carry on living. You're young; it breaks my heart to see you floundering."

The stone that grew in my throat with her words refuses to budge.

"I know," I choke out finally. "But I don't know how."

"Maybe this will help." She pulls out a file stuffed with printouts. Communications between the two of us and the publishing contracts I've had with the house since my career began. "This, here, is the contract you have with the publishing house for the six-book series. And the original deadline for book two was over eighteen months ago. This is your last chance."

Her face is empathetic but firm.

She is kindly telling me this is it. My ultimatum, delivered in a way that only Livvy can.

Livvy's version of tough love.

"This is my last chance?" I repeat.

"Last one, hon."

"Okay." I swallow and tears well. "What if I can't?" I whisper.

"Nope, we are not going there. In fact, I had an inkling you might say that. So, I have a proposition for you."

What on earth? What could she possibly offer that would shift me out of this funk I've been in?

"Do I have a choice?"

She sighs. "At this point, no, not really."

"Okay."

"I'm sending you away to finish this book. I can buy you another nine months to get it done. Not a day more. Since you need peace and quiet and not this bustling city, I have made arrangements for you to stay in a quiet little cottage all on your own. No noise. No distractions. Simply lots of writing. And"—her hand reaches over the desk—"what I think you need the most. Healing."

Her hand squeezes mine. The bridge of my nose prickles, and I scrunch it up, unable to respond. Livvy's plan is sensible. It's the logical thing to do—hide away and write my book. Move on with my life. I mean, it's not that I haven't tried to. Really, I have. But I've lived here all my life, and everything reminds me of my life before the accident. Maybe a change is what I need.

Allie's been trying to get me to do this very thing for years.

I know I should. One moment in time shouldn't define me like it does. I glance at Livvy's frame-lined shelves. Two people, huddled together for the camera in front of magnificent places . . . An island. The same two people who were in the frame I saw earlier. I drag my gaze back to my ever-patient editor. "Okay, when do I leave?"

Livvy smiles at me, glancing at the frames along her shelves that held my attention.

"How's tomorrow sound?"

firefly

Two

CALLUM

"You're getting a wee lodger," Iris drawls.

Coffee splashing over the rim of my cup, I jerk my head up, my eyes burning into my sister's.

"Don't want no company. You know that, Iris."

"Huh. Well, big brother." She swings the tea towel over her shoulder, leaning against the counter of the café she's been running since our parents passed years ago. "You have no choice in the matter. That lighthouse isn't going to pay for itself much longer. Fire Island is the last on the list where funding is concerned from those heritage restoration dunderheids. She won't be much trouble. I hear she's a writer. Probably have her nose stuck in a book most of the time, you know. Besides, that Fresnel desperately needs replacing."

I grunt, returning to my coffee.

Great, just what I need. Something else to look after.

A woman, no less.

"How's that meditation coming along?" Iris prompts, pinning me with a glare. "You could use a few less rough edges."

"It's not." I return the sentiment, my accent not as thick as hers anymore.

"You will be on your best behavior, Callum McCreary. It's not only your hide on the line." Iris levels me with a glare that could sink a thousand ships and see their sailors beg for death. Always dramatic, my little sister. I tell her it's because she was born the decade after me. Nothing to do with her being a woman, I'm not that damn stupid.

Iris continues, "You might have to clear out, let her have the house. That hut of yours with no electricity isn't going to keep a tenant longer than a day, 'specially one from the city."

I let out a string of curses under my breath. The tea towel flings at my head.

"Aye, righto. Keep your hair on. She can have the house. I'll bunk in the slums. You have my word, oh pristine overlord."

Her green eyes narrow, hands planting firmly on her hips. No wonder no man has braved that particular storm.

"You can come and check for yourself, warden, if you like." I drain the coffee cup as the tea towel flies in my direction again. Grunting, I catch it in one hand. "See ye, Irry." I toss the tea towel onto the counter and head for the exit. Folks dip their gazes as I wander past. Errol, the oldest Coast Guardsman ever known to man, throws me a fowl look, pulling down his standard-issue cap.

I shake my head at him, resisting the urge to slap that cap right off his head in my little sister's café. "Hold a grudge long, Errol?"

Just fucking rude.

In our everybody-knows-everybody town, you can't walk fifty feet without having to stop and chat. Not that it ever happens to me.

Not real big on small talk—or talk in general—with anyone other than my sister and my best friend, Emmett. Seems like he's been in my life for eons, at least that's how far back high school feels. Damn, I'm getting old.

Errol sneaks a look out from under his cap. "Don't let the door hit your ass on the way out, McCreary."

"She'll be here in thirty, Cal. Don't you dare leave without her! You gonna make it for Wednesday dinner this week?" Iris calls out as I move toward the front door of the café.

I wave a hand over my shoulder in response. Wednesday—my birthday. Great, another year closer to fifty. Well, forty-three, but who's fuckin' counting?

Doubt I'll be back.

She mutters something like "stubborn ass" as I push

through the café door and into the sunshine. The marina is quiet in our sleepy little town. The gulls are already circling the morning's fish market scraps down by the dock. The crisp winter air, salty on the senses as it always is, breathes life back into my body as I make for the marina. Guess I have to wait for a passenger now.

Christ, how hard is it to be left the hell alone?

I find Emmett striding down the gangway, doing his morning harbormaster rounds. Lucky bastard had the job passed down from his old man, after he graduated from the Corps, and was happy settling with the hand he'd been dealt. He waves when he sees me coming. I take in the boats bobbing in their slips as I make for mine.

"Cal, morning. How's Iris?" Em pays me a fleeting glance as he leans over, checking the rigging on a schooner.

"Same as last fortnight, Em. Bossy."

He chuckles. "Someone has to keep you on the straight and narrow."

"Yeah, I'm a whole lot of trouble, holed up on a rock in the middle of the goddamn sea, minding my own business."

"Your supplies turned up. Loaded them onto her for you. You all set?"

"Nope, gotta wait till the midday bus. Got a lodger."

His eyebrows shoot into his hairline. "Someone is *paying you* to live in that old hut? Man, it doesn't even have electricity."

"House, not hut." I groan at the thought of some

stranger in my space. But desperate times call for desperate measures. Possibly losing Fire Island's only lighthouse is desperate times.

Not a big fan of change. I like my solitude on that tiny island. If taking a lodger on means I can keep that peace a little longer, I will.

Like Em's father did for him, mine handed down his legacy—the lighthouse. Among some of the more stubborn features, our parents also handed the accent down to us. Although it's waned since they've been gone. Now, the inflections, a handful of Scots words, and a few Gaelic phrases my father would use from time to time are all that remain from our parents' homeland for Iris and me.

"Hell, that'll be rough midwinter, bud."

I huff a chuckle. "Survived worse, Em."

His face falls. "Yeah, you sure have."

The pang of the ghost of past heartbreaks haunts me for a beat. Clearing my throat, I compose myself and slap his shoulder as I walk past, heading for my boat. It's not Em's fault. It isn't anyone else's. Even all these years later, it still rips me up. I have managed to ignore it over the years. And time really does mend hearts. But the stitches old Father Time used to put my haphazardly beating organ back together show from time to time.

Footsteps from behind tell me Em is following. Probably to make sure the supplies are secure. And check I'm not going to sail off into the unknown, never to return. He's like my brother. We've always been close. Through girls, sports, college, even my stint in the Navy, he would always be one of the first to meet me at the docks. His father's death. My parents' accident . . .

My morbid thoughts are interrupted when he catches up.

"Cal, you need a hand to get all this sorted?"

I look at the boxes of supplies, the items on my fortnightly list that I drop off first thing when I dock every Friday morning. "No, bud, it looks good. Thanks though, hey."

A soft smile pushes up on his face. His brown eyes are tight. "You know, if you ever get sick of living the real-life survivor episode, the mainland will always have you back."

Tossing the cargo net over the supply boxes, I secure it down. "Nope. Like my peace, you know that."

"How long is this lodger staying?" Em asks, bending over the side of the old fishing trawler to tie off the cargo strap on port.

"Not sure, hopefully long enough to pay for the lighthouse upgrades. The old Fresnel needs swapping out. At this rate, the fishing hut is going to outlive the damn house."

Em chuckles. The memories I have revolving around the fishing hut on the southern end of the island are too many to count. Some of my best days were spent there. The only place I can still feel my father.

"Boss lady got you all sorted, I see." Em's face lights up

with his reference to my tenacious little sister. Rubbing the back of his neck, he opens his mouth to say something. Heels click down the gangway toward us, and he snaps it shut. "Been a long time since you had to share anything with a woman. Sure you're up to it, old man?"

"What're you havering about? A, you're literally the same age as me, asshole. B, she's probably some crotchety old hag who smells like camphor and cats. C—"

Em moves, his gaze looking right past me to whoever is walking toward us. He pulls his cap from his head with a nod. "Or not."

I spin around.

A young twentysomething looks around, confused. Her bottom lip worries through her teeth, black-rimmed glasses on her face. Her long dark hair rests around her slim shoulders and a dark grey cap sits on her head. In a cream sweater and tight dark jeans ending in black heeled boots, she swivels on the spot, as if searching for something.

"Hi!" Em steps forward like a bellhop, hands clasping his fucking hat. "I'm Emmett. You must be here for the accommodations."

"Oh, hi, yes. I was sent down here from the café. A lady called Iris said my ride is here?" Her eyebrows lower over dark brown eyes. "Is it you I'm looking for?"

Emmett steps sideways. "Nope. That would be Callum."

Now her gaze swings to me. "Oh sorry, I didn't realize.

Hi, I'm Eve. Sorry about the short notice. My editor only organized this all yesterday."

Not an old, camphor-smelling crazy cat woman.

Brown eyes stay locked on me, as if waiting for something.

Emmett takes her bag, muttering something under his breath before waving her toward the boat.

"I'm confused, is the cottage up the coastline?" Eve says softly.

So fucking meek.

Great, just as I thought. Someone needing looking after.

Stepping aboard, the old fishing boat moves with my weight. I do a round of pre-start checks, like I didn't already run her in from the island this morning. Em can deal with the crazy lady.

"Is he going to be long?" she says.

"Huh?" Em grunts, settling her things beside the cargo netting. "You're going with."

She stares at Em. "Up the coast?"

"The cottage is on Fire Island. Callum will take you over."

Eve looks like she's about to turn and run back down the gangway. "Oh." Instead, she looks around like a deer in headlights. I busy myself with checking fuel and oil levels.

"You mean . . . over that?" She points toward the sea, now a little choppier than it was on the trip in this morning.

Great, she probably gets seasick. Hell, Iris couldn't vet potential lodgers?

"Typical," I breathe under my breath.

Eve paces in a small circle, arms hugging her chest as she mutters to herself.

Wonderful.

I'm the one who should be worried, about to be stuck on the island with crazy.

"You can do this, Evie. You have to, no other choice now," she whispers before halting abruptly. I roll my eyes and drop onto the captain's seat. I fire up the old girl and let her idle, chugging out water behind us at a low churn. The sound snaps Eve from her partial conniption, and she edges toward Firefly.

"Here, watch your step," Em says, extending a hand.

She stares at his palm before she takes it and steps onto the boat. Forcing a small smile his way, she grabs onto the boat for dear life. "Sorry, I'm not usually this uptight, honestly. It's been—"

I throw the throttle forward. A squeaking noise bursts from her lips as she sways on her feet. Em scurries for the lines, setting us free in quick time. Raising a finger to my forehead in a salute aimed at Em, I steer Firefly out of her slip. Eve drops onto the small bench seat behind me, hands clasped together in her lap. I set my sights on the eastern horizon, maintaining heading.

Twenty minutes later, the rocky shoreline of Fire Island

comes into view. I run an eye over the chop and swell, slowing her as we approach. The weathered jetty stands stoic in the water. Just the sight of it has the tension I felt on the mainland starting to loosen. As far as things a man could want for, peace and a place of my own have always been top of the list.

Loneliness and me have shared a bed for well over a decade.

The sneaky bitch slithered her way in and never left.

Firefly slides in beside the jetty. I kill the engine and throw the lines up. Eve sits frozen, watching. I tie off and jump back down into the boat. With a huff, I snatch up her bag. A second later, I drop it, remembering I need to clear out my house before she steps foot in it.

I step back up onto the jetty and start toward land. The iconic Fire Island lighthouse stands proud and tall on the northern end of my slice of isolated paradise. The white and black paintwork that took me weeks juts into the sky. The small keeper's cottage, mere feet from the oversized structure, shares the same color scheme. But none of the amenities. Well, a fireplace and a bath, a basic bunk—no bed or living quarters. It's an all-in-one type arrangement. And for the next however many weeks, my new space.

Shuffling from behind sees me spin back. Eve is grabbing up her bag, like she's about to hop from the boat and waltz right into my damn sanctuary like she was fucking invited.

Not likely, lassie.

I move toward her and hold up a hand.

Her mouth pops open a little, and she glances between me and the lighthouse. I shove my hand forward, signaling for her to stay put. When she drops back to the bench seat, I make for the lighthouse.

It takes all of ten minutes to clear out my personal effects.

I give the place a rough tidy and walk out the door.

And run right into softness.

Something like jasmine and vanilla shrouds me. Her bag drops to the ground at her feet. I force my gaze up to hers. Frowning, she looks over my shoulder into my goddamn house. When her eyes meet mine again, she says, "Thank you."

Grunting, I leave the doorway, arms loaded with my belongings.

She may have to be here. I may have to make sure she stays to keep this place from being lost forever. But I don't have to like it or her.

And I sure as hell don't have to talk to her.

Three

EVIE

"It's a freaking lighthouse," I utter as my gaze darts around the large circular space. A genuine, real-life lighthouse. Stunned, I stand with my bag in hand. A door slams behind me, and I twist to see Callum pass by the tiny window of the small cottage connected to the lighthouse by a gravel path. He stops in his tracks and tugs a tattered curtain past the frame, disappearing from view.

Okay then.

I spin back, taking in the cozy surroundings. The ground floor has a kitchen, a fireplace, a wide shelf stuffed with books, a worn blue sofa, and a coffee table that looks absolutely handmade. It's full of natural light, with three generous porthole-shaped windows with black shutters. The curved interior walls are whitewashed stone. The light fixtures look like something from an old maritime movie. I guess this is the essence of man living among the sea, so it fits.

That brings me back to the fact I'm alone on an island with a stranger. A man I know nothing about. Surely, Livvy wouldn't have arranged this if he could be a problem, right?

Still, there's nobody else here.

Just me.

And him.

The recent stalker letters have my nerve up, sending an anxious knot tightening in my stomach. Forcing my mind anywhere but fear, I take a second glance at my home for the next nine months. Past the sofa, a spiral staircase leads to the next level. Dropping my bag, I head for the twisty treads. Their black metal glints in the sunshine pouring in. Grabbing the curved rail, I make my way up the treads with my gaze stuck above me.

A moment later, I'm on a landing of sorts. A large spiral staircase curls up the inside of the lighthouse, heading to what I assume is the very top. On the other side is a door. I turn the knob and let it fall open to find the bedroom, wood-paneled and homey. A large, antique-looking cast iron bed sits in the center, made up with a light grey duvet and navy pillows. A porthole window is above the headboard, and two small wooden nightstands flank it. A low-hanging light that looks like something made from a recycled buoy is suspended over the enormous bed. Another fireplace, smaller and on stone tiles, sits in the curved corner space. A small desk stands under the only other window. A rustic wardrobe and an old wooden chair are the only other items in the room.

Crossing the room, I open the window. The round metal-framed glass swings open easily. A great span of sea with choppy waves crashing into the beachy shoreline fills the scene. You can see forever from here. A never-ending swash of blue. The ocean meets the steady blue of the horizon. It's serene. Vast. Making me feel smaller than ever. I inhale and let the sea air flood my lungs.

It's amazing.

Maybe this is the place where I'll finally be able to write. Finally move on.

The desk is neat, mostly bare, only sporting a small wooden cup with three pens and a worn carpenter pencil. A wooden box sits on the other side, its brass clasp shut tight. I close the window, leaving it how I found it, and try the only other door in the room.

It opens to a small bathroom with a pedestal vanity and a clawfoot tub and brass showerhead. Black-and-white tiles that look well cared for cover the floor. A small wooden cabinet, no higher than the vanity, sits between the toilet and the shower. It's quaint. Clean.

Lovely.

I pad back downstairs and stand in the center of the room.

For the first time in five years, the weight on my chest anchoring me down is gone. Like somehow, I escaped out from under it by changing location. Maybe it's the thrill of my new surroundings.

Maybe this is what moving on feels like?

My stomach grumbles.

Damn, I'd been so focused on finding the cottage, I forgot to grab groceries. Wandering to the fridge, I pull it open. Beer, condiments, something in a casserole dish that looks like stew, and a chunk of cheese sit on the otherwise bare shelves.

"Shit," I mutter.

I hunt around the rest of the kitchen, hoping for coffee at the bare minimum.

Nope, no coffee.

A small canister of sugar. Some pantry staples and half a loaf of very stale-looking bread.

Ugh. This means I have to make a trip back to the mainland, and soon. I can barely function without coffee and regular snacks, let alone write a ninety-thousand-word novel with high-concept world-building and an original magic system woven around a romance arc that will knock the readers' socks off.

"Well, that's just great."

I turn back to look around. I'll unpack first. Then go ask about the food situation.

Sounds like a plan.

I haul my bags upstairs, dropping one on the chair and the other by the desk. I start unpacking my clothes. With an armful, I manage to open the wardrobe.

It's full of clothes.

Man clothes.

Double shit.

"Well, this is awkward." I turn to dump my clothes back on the bed. Movement catches my eye.

Callum stands in the bedroom doorway, a crate in his hands and a scowl that would scare the feathers off a gull plastered all over his face.

"This is your stuff? I—"

He shoves past me and goes about tossing his belongings into the crate. I stand rooted to the spot as he clears out the room before disappearing into the bathroom. With his crate loaded, he walks out and trudges down the spiral stairs. I follow, desperate to ask about the food, to apologize for the inconvenience I've obviously imposed on him.

He stalks to the bookshelf, tossing a handful of tomes on top of his already overflowing cargo. Next, he tugs open a kitchen cupboard and takes a handful of things. The last item he grabs is a navy tin mug.

"I'm sorr—"

He flicks me a glance that looks more like a warning than acknowledgement, and I close my mouth.

But I need groceries and to not feel like I've hunted him out of his home. I move a little closer, hands wringing my shirt, and decide to try again.

When I open my mouth to say something, nothing comes as he stalks for the front door.

It slams a second later, and I stand staring at it. No closer to figuring out this mess I have found myself in.

"Great, thanks a bunch, Livvy."

Good lord, it's going to be a *long* nine months.

With a belly full of cold stew and stale bread, I lay on the bed, not game to breach the covers and lay in the man smell that shrouds this room. With a heavy blanket I found downstairs, I huddle up against the East Coast winter. It's been a long, long time since I was among anything masculine. It's heady. A little nerve-racking.

Staring up at the ceiling and studying the design of the upcycled light fixture, I try to outline a plan for the next few weeks. So far, I have three chapters. A measly six thousand words into a ninety-thousand-word project.

Rolling over, I glance at the night sky through the

window. The stars seem as if they are hanging just outside, so low you could touch them. Waves crash outside the open window, lulling me into a mesmerized state. A stark contrast to the noise, the sirens, the chaos of the city.

The lights in the little cottage were out before I even threw together my makeshift supper. I don't recall them coming on at all, now that I think of it. Maybe he's one of those "to bed with the birds" types. Most likely will be up before the sun. A polar opposite to the night owl I've become as a writer.

I roll over without thinking. His scent hits me.

Like a ton of bricks.

Memories of having a man in my bed rush back like the punishing waves on the rocks outside.

Joshua.

The pang that used to turn to unbearable agony stays just that, a pang.

Letting my eyes drift shut, I breathe in the salty air like it can heal my wounds from the inside out.

But my mind won't slow, and my heart thumps heavily. I need to make this work. What other options do I have? Writing is all I've ever done, ever wanted to do. I have no useful real-life skills. Not one. Starting again from scratch would be painful, to say the least.

I toss the blanket off and grab my robe from the end of the bed. With the moon high over the lighthouse, shining its silver spears over the polished wood floor, I take out my laptop and place it on the small desk. My phone buzzes, the screen lighting up.

A text from Allie.

She'd be up still. Always my nocturnal companion.

I lift my phone, and the service disappears.

The screen says SOS. No service.

Great.

I decide to stick with the inspiration that hauled me out of the warm comfort of the bed and ignore her. Opening the laptop, I fire it up and wait for the telltale ping of a trillion emails and updates.

Nothing comes.

I check my phone.

Two bars . . .

I hold it up, moving side to side. A bar disappears. Then both ghost me. SOS stares back at me.

Again.

Shit.

Wait. There's no Wi-Fi?

I didn't even think of that.

Hell.

That absolutely puts a damper on my research abilities. Making my laptop useful for one thing only. Writing.

Huh. This must have been Livvy's plan all along.

How villainess of her. I shove my hands through my hair and let it hang.

Right, so, taking stock.

I'm isolated on an island with a stranger.

A stranger who is a man, and older than me by a fair bit.

I'm down to rations and living in someone else's home.

I have no Wi-Fi or contact with the outside world.

No way off the island, because who am I kidding? I can't drive a car without incident, let alone a boat.

And the one other person on this island hasn't spoken a word to me since we met.

With those pleasant thoughts, I shrink into the only safe place I know. My imagination.

Pulling up my writing project, I'm determined to make the most of this. I keep coming back to the fact that Livvy sent me here. She would have known the lay of the land, so to speak. If she thinks I can get this book done without the distraction of the city, the hustle and bustle, Wi-Fi, and other people, who am I to say otherwise?

I read the last few paragraphs of the last chapter I wrote, pulling my outline up to refresh my memory. Oh, that's right, the two MCs just met. Realized they are enemies. Blah, blah, blah. Okay . . . time to up the stakes. I tie up my hair in a this-means-business messy bun.

My hands fly over the keyboard as the night wears on, the moon rising higher and higher before it finally peaks and starts to plummet.

The small clock on the desk ticks, the only other sound in the dim moonlit room. I shiver and reach over to close the window. The blanket from the bed finds its way around my shoulders, and I write on.

I get caught up in the fantasy world of my characters. The angst and the stakes. The banter and the high-octane emotions. As sleep tugs at my eyelids, I finish the paragraph and scroll up to read it over. Resting my chin in my palms, I yawn. I'll check it over once more and call it a night.

Just once more.

firefly

Four

CALLUM

I enter without knocking. Iris would have my balls. But fuck it. This is my damn house.

It's quiet.

Like *nobody's up* quiet. The sun's been up for an hour already. And it's winter. I pull open the fridge and take out the small jug of milk. Surprisingly, it hasn't been touched. Maybe she didn't realize what it was; it's not in a carton like I'm sure this city girl is used to. Taking a plastic container from the freezer compartment, I toss a spoon of instant coffee in a mug and light the stove.

The kettle is still half full, and I slide it over the heat. The gas stove was one of my later installations after renovating the interior of this old house. Wood stoves are great, but they are a pain to maintain, and wood on an island can become a supply issue. Gas cans are much easier to haul from the mainland, and last much longer.

The kettle whistles and I slide it off the heat. Steaming water splashes into my cup, and still nobody else stirs. I glance up, wondering what she could be doing for so many hours in that tiny room—my tiny room—upstairs. Adding a dash of milk and taking a tentative sip, I ascend the stairs.

The bedroom door is open.

The bed's empty.

A blanket-covered woman sleeps slumped over the desk I made when I first came to live here. Her computer screen is black. Sleep mode like its owner, I guess. Black-rimmed glasses hang off her face, half covered by messy dark hair escaping a lopsided bun. I trudge back downstairs, making a beeline for the front door. Coffee in hand, I track over the small gravel path between the towering lighthouse and small cottage originally built to be storage space.

The wind is up, bitter and cold.

The days are shorter than usual. The workload for this self-sufficient little island is still as long as the summer months. I haul my windbreaker over my arms, shrugging it up around my shoulders. Draining the last of the coffee, I pull on my beanie. My days of solitude have been spent doing chores for as long as I can remember. Living semi off-grid, growing my own food, and building things from scratch takes hard work and long hours. Add that to my lighthouse duties, and my days are full. Just how I like them.

There is so much to Fire Island that nobody else will never see or know about. Like the fishing hut my father built on the southern end. The depths of the small forest filling the land between here and there. Among other things. I flip the collar of my jacket up and stalk my way to the greenhouse.

The inside of the large hot house is stifling. A sweltering contrast to the frigid outdoors. Sitting my coffee down on a potting table, I tug the windbreaker off and tuck the beanie into my back pocket. The large area is defined by four rows of aboveground beds, host to every vegetable, herb, and salad fixing I could get to survive in the salty coastal air. Doing the rounds, I tend to each plant and harvest anything ready for the picking.

With arms full of vegetables, a few handfuls of fruit, and a fresh bunch of garlic, I head for the enamel sink. The water is damn freezing, so I clean up fast. The wind howls outside, and I send my thoughts to firepit nights with s'mores. To summer fishing. To swimming in the freshwater lake at the heart of the island . . .

The door to the greenhouse opens, letting a frigid gust of wind into the sanctuary from the tempest.

Swinging back, I find her standing in the doorway with her arms hugging her chest. She shivers where she stands. I point at the door, the scowl on my face deepening with every second she lets the cold wind in.

She finally shuts the door and moves into the warm space, and I turn back to the cleanup.

Great, just fucking great.

She walks around, slowly, taking in the plethora of plants. Running her hands over the soft tips of the shallots, she stops mere feet from me. "I thought I smelled coffee?"

I turn off the water and scrub the carrots in the sink roughly. I've always only ever picked enough for each day. Waste not, want not, and all that. Now, with another mouth to feed, I guess this morning's haul is warranted. She better not be damn fussy.

My hands burn with the icy water, and I do my best to focus on that and not her.

When I don't reply, she shifts on her feet. "Would it be possible to go back to the mainland? I need some groceries."

I toss the carrots on the draining board and pluck the stems from the tomatoes, tossing the green waste into a container for compost. With a sigh, she turns on her heel. The gravel-covered ground crunches under her feet. The sound fades, and the door opens and closes, and I hang my head.

The last thing I wanted was company.

Let alone nine months of it.

But over my dead body are they decommissioning this lighthouse. It's been the biggest part of our family legacy for so long. Then the thought hits me. If I make her uncomfortable, she's going to leave.

Along with the money her publishing house pays for her to accommodate my home.

With a grunt, I bundle the day's pickings into my arms. Running through the options of how to ensure she stays, preferably with minimal interaction, I push through the cottage door and dump the food on the small table under the far window.

This lot should be in the fridge, in the house. Not sitting around here to wilt.

Reluctantly, I gather my load up and cross the path to the house. Remembering the house is not my own at the moment, I turn and knock with my elbow, trying not to lose my load in the process.

A moment later, the door opens. Soft brown eyes find mine, a small, nervous smile pushing her lips up briefly. Still bundled up in a sweater, jeans, and boots, she's added a scarf that's wrapped around her neck.

I nod to the load in my arms, and she steps aside, allowing me inside.

I deposit the fruit and vegetables in the fridge. Rummaging through a drawer, I find string and tie the garlic to the curtain rod over the sink. She watches me as I work, leaning on the small dining table. "You grow all your food?"

Her small talk could use some work, since she was literally standing in the greenhouse moments ago. Not responding, I head for the door. Her arms unfold from her chest, her hands hanging by her sides. Fingers pale and the tips of her nails blue—she's cold. The fireplace has died down. Probably got no idea how to stoke it.

With a sigh, I wander to the wood rack and pluck up three logs. Opening the fireplace door, I toss them in. With the fire iron, I poke at the coals, and the logs catch. I shut the door tight and open the flue a little way to get the flames higher. When it's crackling away, I rise to my feet and adjust the settings again. No need to burn the fuel up too fast. I'll only have to come back in that case.

Glancing around the living room and kitchen, I make sure the windows are still shut tight. A little frown pulls her face down, her bottom lip between her teeth. For a moment, I take her in. The long dark hair that flows over her shoulders, her pretty face, the curve of her hips that rise to a slim waist. Jean-clad legs that go for damn days . . .

Clearing my throat, I head upstairs and stoke the fireplace in the bedroom. Footsteps close in behind me as I shut its small glass door.

"I'm sorry I'm in your home," she offers. The words are tentative. Like she either doesn't believe them or that one sentence took more bravery than she could muster. I turn back to see her shifting on her feet like she's about to bolt, and I know it's the latter.

She's like a porcelain doll. Pretty to the point of elegant beauty, but meek and timid. One of those introvert types.

This might work out, after all.

I walk back downstairs, but this time my shadow stays put upstairs. I take the opportunity to put together lunch for later, pulling out a baking dish and seasoning some veggies before covering the bowl with a plate and placing it back in the fridge.

A throat clears behind me.

I wash my hands in the sink and dry them on a tea towel. She moves into the kitchen, hands shoved into her back pockets. The scarf is gone; she must be warmer.

"I really do need to get back to the mainland for supplies," she says, eyes pleading.

Not ready to engage, I simply point at the calendar by the bookcase. Turning toward it, she figures out what I'm indicating. Walking to the wall by the bookcase, she runs a fine finger over the dates. Her mouth pops open when she realizes my meaning.

Every fortnight, I go back as proof of life for my sister, and sometimes for supplies the island can't afford me.

The only other reason I will leave this island of mine is if Iris makes me. Which is only a few times a year.

"But that's almost a fortnight, Callum."

Something snags close to my heart at her using my name. I don't like it. Not one bit.

"Shit," she utters under her breath. Realizing I heard, her cheeks flush crimson.

I fight back the smile wanting to split my face at her

discomfort from using a curse word. Is shit even considered a curse word?

Hell, how would I know? Curses are normal words to me. At this point, with conversation being a rarity in my life, I'm sure she'd do better at holding one than me.

I make myself busy, checking the windows are in fact closed and sealed, with no drafts slipping through. Her gaze follows me as I move around the house, tugging each one to check. And, momentarily, I feel bad for not being more accommodating. I could have very well ended up with a much worse lodger.

Nope.

Not going there.

We're not going to have long conversations, take in sunsets, or become damn friends. She's at least fifteen years younger than me. The last thing I need right now is more complication in the shit show I call my life. Passing the fridge, I tug it open and snatch out the coffee from the small freezer section and dump it onto the counter.

The small label that says *coffee* catches her eye.

She's a writer. Smart enough to work out the gas stove, I'd guess. With that thought, I hightail it out of my own fucking house and into the frigid gusts outside. I don't bother closing the door behind me.

The pretty twentysomething can do that, too.

Five

EVIE

After days of living off Callum's leftovers, which he graciously leaves in the fridge without a word, I'm at my wits' end. I haven't been able to write a word since that first night I arrived. Apparently, all this nothingness is not conducive to productivity. I need to get to the mainland.

I wander around the lighthouse, exploring. It's not as cold as it was when I first arrived. The sun is actually warming my face. There are other outbuildings tucked away near the tree line. I cross the swaying grassy area. The weathered wooden doors are all shut tight. No doubt the warped frame is keeping them bound in place.

I pull on the long metal door handle of the first building. It doesn't budge. My imagination takes hold, coming up with what these mysterious shacks could hold.

The steady rhythm of an axe hitting wood floats over the island. Callum is out in the sunshine as I am. His chores keep him occupied. So much so, I rarely see him unless I go out looking for him. Which I have done all of once and never again. I don't understand the no-speaking thing. Has he been alone so long that communicating is something he doesn't participate in anymore?

But then, I saw him talking with the harbormaster. I think his name was Emmett. So it's just me, then.

Brilliant.

I scoff at the thought and harrumph at the stubborn door. This is not getting me any closer to the mainland. With no hope of getting into the writing zone, I need to find a way across the water. I can't wait another week. Between the man not speaking to me and having him trudge through the living space multiple times a day to tend to the light at the top of the lighthouse, I'm harried at best.

So much for Livvy's plan.

What I wouldn't do for a minute or two of Wi-Fi.

Spurred on, I decide to walk the shoreline of the western side of the island. Maybe I can sit on the jetty and inspiration will strike.

Stranger things have happened, right?

I make my way toward the rocky shoreline. And it's when I'm almost at the jetty that I see a gravel path that swings left, heading south. The curious writer in me can't resist. I duck down the path and pick up the pace. A hundred feet or so along I find a smaller ramp jutting out into the water. And tied to it . . .

A rowboat.

Now *this* I can manage.

Who doesn't know how to use a rowboat?

Not that I've ever captained one before. Is that the right word? Do you captain a rowboat, or is that too ridiculous?

Two oars lay in the center of the most seaworthy-looking rowboat I've ever seen. Its white hull and black-trimmed outline floats to the steady swell of the waves that softly caress the little cove it sits in. The name *Lassie* is in hand-painted black script letters.

Excited, I rush back up the path and into the house. I gather up my bag, phone, and my cap, just in case. Running out the door, I tug my coat from the hook and slam the door behind me.

Shit. So much for being covert.

I speed walk down to the rowboat and throw my belongings in before stepping down into the small vessel. I untie the two ropes holding my only hopes of escape in place. Sinking onto the bench seat, I run a hand over the handles of the oars. I can do this.

I send my heroines into raging battles with only their wit and a sword. Surely, I can handle a rowboat. If it took twenty minutes in Firefly to get here, I'm guessing it will take me an hour or so to row to the mainland. But math has never been my strong suit. In any case, I need to get off this island. I need supplies, and if Callum can't be bothered to help, I'll make my own way.

Sliding one oar over the edge, I hook it into the oarlock. It sinks up to its metal casing, securing it in place. After doing the same to the other oar, I lean over and push a hand against the ramp, sending the small boat away in the water. The thrill of something akin to main character energy at the start of an adventurous journey slips through my veins. I smile to myself, feeling in control of something for the first time in a long time.

I row the oars in synchronous movements through the water. And in no time, the ramp is behind me and I'm heading out into the stretch of sea between me and copious amounts of coffee and snacks. Thoughts of writing hordes of words completely sugared up spur me on faster.

Pretty soon, my arms ache. My grip aches, and I slow my pace. I look back, gauging how far I have come . . .

Around fifty feet from the shoreline. Ugh.

I am *not* giving up.

If this was my heroine, she would double down, summon her dragon, and get this done.

Wishing I had an actual dragon right now, I plow through the choppy water with so much determination it sends a hum through my ears.

As the hum turns to the drone of an engine, I swing my gaze over my shoulder.

Shit. Shit. Shit.

Firefly roars up beside the rowboat, rocking it as I pretend not to notice his presence. I keep rowing. Gritting my teeth, I send the little boat faster. No way am I going back. I'm getting those supplies if it kills me. Studying the horizon and finding no sign of the mainland, I realize it absolutely could.

A rope flies onto the stern of my small vessel, circling the small hook. We slow to a halt, the rowboat bumping into the fishing trawler.

Heat floods my cheeks, and I scramble forward and toss the line off. Before I can grip the oars and row to my escape, Callum lands feet first in the boat. He ties the rope off and tugs me up from the bench seat with a harsh grip, curling his enormous hand around my upper arm.

"Of all the harebrained, half-witted, idiotic ideas." His face is feral, his jaw clenched.

"Get your hands off me!" I tug furiously, wanting out of his grasp. My arm doesn't budge. I twist and try again, only succeeding in ending up almost wrapped around him. His scent smacks into me. The same masculine essence that's soaked into his bedding, into his pillows that I sleep on every night.

Something low in my belly flips, and I frown as the air in my lungs peters out.

He hauls me toward the cruiser, shoving me up the side ladder, his hand unceremoniously on my ass pushing me upward. With a squeak, I land inside the trawler on my rear. He's on deck a second later, tying the rowboat behind Firefly. Scowling, he turns us around and heads back to shore.

Dammit.

He says nothing as we moor, and I climb onto the jetty as my bag is tossed in my direction. I catch it, faltering on my feet as awkwardness sinks in. Standing like a stunned idiot as he hauls the rowboat from the water and onto the jetty like it weighs nothing, I close my gaping mouth.

All I can think of as he stalks past me, heading for the lighthouse, is *he spoke to me.*

I got seven words out of Callum McCreary.

And the fact that I was hauled against him, my body against his, surrounded by his body. Literally hanging from his big bear hand.

Intrigued and breathless for reasons I can't pin down, I follow at his back all the way to the house. He disappears into his cottage, and I pad inside the lighthouse. When I shut the front door behind me, I lean against it, reliving the last five minutes on repeat. It's been an eon since I touched a man. Since one touched me. It's only natural to have some sort of physical reaction. He's all grabby-grabby, and I'm like a rag doll in his hold.

I shake my head, dislodging the thought.

I have no intention of getting anywhere close to Callum McCreary.

Big bear hands or not.

Handsome damn scowl face, my ass.

I'm here to write.

Nothing else.

The door to the cottage slams and I flinch. I walk to the kitchen window, only to see him stalk his way toward the tree line of the small forest that takes up the center of the island. Good. That's good. *The further away, the better, grumpy ass.*

Defeated and no closer to fixing my food problems, I sink onto the sofa. Running my gaze over the bookshelves, I study the tomes that Callum deems worthy of his small library. Some reference texts, some nautical, other generic encyclopedias. A small section of thrillers sits on the bottom shelf. A few classics, like Charles Dickens and Mark Twain, take up space on the higher shelves.

The rest of the shelf houses gadgets. Something that looks like a sextant. A wooden box with the lid open holds a brass compass that looks antique. Curious, I rise and move to the shelves. I run a finger over the brass, marking it with a fingerprint. "Dammit."

Plucking up the hem of my shirt, I polish it back to a shine. Everything about this place has my back up. Like I'm an intruder.

I guess I am.

Guilt follows me with every decision I make. Every meal

I eat that should have been his. Every night I sleep in his bed. Dwell in his home. I wish I could give something back, make amends for the intrusion in some way.

Then I remember the fire in those eyes, the way he looked at me like I'm the stupidest girl in the world when he hauled my ass out of that boat. The branding touch of his huge mitts on my ass. My face flushes again.

Groaning, I flop back on the sofa.

Deep into my wallowing stage of self-pity, I lie there, staring up at the ceiling.

The front door opens, and heavy footsteps trod toward where I lie.

"Please leave me to my humiliation, Callum."

He doesn't.

Of course he doesn't.

Instead, he plants himself at the end of the sofa, arms crossed, scowl firmly fixed as his eyes burn into mine.

"Seven a.m. Sharp. Jetty. If you're late, I will leave without you."

Without another word, he stalks from the house, slamming the door behind him.

I rub my hands down my face before rolling over and burying my face into the plush blue upholstery. I scream and smack a fist onto it. My hand hits something solid. Slipping it between the cushions, I produce a tattered journal of some sort. The words *Weather Log* are gilded and embossed into the leather cover. I toss it on the coffee table and glance at the window as he walks past it.

Most infuriating man on the planet.

No, the whole entire goddamn universe.

He better not leave without me.

firefly

Six

CALLUM

I slide the throttle back, slowing the cruiser as I approach the jetty. The mainland was bustling. Not that Eve would know. She didn't show . . . or was late. I left at seven sharp. Now, three hours later, I make out her pacing, huffing figure on the end of the jetty.

I chuckle at the sight of her all wound up.

She could have just showed up. Being on time isn't hard. Firefly bobs up to the jetty, and I throw a line over and anchor her to the structure. The harsh click of heeled boots flies toward me. I tamp down the smile that wants out at her pouty fucking face. This ought to be good.

"You utter ass, I was here at seven oh five! You left without me!"

The meek, shy girl is nowhere to be found. And I can

only assume her permanent state of hangry since she arrived has set in.

She should have been on time.

"I left at seven. Told you that."

She crosses her arms over her chest. "You have to go back. I need provisions." She looks like she's about to cry.

Fuck.

I toss a bag of *provisions* at her and she catches it, fumbling the bag a little.

"What's this?"

"Iris sent some things."

"Iris did?"

"Yep. Try not to be too grateful."

Her mouth gapes open but she slams it shut, unrolling the paper top and peering inside. A little gasp leaves her lips, and her eyes shoot back up. The way she goes from night to day in a split second over a chunk of damn cheese is hilarious.

"Tell her thank you . . . but I do really need to get back there. I have things I nee—"

"It can wait till Wednesday."

"No, no, it can't."

"Has to."

Giving me the poutiest twisted face she can manage, she turns on her heel and walks back up the jetty, holding her one paper bag of groceries like it's her prized possession. I won't tell her Iris actually sent three bags. I'll leave them at her doorstep. Ought to light them on fire before I do.

Fucking brat.

At least she's sticking up for herself. A far cry from the conservative, shy girl that breached these shores that first day. I kill the engine and secure the boat before hauling the two remaining bags and a few things I needed back up the path. I drop the bags at the house front door and make my way to the cottage. My few pickings, grabbed while I waited for Iris to shop for Eve, are wrapped in a smaller bag.

My stomach rumbles as I stash away the few essentials—soap, toothpaste, a new novel. God knows the few on my shelves have been read a thousand times. A small knock at the door sends it creaking open.

Eve stands at the threshold, her hands wringing through themselves.

"Thank you." The words are too soft.

And the meek, shy girl is back.

I think I preferred her with a little fire.

Hell, I know I did.

The way my gut flipped, the way my cock twitched at her pouty fucking face and blazing eyes trying to shred me to pieces where I stood.

"Nope."

"Pardon?"

"Not me you need to thank, remember?"

"Oh, yes, of course. Thank Iris for me if you would, please?"

I move toward the door where she stands, slapping a hand onto the frame. I'm almost in her space. But hell, she's in mine, so it's only fair. Her cheeks are flushed as her eyes dart around the small cottage. And her frown deepens with every moment that passes. "This is . . ."

"My space."

I slam the door in her face. The echo of a little gasp hits the other side, and I scoff a laugh before turning back to put away my few items. Gravel crunches under her footsteps as she walks back to the house. The last thing I need is for Little Miss Meek-and-Mild to feel fucking sorry for me.

That ain't happening.

Sand sprays up from each heavy footfall. Sweat beads on my forehead, trickling down my face and neck before soaking into my T-shirt. The sweatpants I wear are threadbare at best, letting plenty of the wind's chill through to my skin. I pump my arms harder. The waves lap at my right, sending me faster. I've run for as long as I can remember. Whenever I have something I need to work through, that is.

Right now, I need to get that meek twentysomething's

pretty face out of my head. Those soul-eating deep browns of hers don't belong there. *She* shouldn't be there. The last time a woman got under my skin, she came off worse for wear.

Understatement of the century.

A familiar burn lances through my chest. I push my body faster through the sand that becomes denser as the tide comes in, but I fail to sidestep out of its way. Sands and foaming water slosh through my toes. The sun warms my right shoulder. Its slow rise is the only way to tell the earth is still spinning and the rest of the world still exists.

I have been content living on my own on this small piece of sandy land for over a decade. After everything that happened, it was a welcome solace. It still is, in a way. But having Miss Twentysomething here is a change I thought I'd hate. Surprisingly, I don't.

Not getting attached to that idea. No fucking way. You get attached; people leave. One way or another.

That's the only true thing left in this life.

I take a sharp left and power up the slope of the dune that meets the grassy island by the lighthouse. Air barreling through my charred lungs, I fold over and grip my knees at the top and let each breath sear me however it sees fit. I like the burn—reminds me I'm still here. The sun heats my back, the sweat cooling with the easterly, where my shirt clings. With a long, slow inhale, I stand up and walk toward the hut.

The fragrance of coffee swirls through the air on the breeze, and . . .

Is that bacon?

Not my bacon.

Not my house, currently.

With a sigh, I push through the small weathered door to the hut. God, I could use a shower. The small, chipped enamel tub I have to fill from the only running water at the vanity stares back at me. The scent of cooking bacon wafts through my tiny window.

"Right, that's it."

I grab my towel, toothbrush, and soap and stalk my way to the house. Without knocking, I stride inside, through the living room, and head for the stairs. In my periphery, I see a stunned twentysomething with a messy bun, her PJs still on under a long cardigan that reaches her knees. One of her shoulders is left bare as the cardigan and top slip when she turns suddenly with her mouth agape. The thin material covering her chest doesn't put up much of a fight as the cold morning finds her skin, and her nipples pebble.

Eyes anywhere else, McCreary.

Fuck me.

Taking the treads two at a time, I pull my shirt off with one hand as I ascend. It clings to me, and I bump into the rail as it snags on my head and one shoulder, my arm up as I traverse the last few steps and make the landing of the first floor.

My house, my shower.

It's been too long since I had a hot one. Despite being sweaty from the run, I could use the heat on my muscles. The bedroom door is open, and I stride through and into the bathroom. Kicking the door mostly closed, I lose the rest of my clothes and dump the towel and toiletries where they belong.

The taps relent and, soon enough, steam curls through the small space. I can't help the long, weighted breath that falls away. My shoulders are a little lighter, even with just this, a simple hot shower. Being back in my bathroom. I'm surprised by how much I missed it. But logical thoughts of funding and needing to start somewhere new douses the kindling of yearning I have for my house. I won't have it at all if I can't raise the funds for repairs and the new Fresnel lamp.

I step into the tub, and the instant the hot water rushes my head and shoulders, I groan. God, who would have thought something so simple could mean so much to a man.

"Hello?"

"Fuck," I mutter, double-checking the curtain is closed well enough.

"I-I . . . Did you need something?" A huffy, strained sound filters through the steam. "I mean, other than a shower?"

What the hell?

"I think I'm out of shampoo, just so you know," she adds.

"I'm fine." The words are short. The sentiment is true, if not a little loaded.

"Okay . . ." Footsteps fade away, then stop.

A moment later, they return, coming to a halt at the bathroom door. "Are you hungry?"

Letting the water wash over me, I rake my hands through my hair. Willing my mind to go anywhere but where it's currently headed—the twentysomething barely feet from me. In the fucking shower. I obviously did not think this through.

And I'm hard.

"Shit," I utter, turning toward the wall a little, like that will damn well save me.

"Sorry, is that a yes?" She steps closer.

I drop my forehead to the tile and send the worst thoughts I can muster through my mind. Rotting fish. Errol's naked body, as I imagine it . . .

"Callum?"

I tilt my head. My name on those elegant lips is not helping my current problem. Instead, I pluck up the soap. "Aye, gimme ten."

"Good, okay. See you downstairs."

She sounds fucking happy.

Dammit.

My body latches onto her floaty words, wringing them out for what they are—feminine and sweet.

It's been way too long since I've gotten laid. That has to be it.

No other explanation is going to fit. Not her. Not now. Not here, and certainly not with me.

Something bangs downstairs. A small cry winds up the stairs, barely audible over the running water.

I kill the water, standing dripping, and listen.

"Shoot!" A pained whimper follows.

Good lord, what now?

I snap the curtain to one side and step out. Drying off quickly, I wrap the towel around my waist and run downstairs. The last thing I need is a hurt tenant. They don't tend to stick around.

At first, I don't see her. Then, my gaze catches onto scrambled eggs scattered over the floor. A foot sticking out from behind the small kitchen counter.

Jesus Christ.

Rushing around the counter, I find her sitting up against it, nursing her hand. The pan, which I am assuming she cooked the eggs in, lies beside her on the floor.

"I burned it." She nods to her hand. It shakes as she holds it.

"Christ, lemme see." I crouch at her side and take her hand.

Her eyes wander my face before falling to my bare chest.

They widen, and I remember I'm only covered by a towel. And by the look on her face before it turned bright crimson and quickly snapped to the side, the towel isn't doing much to cover me. Standing, I adjust the towel and drop my hand down to help her up. She slides her good one into it and pushes to her feet as I take her weight on one fucking arm.

"Sorry, I get a little lightheaded on low blood sugar. The pan was heavier than I thought. Then I tried to save it mid-fall . . ."

Even injured, she's apologizing. I grind my molars at her lack of self-preservation.

"Here, under the running water." I turn on the tap and she moves to the sink with me as I slide her hand into the cold stream of water. So close, her scent clouds around me. Her upper arm presses to mine, her fine collarbones still exposed, her sleeve hanging off her shoulder. The slight curve of her upper breast pushes out the soft fabric.

Damn, this close I . . .

Evie closes her eyes, leaning on the sink, her good hand grabbing the edge.

"Eggs looked good," I grunt, desperate to focus on anything but the way her body molds against mine.

She huffs a shy laugh through a slim smile before opening her eyes. "Yeah, I'm starving."

"Keep your hand in here. I'll make eggs. But you eat them how they're made."

She nods and I clean up the eggy mess before working

my way through the kitchen. I return the pan to the heat and add a wad of butter. Cracking four eggs into it, I shunt them around when they start to cook. It's only when I turn back to plate the food that my body washes with goosebumps.

Hell, forgot I'm only wearing a towel.

As the chill sinks in, I adjust the only cover on my body.

Evie's gaze hasn't left me. Her hand is still in the sink, but it's moved out of the water stream, like she's forgotten about it.

I clear my throat. "Think you can manage to toss this lot onto a plate while I get dressed?"

Her mouth opens, then closes.

I turn off the heat and give the eggs one more push around.

"Yes, I can do that," she finally says, her face gone from slack to all business.

"Back in a minute." I leave her with the food. By the time I make it to my hut, I'm hard as a fucking rock again.

Seven

EVIE

One would think after our encounter with the shower and then the eggs and bacon, some kind of progress would have been made between Callum and me.

I mean, not like there's a Callum and me.

Just, that . . .

With a sigh, my forehead hits my keyboard. The one I've been staring at for hours only to get down a whole one hundred and twenty-eight words. Fire Island can be kind of lonely, even for a hermit like me. And that little burst of time we spent together over a fortnight ago felt like something I can't explain.

It was . . . nice.

Comfortable with an undercurrent of something intense that I haven't yet been able to place.

Then it was like it never happened.

He never came back for breakfast that morning, and I cleaned up and ate alone. And just like that, that spark of life, of connection that would make my stay here more bearable, has gone up in a puff of smoke, along with my words. Callum hovers around, tending to the garden in the greenhouse and maintaining the light above my small room. He's good at keeping busy. Then, he went to the mainland without me last week. Again.

And we're back to square one.

So, now, I find myself alone once again with writer's block that's kicking my butt.

The plot is all over the place, the characters too shallow, and the world-building as thin as Saran Wrap. And the chemistry between the hero and heroine? *Nonexistent*. I haven't managed to write anything romantic since the accident. It's like every bit of lust and love that I ever possessed stopped breathing the minute Joshua did.

Maybe some research could help?

Groaning, I push off the desk, adjusting my glasses before deciding I need some fresh air. Maybe that will kickstart this stupid, stuck head of mine. Revive this aching heart. The weather has started to warm up and I change out of my PJs and into a yellow sundress, plucking out a cardigan just in case. A long, slow walk on the beach on the eastern side of the island should help.

Here's hoping.

I'm out the door before my never-touching-grass brain can catch up. The gravel of the small path around the lighthouse crunches underfoot, and I take in the magnificent grass-topped rock I'm lucky enough to live on, even for a while. Making my way toward the sheds and the eastern beach, I wonder what it would be like to live here as long as Callum has. And at which point the loneliness would find me.

The grass ends, giving way to a dark rocky border before the beach spills out around me. The waves on this side are wilder than the mainland side. The tide is out. I kick off my slip-ons and pad toward the roiling ruckus. The sand is still cold, like this is only a brief pocket of warmth, not the turn of the seasons I hoped it would be.

The ground is awash with shimmering sand, clusters of shells, small ocean debris, and the odd scurrying tiny crab. The ocean breeze steals my hair, tangling it behind my shoulders at my back. I close my eyes and hold my arms out, letting the rushing water, briny scents, and wet, wet sand that sinks between my toes swallow me.

Inhale.

Exhale.

The world quiets for a beat, letting my racing, harried mind slow the tiniest bit. The morning sun kisses my skin, my arms and legs and shoulders tingling with the welcome rays. My lungs stretch with each breath. All thoughts of fantasy worlds, mythical creatures, worlds too big to be contained in one mind melt away. For this very moment, I'm right where I'm meant to be, even if only for a while.

A gull cries overhead, and I snap my eyes open. The waves are biting at my feet. The tide is shifting. I turn back and wander along the beach. The waves eventually chase me up the sand and to the rocky edge. It's been forever since I spent hours outside with nothing in particular to do but wander.

So I do.

Stopping at the shed, I skirt around the outside until I find a window. Pushing up on my tiptoes, I peer inside.

There's boxes, old pieces of furniture. Some covered in sheets, others with only a thick layer of dust for cover. Rusted items hang on the wall. Something big sits at the end of the shed, covered, with smaller boxes resting on top. Some of the furniture looks antique. A box sits on a bench by the opposite wall, next to another labeled *clothes*.

It's like someone moved out and left their things behind. Maybe the lighthouse keeper before Callum?

"Find what you're looking for?" a harsh voice snaps from behind me.

I stumble away from the shed to find a stone-faced Callum, his arms crossed over his chest. Eyes burning into me, like if he only stares hard enough I might burst into flames.

"I was exploring," I say, too quietly.

"Taking a man's home wasn't enough? You gotta snoop over every inch of the island as well?"

My mouth gapes.

"No, I wasn't snoo—"

"Yeah, you were. Don't you have a novel to work on?"

My brows drop, but I take a step sideways, toward the lighthouse. His eyes track the length of me, taking me in.

"Go on, then." He nods to the house.

Ass.

Giving him the poutiest look I can make, I stalk toward the lighthouse. The wind plays with the hem of my dress, flipping it about. All of a sudden, the frigid bite of the wind finds me.

Right now, I couldn't care less.

"You always do what you're told, princess?" He chuckles from behind me.

Ugh!

I spin back and march right back to where he stands. My finger is in his stupid face a second later. "Don't call me that, *ever.*"

A smirk pulls up on his stupid, handsome face as his blue eyes light up. "What can I call you, then?"

His demeanor has changed from a minute ago when he was accusing me of snooping.

"Eve. You get to call me Eve. That's it."

"You sure?"

"Absolutely."

"Okay, Evie."

"Urgh!" Only my family and Allie call me Evie. You know, the close friend and family I love. Not *him*; he doesn't get that. I turn back and walk for the house.

A large hand wraps around my wrist a heartbeat later.

I stop dead still.

"Eve."

"What?"

"You can't go wandering around the island alone."

"You do," I say, turning back. His hand on my wrist burns, sparks flinging up my arm like damn wildfire, settling in my chest.

His gaze drops to where he's still holding me to the spot. His grip softens before he pulls his hand back. I stare at the place his fingers had just covered my skin, willing my body to calm the hell down.

His face softens, and he sets his shoulders back. "Just tell me where you're going if you wander away from the house."

"Sure thing." Sarcasm drips from every syllable.

Who the hell am I?

This man is infuriating.

A hint of a smile ghosts across his lips, and he walks away. But he glances back. "Don't get too used to the warmer days; the last cold snap will be here"—he nods to the sky—"any day now."

Watching him, I'm rooted to the spot. The bundled-up man from a month ago is down to jeans and a T-shirt. A broad back with musculature that would make a Greek god cry . . .

His hair is ruffled, like he's been out in the wind since he woke this morning.

My mouth is gaping.

Shit.

Good lord, Evie, snap out of it.

I jerk, spinning back to the house. I'm guessing any man would have that effect on a woman who's been starved of human touch for five years.

Yes, that's it. He could be anyone.

I'm certain of it.

Safe inside the house, I kick off my shoes and pad to the kitchen sink. In a daze, I find a mug and fill it with water, drinking it down like I'm dying of thirst. I lean a hip on the sink and refill the mug. Movement from beyond the curtained window catches my attention. I sweep the pale-lemon cloth aside, holding it back.

Callum is stacking wood. Corded arms and working shoulders manhandle the timber. He tugs the axe from the chopping block and bends down to pick up a short round log. The mug meets the counter, my hand still wrapped around it.

The axe swings, smashing into the log, his hands wrapped around the handle. The log splits, one half falling to the ground while the other teeters on the stump. Fore-arms flexing, he adjusts the split half and swings again.

It splinters, but the blade is stuck deep into the wood.

One large hand wrapped around the wood, he pries the head of the axe out. I swallow, chest heaving, as I lean closer to the window. Lips parted, each breath I take rustles the curtain, its fabric now white-knuckled between my fingers.

With the wood down to size, he tosses it into a pile to his right and bends over, swiping up the other half. As if my gaze is burning his skin, he turns toward the house. I jerk back, letting the curtain fall.

"Oh god." The word is breathy, and far too guilty.

Frozen to the spot, I stall the air in my lungs. Eventually the thwack of the axe takes up again, and I relax. Fumbling the mug in my hand that's warmed in my hold, I drain the last of the water and place it in the sink.

Words.

Right, I have words to write.

Surely after seeing the only other person on this isolated island working in the sun, my imagination has been stoked. As I climb the stairs and wind my way up to my room, I can't help but think that my words aren't the only thing I have rediscovered today.

I slam the laptop shut. *Well, so much for that theory.* Watching Callum work did something, but unblock my writing was not it. I slide the desk drawer open and pull out the old, tattered *Weather Log* journal I found in the sofa days ago, flipping through the pages to read a few entries. He writes about Emmett's problems and possible solutions. Iris and her life. The words are selfless and so . . . kind.

I'm warming up to him more with every turn of the page. Every entry I read gives me a privileged look inside Callum McCreary. His thoughts, his life.

The door shuts with a thud downstairs, and I rise from the chair, slipping the journal back into the drawer. It should be weird, him coming and going as he pleases, but it's not. Heavy footsteps tread upward and bypass the open bedroom door.

Curious, I follow. Outside my room, I glance up the spiral treads that continue to the very top. The lantern room. Callum disappears into it, and I hurry after him. I've never been up there. I'm not sure I'm allowed. Maybe I could put it down to research? Surely there could be a lighthouse in my fantasy realm? Magical pirates and all . . .

World-building research, that's what I'm going up there for.

Not the long-lost chemistry I can't seem to pin down, no matter how hard I try.

"Callum?" I grip the last of the rail before the room's threshold.

"'Round front."

Well, at least he didn't accuse me of snooping this time. I step into the room. It's bigger than I imagined. A curved, slatted cage fences the enormous light in. Everything is bright white or transparent. The lamp itself is silver and reflective. The round room is topped with a small dome. Interesting.

"You needing something?" a gruff voice rumbles from behind the lens.

I lean around it, but the apparatus is too big. Carefully, I step around until I find Callum squatting down, a white rag in one hand, a long brush in the other, and a scowl on his face.

I sink to the floor beside him, and he looks at me. A curious but entertained look flickers over his face and his blue eyes don't leave me. I train my eyes up to the huge light that's currently stationary and turned off. "It's so big. The light, that is."

He chuckles, continuing his cleaning. "That it is."

"Did you always want to do this? Live out here by yourself?"

He drops to his seat and leans against the slatted wall behind him. The rag comes to rest between his hands over his knees, now bent up. His face falls a little. "It wasn't my first choice. But the best one at the time."

"Oh," I mutter. I can't seem to close my mouth. He runs a hand over his short-cut beard and licks his lips, and I'm mesmerized. Clearing my throat, I drop my gaze to my hands. My idle, useless hands.

"You always want to be a writer?" he returns.

Surprised at the question, I look up with a strained chuckle. It's odd, these little pockets of easy we find ourselves in between the otherwise strained existence we have here together.

"I guess. I had the idea in high school and never really worried about looking any further."

He simply nods. "Sometimes you just know."

"Yeah, sometimes."

The conversation is easy, if not a little stifled. It's the first time we have talked like this. Who knew all I needed to do was corner him in the lantern room? And it's refreshing; it gives me hope. Maybe life isn't as bad as I think it is. Maybe the grey, lifeless days I endured were meant to give me a fresh start. Maybe not here, but this is like a precursor, a way to kick the tires. This is me, dipping my toe in the waters of change. Changing from the life I have in the city to something different. Anywhere different. I can take my writing anywhere.

Maybe I should.

The deep-seated thought of my heart's work resurfaces for the umpteenth time since I started my writing career. Fantasy isn't what my heart wants. It fills the void most days, but it far from lights me up. To be honest, it stresses me out. The world-building and magic systems. I haven't had the guts to tell Livvy.

"...down?"

I flip my focus to Callum's frowning face. "Sorry, what?"

He gives me a quizzical look that ends with a genuine smile.

And, oh my god, he's stunning. A wide smile that lights up his eyes the way I imagine this lantern room illuminates the ocean. His throat works as his chuckle peters out, and the room is far too small all of a sudden. My heart flings against my ribs, and I can't help it when my eyes lift to find his mouth.

Shit.

I scramble to my feet and look anywhere but at the man below me. He stands, shoving the cleaning rag in his back pocket. "We should go down before the afternoon sun finds us."

"Ah—yeah—sure thing." I grab the rail and descend faster than is safe, my cheeks aflame, my body doing something ridiculous. When I hit the first floor, I dart into my room. Shutting the door behind me, I lean against it. My head thumps backward onto the wood and I slide down to the floor. Knees hugged in my arms, I groan.

What the hell was that?

firefly

Eight

CALLUM

My bones rattle as I lie on my small bunk in the hut. May as well be a fucking igloo. Just as predicted, the cold weather did a hairpin turn. Grinding my jaw shut to stop my molars from busting from the chatter, I roll over and try to ignore the ache that's slowly consuming my body.

Goddamn winter. It's been a long time since I've had to rough it. I duck my head under the blankets, hoping each steamy breath will warm me in my cocoon.

The cloud of steam that puffs with each exhale fades and cools miserably. My hands start to cramp.

Fuck me.

Must be below freezing this time.

Not unusual for the East Coast, just unlikely.

At any rate, I refuse to go to sleep and freeze to death.

Tossing the covers from my half-seized body, I roll off the bed and to my feet. Huddled in a coat, I shove my socked feet into my boots and brace for things to get worse before they get better. I swing the hut door open and make a run for the house.

Inside is warmer. Not warm.

I glance to the fireplace. Fire's died out.

Fuck.

With stiff, aching fingers, I pluck up logs and toss them in. Grabbing the fire iron, I shunt the coals about until the wood catches. As it flares back to life, I close the door and open the flue. If this one's gone out, has the bedroom one also burned down?

I take the stairs two at a time.

The hollow of the stairwell in the cylindrical space is freezing. The cold air is sinking. And it's going to roll into whatever space it finds. With the bedroom door pinned back, Evie must be freezing, too.

I pad into the room. She lies on her side, facing the fireplace. Her body shivers. The duvet and the one thin blanket she has on are not nearly enough. I close the door to stave off the sinking cold and make my way to the small fireplace. As quiet as I can, I stoke it, gently sliding the logs over the coals. When they catch, I adjust the flue and shut the door.

Evie doesn't wake but still shivers. From the old cupboard, I hunt through the hanging clothes to find the extra blankets on the bottom. Plucking up two of the heaviest, I unfold one and lay it over Evie. After adding the last one, I tug off my coat, toe off my boots, and slide in under the covers.

Evie's shivers shake the bed. Hell, how she hasn't woken up is beyond me. Lying on my back, I stare at the light fixture. She's going to be pissed when she wakes up. I bet the look on her pouty little face will be worth it, though. That, and not freezing to death in my sleep. I raise my arms, tucking my hands under my head.

Turning my head, I watch her sleep for a while. After ten minutes, her shivers subside. She murmurs and rolls onto her back, and I take one last glance at her. Those elegant angles and perfect damn lips. I roll over and the warmth of being tucked up with the fireplace and extra blankets is stifling. I tug my shirt off and settle in.

This is a much better way to die.

I fall asleep with a smirk on my face, imagining how tomorrow morning is going to go.

"The hell!" The screech reaches my ears before I register where I am. "Holy shit!"

The bed rocks, the blankets shifting sideways in a violent sway. Cracking one eye open, I squint against the stream of golden light pouring through the porthole window. A harried, flannelette-clad woman, brown eyes burning, seethes, where she stands by her side of the bed. I resist the urge to chuckle. Sitting up, I sweep both hands down my face.

The blanket, or what's left of it on my side, falls into my lap. My naked, bare lap.

Fuck. That's right, I got hot and stripped off.

"Callum! Why are you in my *bed*?"

I groan. It's way too fucking early.

I barely slept.

And I can't decide if it's because I was next to Evie all night or because I wanted to make sure the room stayed warm. I'll go with the latter.

"First of all, this is my house. My bed. Second, how about a little gratitude for not waking up dead."

"What? That doesn't make any sense. You can't wake up if you're dead . . ."

Evie looks to the fireplace, still burning away nicely, then lowers her gaze to the bundle of blankets on her side. She hugs her body, inching forward, as if she's cold again.

My eyes drift to her pert nipples, before my proper brain has a chance to catch it. Yep, she's cold. I pull the blankets back on her side. "Hop back in before you freeze."

She gapes, nodding at what I assume is my naked body, somewhat covered by the blanket now.

"Don't get your panties in a knot, I'm getting up. Fire needs more wood downstairs by now, anyhow."

I make to rise, and she spins around awkwardly, hands flying over her face. I roll my eyes. When I stand and pull on my pants, I see her socks pulled halfway up her calves, the pajama pants tucked into them.

It's fucking adorable.

A moment later, she turns back around. Her mussed-up hair sits tossed around her shoulders, that bottom lip tugged through her teeth. Brows lowering, she opens her mouth to say something, but the words disintegrate into a breathless silence.

Heat blooms in my chest, sending blood south.

Time for me to leave.

I head for the door as I grunt out, "You're welcome."

She tilts her head as if in apology as her eyes soften further. And I stalk down the stairs, pulling on my coat as I go.

With the cold snap well and truly behind us, and a week of awkward nights in the same bed, we venture off the island. Evie sits on the bow of the cruiser, hair whipping about her face, head hanging back, hands planted on the bow behind her as her face tilts toward the sun. Seeing her like this has me thinking thoughts, processing sensations I shouldn't damn well have about a twentysomething. Still, my gaze rarely wanders from her lithe form draped over my boat like she fucking belongs here.

It's good to see her unwind, come out of her shell. She spent the first month here tucked away, as if she was punishing herself. I hated it. Hated that she felt the need to shrink herself. Nobody should be made to feel *that* is their only option to fit with this life.

Especially not a woman like Evie.

Firefly buffets over the waves, but the ride is pretty tame compared to some days. Spray shoots up and falls like rain over her. She squeals, rolling onto her hands and knees before she crawls toward the cabin. I chuckle at her yelp, but when she tilts her head up, her soaked hair hanging around her shoulders, her deep browns meeting mine, it dies out in my throat.

Air lodges, stuck solid for the second that her lips part. She stills, realizing she's crawling toward me. I white-knuckle the steering wheel. Every inch of my deprived being zaps to life. I can't take my eyes off her. Still, the boat rocks over the water, pushing forward.

Shaking her head, she dips her face and climbs to her feet, having made it to the railing. I set my gaze on the horizon. Where it should have been all along. Where it should *stay*. The engine whines, and I check the gauges. Plenty of fuel. Everything looks normal. I throttle back a little way as a precaution. Don't want to overheat the old girl. I tap the radio and the screen blinks.

Good.

Evie makes her way into the cabin, wringing her hair between her hands. Her face is bare. And god, it's like the first time seeing her. Those big brown eyes that held me captive moments ago are stunning. Her face, with plump ruby lips curled in a smile, is perfect symmetry.

Her glasses sit on the boat's console dash. She plucks them up, sliding them on.

Eyes on the horizon, McCreary.

She leans against the cabin wall, turning her head to one side to look ahead. The smooth, delicate angles of her neck and jaw fill my periphery. Her scent shrouds the small place, rising with the tang of the briny water she's doused in. Her pale-blue V-neck shirt clings to her body. And it takes every bit of propriety this man has to cement my focus on the horizon.

Where it damn belongs.

"Are we there yet?" Evie says.

I pay her a cautionary glance, and mirth lights up her eyes. *Fucking brat.*

"Nope," I grunt out.

But she doesn't respond, only sighing as she studies the same horizon I am fixated on. The boat lurches with a larger wave.

"Ah!" Evie yelps, her hands snapping around my biceps. They barely wrap around it.

I raise an eyebrow at her, and she worries her bottom lip through her teeth.

Christ's sake.

After a beat, she releases me and reaffirms her grip on the console, stepping into it to face forward. Doesn't like surprises, I guess. I double-check the gauges, and we travel in some sort of silence. I wouldn't call it comfortable. Maybe more like pleasant silence with an undercurrent of lust, at least on my part.

Fucking hell, maybe I should stay over this trip. Sort this needy shit out. I'm sure I could find a willing participant at the local tavern. Wouldn't be the first time I've had a one-night stand. Only, the potential aftermath of Iris's wrath when the gossip mill gets back to her stops me from taking that particular little plan any further. I've never been this town's favorite son. After everything that happened back then, there will always be some folks that will never come around.

Serves me right.

The engine splutters. With a loud clunk and grind, we slow to a halt. The water slaps into Firefly, shunting her side to side.

"What was that?" Evie says softly, worry creasing her face.

"Hell." I squat with a grunt and fling open the console panel. Nothing amiss with the fuse panel. "Stay here."

A strained giggle slips through her lips. "Where would I go?"

She has a point. I stalk from the cabin and pull up the deck trapdoor to the boat's engine. The acrid tang of electrical burning wafts up, spilling out over the deck.

"Fuck."

I hold the back of my hand to my nose as I wave the fumes and smoke away. Dammit, this will be an Emmett job. And we are stuck halfway to the mainland. I slam the trapdoor shut.

"Can we fix it?" Evie comes to my side, peering at the floor, like she can see right through the wooden deck.

"Nope." I move back into the cabin, and she's hot on my heels. I grab the radio and turn the knob up a little. "Bay Shore Harbor, this is Firefly. Over."

The VHF crackles, and I turn it up.

After a minute, I try again. "Bay Shore Harbor, this is Firefly, please respond. Over."

The crackle squeals and a voice as familiar as my own snaps through the small speaker. "This is Bay Shore Harbormaster. Over."

"Emmett, you dolt. Busy doing nothing, buddy?"

A heady laugh echoes through the line before he says, "Yep, all slow days and leisure, my friend. What can I do you for, Cal? Over."

"Engine's out. 'Bout four miles out. Over."

"Now who's the man of leisure? You need a tow, or can I settle it out there? Over."

"That's your call, man."

"Be there in—oh, shoot. I got a ferry coming in and a supply run after that. How does before sunset sound? Over."

I hang my head. There goes my day. But Emmett will be here as soon as he can. He's always been that way.

"Sure, man. We'll take in the scenery. Over."

"We? Oh, Evie's with you? Over."

"Yeah, bud. Two S-O-Bs."

The radio is silent for too long before he comes back with, "No rush then. Over."

I roll my eyes at him. Christ, that man and his damn soft side. Probably thinks if we're stuck out here together long enough, I'll cave on my long-standing no relationship, no women getting tangled up in my life rule. Look how that turned out last time.

"So, he's coming eventually, then?" Evie says. Her pretty face is still carrying worry, although not as intense as before.

"He'll be here when he can. Might as well make yourself comfortable. It'll be a while."

The radio whines. "You still there, Cal? Over."

"Yup. Over."

"Hang tight. Be there as soon as I can. Over."

The lilt in his voice doesn't have me convinced.

"Ten-four. Over and out."

I hang the handpiece back on the radio body and drop into the captain's seat, running a hand through my hair. Evie walks the deck, looking out at the gentle, rolling water. At least the weather is mild. Be a different story if a storm rolled in. With nothing better to do, I wander to where she stands at the stern. The ocean's constant breeze plays with her long dark hair, and her clothes have dried already in the morning sunshine. But she shivers with her arms wrapped around herself.

"How's the book coming along?" I ask.

She turns to face me and offers a small smile. "Okay, I guess."

By the way her smile falls, she doesn't believe a word she said.

"What's it about?"

Now, she scoffs. "You don't want a rundown. It wouldn't be your genre."

I fold my arms over my chest and tilt my head to one side. "Try me."

She drops her gaze to the deck and sucks in a breath. Damn, woman, not this timid bullshit. Not again.

If there's one thing I could give her during her time on Fire Island, it would be to lose the Miss Meek-and-Mild and harness that feisty side of hers. The streak of the fiery girl I've seen only a few times. It's addictive. Maybe it's a good thing she's not like that all the time. Make my life a hell of a lot harder, not being to be able to control the effect she has on me.

Luckily for me, she stands unsure and fidgeting like if the real world can see who she really is, she'll fall apart.

"Romance, then?" I ask, hazarding a guess.

"There's romance in it," she says, shifting on her feet.

"What's the main story?" It's like getting blood out of a stone.

"Um, fantasy. Pirates and all that." She waves a hand in a half circle, not looking at me.

"Sounds fun?" I raise an eyebrow at her again for the second time in an hour. And if her chest wasn't rising and plummeting like she's about to have a panic attack, I'd push further. But I'm not that man, the one who gets off on making women feel small, so I don't.

Not that the small town I grew up in would verify that statement.

"Not really, not anymore," she says. She sounds defeated. *Not anymore.*

Her words take me aback.

Like it's something that she loved once before but no longer does. "What changed?"

Deep for a conversation between us, I guess. But what else do we have to do?

Now, brown eyes flick up, and she purses her lips before folding her arms over her body. She looks like a deer caught in the proverbial headlights, and I hate it. A stone grows in my airway, and I have no idea why I am feeling this way over a woman almost half my age, who I have made a point to stay away from.

A woman who is temporarily on my island. Temporarily in my life.

Old wounds, scabbed but never fully healed, seep through my soul, burying their way into my bones. Some days are better than others, but right now, the ache blooms to life as I watch her work through whatever is going through her mind.

"It's okay, you don't have to tell me. Just killing time."

I wander to the cabin and open the small cooler, fishing out two sodas before returning to the stern and handing her one.

"Thanks," she breathes.

I crack mine open and swallow the first few mouthfuls down. We stand in silence, simply staring out at the water, and a million things I want to ask—and a few things I want to say—fly through my mind. Staving off the need to fill the quiet, I continue drinking. Evie nurses hers as she moves to sit on the side of the boat and trails a finger through the condensation on the can. Her elegant digit tracks the logo before rounding the bottom and gripping the cold can between both hands.

"I used to love writing fantasy and romance. Romantasy, they call it." A sad smile slips over her face.

"Yeah?"

I sit beside her, leaving enough deck between us that we don't touch. Just.

"But . . ." She inhales and closes her eyes briefly. "Then, my husband died."

My mouth slackens, and I can't catch my next breath. *That*, I was not expecting.

"Shit, I'm sorry," I say quietly.

Evie huffs a laugh, but it's as sad and strained as the look that now claims her face. "Me too." Downing the last of her soda, she meets my gaze. "It was five years ago. Car accident."

"Fuck, that's terrible."

"It was that and more. My wedding dress was ruined," she says with a forced lilt, eyes lifting to the sky.

As the words register, my gut sinks, lungs stalling out. "Christ, Evie."

She scrunches up her face, desperate to stem tears. But it takes her by surprise, and one falls.

Fuck.

Swiping the moisture from her cheeks, now pinked, she shakes her head. "I haven't talked about it with someone I hardly know before. Guess it feels different telling you. Somehow it doesn't feel as hard."

My heart aches for her.

Because I've been where she is. Was.

No car accident, something slower. More preventable. Something I took the blame for, and still do.

I resist the urge to hug her. It won't help, if experience has taught me anything. Being wrapped in sympathy only serves to prolong things. Who in their right mind would want to prolong a grief so deep?

"Now, you tell me yours." Her eyes hold me to the spot.

"Mine?"

"Yeah. The reason you're holed up on an island by yourself, in the prime of your life."

A huffy laugh escapes my lips. *Prime, my ass.*

"Just the consequence of many choices—some good, some bad."

"You ever think about leaving the lighthouse and rejoining civilization?"

"Not too often, no."

"Really? You don't get lonely?"

I didn't. Not before she turned up on that damn marina dock. Now, the thought of going back to me, myself, and I seems more wrong than it should.

"Nah, I enjoy my own company. Besides, the conversation's always on point."

She raises one elegant brow. "You talk to yourself often?"

"About as much as you do," I say, throwing her my biggest shit-eating grin.

Her cheeks pink again, and she shifts her gaze to the water. I hear her talking to herself in the bedroom. Testing out lines of dialogue and reading out loud when she thinks I'm busy elsewhere.

Shaking her can, Evie rises and takes mine. Her fingers brush over my knuckles, and my skin buzzes to life.

"Trash?" She looks toward the cabin.

"Left console cabinet. Thanks."

She disappears into the cabin, but not before I lock eyes on the sway of her hips. Those long legs, that hourglass shape, her narrow waist. It's all my imagination needs to take off at full speed. I need to readjust myself in my jeans when she bends over, putting the cans in the trash, and her jeans slip down. The red band of her panties peeks over the top.

"What's this yellow device by the trash?" she calls back.

"EPIRB. The emergency position-indicating radio beacon. It activates when it gets wet. So, if you—"

She returns, excited and flushed. "You sink. If you sink, it activates?"

"Yep, that's the idea. The front portion is removable if you're ever in crisis and need immediate assistance."

Evie frowns. "Isn't that what mayday is for?"

"That too."

"Oh, okay."

She drops down beside me, bringing that damn scent of hers that floods in around me. Soft brown eyes study my face as she offers a small smile.

It's going to be the longest few hours I've endured since forever.

Hurry the hell up, Emmett.

Nine

EVIE

Killing time has never been so freeing. No idea why I blurted out 'my husband died' to Callum. I rarely talk about Joshua, unless it's with my family or Allie. And even then, I try to keep my emotions in check. But something about being on this boat in the middle of the wide blue ocean has cracked my heart open. It's a relief to finally say it and not need to relive the entire experience.

Callum listened; he didn't push. Didn't ask for details. It's almost as if he's been there and understands how much it hurts to have to keep repeating the worst moment of your life. That right there is another chink in my armor of staying indifferent to the man who's given me his home, fed me, taxied me back and forth, and kept me warm with a constant stream of firewood in the last few colder days.

I force the memory of him naked in my bed from my mind.

The sun is starting to set when we sit on the deck, backs against the port side of the gunwale. This old tuna trawler is simple, but it's sturdy. Engine troubles aside, it's been reliable over the last few months. As we wait, we exchange childhood stories and details about our families. I now know how important Iris is to him. His parents are no longer here, but it sounds like they had a great relationship before.

Similar to me and mine, I guess.

Although my parents are still alive. Living their best life in the city. I also learned he is almost eighteen years older than me, has had one serious relationship, and that he and Emmett have been friends since high school. My back aches and I stretch, arms over my head. I turn on my seat and lay on the deck. The pain in my lower spine fades instantly. I moan as the release sinks into my muscles.

Callum stares straight ahead, his throat working.

Eventually his gaze lowers to wander over my outstretched body. His throat bobs again, and I train my attention to the pink and orange sky. It's brilliant. "You should see this, Callum. It's incredible."

I'm sure he's seen it many times before. The wonder is probably lost on him. But when he groans and moves beside me, laying down, I smile.

"Which color do you like best, the pink that keeps

getting lighter, or the orange that is set on turning gold?" he asks.

"Can I say both?"

"You can make whatever choice you want."

I chuckle and glance at him. "Both. I choose both."

"Rebel."

His face breaks into a grin, the blue of his eyes lighting up. It takes everything I have to stop myself from letting my fingers wander to his jaw, over the short-kept beard, his mustache. What would his lips feel like under my fingertips? This softness about him is new. And I wonder if opening up about my life is the reason. I turn onto my side to face him, sliding my hands under my head. I take him in for the next moment. Then the one after that.

His eyes don't move from the colorful sky, but his hands drop to his sides, mere inches from me. I swear his nostrils flare as he says, "Em should be here any second."

Like some freak telepathic event, the drone of another engine fades into range. The sinking feeling of disappointment is heavy in my gut. On an inhale that's sharper than the last, I clear my head by slamming my eyes shut, reminding myself of my reality.

I'm here to work. To get the slip on my stalker.

The torment-free weeks have been bliss. The fact that I'm literally isolated from the rest of the world has let me relax for the first time in I don't know how long. No more looking over my shoulder. Making sure I'm always with someone else, mostly Allie.

Callum pushes to his feet, and I make my way up to mine in twice the time.

A huge Coast Guard vessel adorned with an abundance of equipment of all sorts peters to a low growl as it closes in on us. The man behind the wheel sends her sideways before tossing a rope over. One that Callum catches and ties off onto a double-ended lug-type thing. The two boats bob on the water, now side by side. Emmett, I assume—I didn't pay much attention to him when I first arrived—leaves his boat idling as he boards Firefly.

"Cal." His arms have Callum in a man hug a second later.

"Hey, bud. She just crapped out."

The Coast Guard officer slides his beanie from his head with a nod to me. "Miss Eve."

I chuckle at his formality. "Hi, Emmett."

"Picked a good day for it, at least." He nods to the trap-door in the deck floor, his dark brown eyes narrowing.

"Yeah, right. Had plans today," Callum grunts.

I suppress the need to roll my eyes at his quick change of mood. From lying on the deck with me, shuttling back and forth stories, to all business and gruff. Not that I don't enjoy both. It's the transition that gets me.

"What plans you have?" Emmett shoves him and drops to his knees, flipping the door open.

The stench of the electrical burn is worse, I swear.

"Shit, Cal. You're lucky you got as far as you did." Emmett waves a hand over the opening, leaning back a little. "Debris in the heat exchanger. It's overheated then melted anything within six inches around it. Hell."

"Dammit." Callum runs his hands through his hair. It stays messed up as he drops his hands and sinks to his knees by his friend. "Any chance of fixing it now?"

Emmett shakes his head. "Nah, even if I clear out the heat exchanger, your wires are exposed. You're going to have worse problems if you try to run her like this."

With a heavy sigh, Callum pushes back to his feet. "Give us a tow back to the island, then?"

"You sure? You'll both be stuck there till I can get back out to fix it." Emmett's stare swings between Callum and me.

"It's okay. We'll make do," I offer. The last thing I'm going to do is be a burden to one more person.

Callum holds my gaze for a beat before nodding.

"Tie her off up front. I'll take it steady." Emmett jumps over, back into his boat. He sends her forward. Next thing, he is tossing a rope to Callum, now standing on the bow.

"Sit down and hold on, Evie," Callum calls as the rope pulls out, wiggling out some of the slack.

He's back in the cabin before I find a place to sit. As my butt hits the deck and I lean against the port wall, the slack disappears, and we're tugged forward in the water with a bustling jerk. The Coast Guard vessel is bigger than ours. This old fishing tub against Emmett's shiny service boat. Callum glances over his shoulder, as if checking I'm still on board before flipping the radio to another channel.

"Coast Guard One, do you read? Over."

Static hums back before Emmett says, "Coast Guard to Firefly, copy. Over."

"How long will the parts take for this old girl, Em? Over."

"Maybe three weeks. Depends on stock. This is what you get for your lack of mechanical skills."

Callum scoffs a laugh. "Yeah, right. What else would you be doing today, bud?"

The formal vernacular between the men drops to the wayside.

"For your information, McCreary, I had plans, also."

"Yeah, with who?"

"Not over the radio, you idiot."

Chuckling, I turn my face away. For two burly grown men, they are ridiculous. It's hilarious. I rock with the boat as we slowly make our way back to Fire Island. Something familiar blooms in my chest when the lighthouse comes into focus. Maybe it's because this place is the first to feel safe after so long. Or maybe it's the unfiltered, uncomplicated company I keep out here. Either way, content is what I am when we slip up beside the dock.

No! No. No. No.

Ugh. I push my laptop away and screech an unflattering sound as I jolt out of the chair so fast it topples backward and hits the floor.

Why can't I get this?

How is something so simple, something carried out by millions of humans every single day, evading me with such intensity?

I mean, come on! How hard is it to write a freaking sex scene?

Pulling at my hair, I pace the room. Everything I write is either cliché or like porn that your deviant hermit cousin wouldn't even want to read.

Sweet hell on earth, this is killing me.

I stalk back and forth past the window, and jerk with a start when a concerned Callum flies through the doorway, breathing heavy.

I—

Oh . . .

"What was that damn noise?" he snaps, his gaze tracking to the upturned chair near the desk.

"S-sorry." I pluck it up and shove it under the desk. His eyes track the full length of my body, assessing for what I assume he thinks is damage. I feel exposed. After hours of trying to write one *particular* scene, it's all I can do to not combust where I stand under his heated stare.

"You okay?" he rasps before his Adam's apple bobs on a swallow.

"Yep," I say, too fast. "All good here."

He raises a brow, leaning a little to one side to look at the desk. "Right, well, if you got a minute, I want to show you something." Shoving his hands in the back pockets of his jeans, his tight T-shirt stretches over his chest. Straining over his broad shoulders. Around bulging biceps . . .

I huff a wobbly breath. "Sure, what is it?"

"You'll see." His face lights up. "Come on, it's outside."

He disappears back through the door. After a beat, I suck in a breath and follow. I find Callum waiting outside the front door. I swipe up my sun hat from the hook by the door and pat down my shorts before folding the collar up of my blue-toned checked shirt. I always get burned, and it's the middle of the day.

Callum's boots scrunch on the gravel as we make our way toward the greenhouse. The day is stunning. With that last bitter cold snap gone, it's all blue skies and soft ocean breeze, the call of birds echoing out from the small island forest. The one place I haven't ventured into yet—the forest and beyond to the south end. Maybe one day . . .

Callum stops at the doors to the greenhouse and turns back. "Close your eyes."

"What? No."

"Evie," he hums my name in a deep sound that travels the length of my body.

With a huffy sigh, I relent. "Fine."

I close my eyes and raise my hand in front of my face. His warm one closes around mine, sending something ethereal through me.

"Don't worry, I won't run you face-first into anything hard." The lilt of his words almost makes me want to crack my eyes open.

With a gentle tug on the hand connected to his, we move forward. From the warm air that swallows me, I figure we're inside the greenhouse. The scent of fresh earth, plant life, and fertilizer turns pungent. It is dead quiet, apart from our footsteps. We finally come to a halt, and he drops my hand and manhandles me by the shoulders, turning me to the left.

"Where are we?" I say, eyes still closed.

"At the back of the greenhouse, where the herbs and edible flowers are. Spring has officially sprung, and I wanted to show you this. You can open your eyes."

My eyes drift open to find bursts of color. All of a sudden, I can smell every herb, smell the scents of the roses, nasturtiums, and other delicate-looking flowers. And they are covered in something yellow, flat . . . Flitting. Busy as a—

Buzzing, or something like it, floods every limb.

"Watch this," Callum says. He steps forward and claps his hands.

Hundreds of lemon-colored butterflies burst from the plants, rising in a cloud of wings.

I stagger backward.

Air leaves my lungs and I choke, trying to catch the next breath. Griping my body tight with both hands, I splutter out a small cry before spinning back and running from the greenhouse like he just let off shrapnel, not elegant insects.

A strangled moan works my throat as I rush to the house, trip up the spiral staircase, and fall into the bedroom.

Knees to my chest, I slide backward until I hit the bed.

What the hell is wrong with me?

firefly

Ten

CALLUM

What the hell?

I stand in a cloud of yellow wings as the butterflies flit their startled way around the warm space, hovering like they're unsure if it's safe to come back down. Not dissimilar to what I witnessed cross Evie's expression. Before terror took over her beautiful face, that is. That shakes me from where I stand. I stalk from the greenhouse and into the house. The living room is empty.

Taking the stairs two at a time, I strain to hear what she might be doing, where she might be. Hesitating short of the threshold of the bedroom, I run a hand through my hair when I see her on the opposite side of the bed. Evie sits on the floor, shoulder pressed into the side of the bed, head bent. Her shoulders shake.

Fuck.

I lean on the doorjamb and close my eyes, listening to her ragged, too-quick breaths. Nobody has a reaction to butterflies like that without some kind of trigger. I'm no shrink, but even I get that. What could she possibly associate the tiny insect with?

Her exhales choke out like an old steam train short of coal. Lead sinks in my gut, burning a hole through my chest.

Like that makes any damn sense.

"Evie?" Her name is a low, raw sound.

She hiccups through a rough gasp.

"I-I'm . . . " Her head lifts before her hands swipe at her face.

Christ's sake. "If I'd known . . ."

Head shaking swiftly, she says, "How could you?"

"Yeah, I guess." I push off the jamb and step into the room. "Need a hug?"

What the hell, Callum? Where in the devil's diaper did that come from?

But listening to her distress is tearing my insides up something fierce. I've developed a soft spot for this sweet little author. Which is, by anyone's count, a dangerous thing to hold when we are literally isolated on this island for months together. To my surprise, she wobbles to her feet and faces me.

Her face is all blotches and red eyes, and I grind my molars at the sight. Before I know it, my arms open wide and she closes the distance, pressing herself against my body, her head sinking into the crook of my neck. I still at the proximity.

Shit, this wasn't my brightest move.

I will the blood rushing south to retreat.

She sniffs and her hand lands on my chest, somewhere over my heart, and I can't help what happens next.

My arms fold around her.

Enveloped in my hold, she softens further. The overwhelming tangle of need and the desperation to keep her from harm play parlor tricks on my mind. Her breathing steadies, and we stand wrapped together like it's the most natural thing in the whole damn world. The moment burns a little against the memory of the last time I embraced someone I held dear right here.

I release Evie and step back, my breathing now escalated.

"Sorry, I—" I grab the doorjamb, swing through the opening, and plummet down the stairs. A heartbeat later, sunshine hits my face. I suck in air like a drowning sailor with one last hope of survival.

That was way too close. Way too real.

My first plan was the better one. Where I keep my distance. Where she writes her book and goes home.

Where I keep my loner existence. And the rest of the world can keep their grudge.

Hell knows it was well earned.

After a light meal and a sit out under the stars, I rise from the outdoor chair with a groan. This old man is ready for bed.

"I'm calling it a night," I say to Evie, who is currently reading a novel in the dark outside with a night-light, wrapped in a blanket.

She doesn't respond, so I head for the house.

"Where are you going?" She looks up, confused.

She didn't hear me. Must be a good book.

"Bed. You coming?"

As if we're an old married couple. Not likely, but after that freezing night, she insisted I sleep in the bed and not on the bunk in the hut. I think she felt bad. Hell, I know she did. Who am I to argue? Being back in my own bed is heaven.

Catching the sarcasm, she frowns, staring at me for a beat before saying, "Just one more chapter."

"Suit yourself."

When her gaze returns to the novel in her hands, I push through the door and head upstairs. Stripping off, I make quick work of a shower and tug on my boxers and a T-shirt. I grab up the book on my nightstand and open it to the place the bookmark holds.

I start to doze off, and the old tome slides from my hands as I hear footsteps ascending the stairs. With a yawn, Evie walks in, novel in hand.

Hell, we *look* like an old married couple.

The pillow wall dividing her side of the bed from mine knocks that notion out of the park. And when she pads to the bathroom to change and reappears in a summer nightie, I pluck up my reading material and stare at the black marks over the pages.

Words.

Look at the words, Cal. Not at the nightie that barely makes it past her ass. The satin material that sticks to her curves. Christ's sake, at this rate, I'm going to have to hide a raging erection behind that goddamn pillow wall. Or use the book for a tent. She climbs into bed, rubbing moisturizer over her arms. Setting my novel on the nightstand, I get up and shut the door, not wanting the cooler morning air to tumble down and roll into the room tomorrow.

Half-erect, I shoot back under the covers before she can catch a glimpse. Sitting up, I lean my head on the headboard as she dons more lotion. Grinding my jaw shut and closing my eyes, I think of every horrid thing my mind can drag up.

Something drops. The mattress moves, and I open my eyes. She's leaning over, the nightie ridden up to display the lacy red panties that cover her ass.

Sweet Christ above.

"You good?" I rasp.

"I dropped the lid . . . I think it rolled underneath?"

I slip out of bed and round the end. Dropping to my knees beside her, I duck down, searching for it. Sure enough, it's sitting under the bed, right in the center. Swiping at it, I manage to grasp it. Ducking back up, I smack my head on the frame.

"Fuck!"

I rub a hand over the spot, the ache blooming.

"Oh, are you okay?"

Something red and silky comes into view. A hand brushes my forehead. Brown eyes laced with worry drop to find mine.

"Fine," I rasp.

She's too close.

"You want me to go grab some ice?"

"Nope, all good." I go to rise, but her hand settles on my shoulder. We are inches apart. The lace-trimmed V-neck of her nightie and spaghetti straps expose her. But it's my chest that's plummeting with every fall. She's too sweet. Smells too fucking good and . . .

She is far too close. I wrap my fingers around hers and remove them from my shoulder. "Go to sleep, Evie."

"Oh—yeah, sorry."

A nervous laugh slips past those delicious lips of hers.

I clear my throat, desperate to put distance between us.

"Here's the lid." I hold it out, and she takes it from my

fingers. The slightest touch douses my lungs in fire before the heat dives lower.

I round the bed and crawl into my side. Patting the pillow wall for good measure, I lie back and get comfortable. Satisfied the blankets are hiding my rock-hard cock, I slide a hand under my head. The other is still draped over the pillow wall. Like even my body can't stand the idea of not being near her.

She turns the lamp off and we lie in silence, listening to each other's labored breathing.

Fine fingers lace through my hand. "Sorry about your head."

I want this pillow wall to fuck off for good so I can rip that scant little nightie from her body. Instead, I give her fingers a squeeze before reclaiming my hand. "Forget about it. Night."

She sighs, rolling over. "Night, Callum."

Legs for days, crossed one over the other, lie bare in the spring sunshine. Evie lounges on the outdoor Adirondack chair, her laptop on the small matching table beside her, sunglasses on her face, and arms draped over the sides of the chair. Her eyes are closed, her music so loud I can hear it over my own hard breathing as I chop wood.

I ignore her.

The threadbare T-shirt she's wearing may as well be nonexistent. Those tiny fucking shorts . . .

I swing the axe above my head, trying to get my mind homed in on the task at hand before I lose a limb. The price you pay for being distracted around a sharpened tool like this one is high. My tools are always kept in pristine condition, like my dad did before me. With that memory, a thought flicks through my head. What would he think of Evie?

Why am I asking that metaphorical, pointless question?

She's far too young.

She's leaving.

She's better off far away from Fire Island. And its damn lighthouse keeper.

I swing the axe into the stump, as if to prove my last point.

A soft moan sounds from behind me. I miss the block entirely, and the head of the axe ghosts past my leg with a brush of air.

"Fuck me."

I let the axe hang in my hand, my head doing the same as I swipe the other hand through my sweaty hair. Dropping the axe, I tug my shirt from my back and pluck up the tool, not bothering to look over my shoulder at the cause of my distraction.

"Get your shit together, McCreary," I mutter.

"Did you say something?" Evie calls, too loud. My guess is her headphones are still on.

"Nope!" I grunt and shake my body out, as if that will dislodge the pent up whatever-the-hell-it-is that's eating at me today.

Well, that's been eating at me since that fucking hug, if I'm honest. Every night I've slept beside her. With the goddamn pillow wall.

Knew that nice-guy bullshit would come back to bite me in the ass. Should've let her cry alone.

That'll be the last time I fall for those pretty brown eyes. That soft smile. The elegant shape of her—

Nope.

Shut it down, bud.

I all but groan at myself. Christ, this is pathetic. I'm forty-fucking-three years old and I'm up in my head like a teenager with his first boner over the girl next door.

Just when my problem couldn't get worse, those long legs, now a little more tanned than the first day they saw sunlight here, move into my field of vision. "Need some help? I could work in the garden . . ."

I glance at her. Headphones around her neck, the soft pads resting on her collarbones. That useless T-shirt, tied into a knot at one side, is hugging every curve of her chest, dipping low. A slim section of belly peeks between the shirt and shorts. She palms her long chocolate locks, dragging them around her neck. They tangle and fall over her breast by the headphones, and I slam the axe into the chopping block. "Go back to your writing."

The words are too harsh. And it shows as shock and a little hurt twist her face.

"Oh, okay. Sorry I bothered you." Her face falls to something impassive, and she turns and heads back to the outdoor chairs. She rounds the firepit when I release a long sigh.

This girl is going to be the death of me.

Jesus fucking Christ.

"Why do you do that bullshit?" I snap at her back.

Arms folded around her body, she spins back to me. Her lips are smashed together as her brows lower and she ponders my words. "Do what, Callum?"

"That." I wave a hand at her passive posture. Her retreat from something she wanted at the first sign of discomfort. She wanted to garden, but just gave up at the first sign of resistance.

The image of her running from the butterflies springs to mind.

"I have no idea what you're talking about." But her hands drop by her sides. As if her understanding doesn't align with her words.

I stalk to where she stands and tilt her chin up, forcing

her gaze to mine with one finger. "This timid-little-mouse bullshit. You like it when the world makes your life miserable, Eve?"

Her mouth gapes.

Hell, I've been wanting to say these words to her since the day she arrived here to find herself squared away with a man she'd never met in the middle of the fucking ocean. With no Wi-Fi, rare cell service, and no way off this rock without me. A normal person would have a fit about this situation, especially if it was forced on them. But she swallowed it like a good girl. Simply laid down and let Livvy walk all over her.

"You're here with me. You don't want to be. You always do as you're told?" I bite out.

Her face curls with annoyance.

That's better.

Her arms snap back over her chest, and she jerks her head sideways, away from my touch. "Don't touch me."

"You sure? You like doing what everyone else tells you."

She gasps. Her breathing kicks up. "You are an utter ass, you know that? To think we were friends!"

I scoff an incredulous laugh. I could never be her friend. Not anymore. Not after the last time I touched her.

"We're not friends, so get that out of your head right now."

Hurt claims her face, and she tamps back a sob. I may as

well have stabbed her through the heart, by the look on her face.

She takes a step back. Typical.

I'm out of bounds with my behavior. And I laid inches from her last night for hours, willing the feel of her in my arms, her scent that soaked into my shirt, and her timid damn heart that's sunk its way under my rib cage to be anywhere but near me.

With a grunt, I hang my head, peering up through my lashes as she walks back to the house. Her things sit in the sun where she left them.

Suppose that's for the best, because if she turned back and handed me my ass right now, that would be the last chink in my armor with this girl. As it stands, I have spent the last months convincing myself I don't want anything from her. From anyone else. No woman would ever need to live through Callum McCreary again.

Not if I can help it.

I walk back to the chopping block, feeling like the biggest asshole on the planet. Mid-swing, I groan. I took it too far. Serves me right. Should have kept my distance from the start, not going around telling childhood stories and holding her in my arms mid-panic attack. Awareness pings through my body at the mere thought of holding her.

The gravel crunches, and I turn too late.

Something hard hits my shoulder. Evie stalks toward me, brown eyes blazing. She stands, shoulders shaking, chest heaving. Her gaze drops to the item that hit me and fell to the ground, and I follow it with my own.

My journal sits open, pages down, gravel dusted over the cover.

I forgot about the old book. It's been months since I wrote in it. Before Evie arrived, I penned the last entry. The ones in there cover the last three years or so.

"Where is he?" she growls. Her finger points at me and eventually lands over my heart as she closes the space between us.

I glance at the journal.

He?

"Where is the man in this journal?" She glares at me.

"He—I—"

"The kind, smart, generous man in these pages. What the hell did you do with him, Callum?"

Fuck me.

I can only stare at her. Her fire is stunning. Brown eyes lit up with more life than most people could ever wish to hold. It's all I can do to think of what Evie would be like if she opened up. Really walked into her light instead of cowering in the shadows like she's been doing since she got here. Since who knows how long.

She's so close. "Answer. Me."

My body vibrates at her proximity. Blood having well and truly left my brain, every drop is holed up south. My cock aches relentlessly. So I do what any man who's stupid crazy over a girl would do. I wrap my palms around her face and crash my mouth over hers.

She jerks backward, hand flying up and pressing over her mouth.

I don't move from the spot. Couldn't if I wanted to.

Which I damn well don't.

I wait as she processes the line we just crossed.

Her hand drops away from her face and she steps up to me, sucking in a breath. "What was that for?"

"Because I felt like it."

A beat passes before she responds, "Wrong answer."

Evie's eyes burn into mine as she invades my senses. Her closeness. Her scent, all flowers and spice. The tension that hangs between us like party lights swinging in the breeze as a storm rolls in to drench the unsuspecting guests. The glass bulbs, our fragile hearts. The cord, the choices we made that brought us right here in this moment.

She raises to her tiptoes and inches closer, her breath hitting my face. My palms burn to claim hers.

Her gaze drops to my mouth.

Each breath that cycles through me singes a little more than the last.

She raises her hand, fingertips brushing over my jaw. My eyes shutter closed.

"Callum?"

Eleven

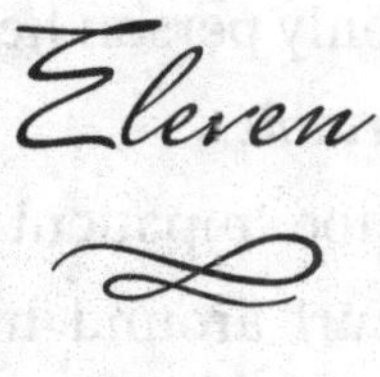

EVIE

Hell will freeze over before I find myself in another relationship. At least, that's how I've seen my life for the last five years. My fingers sweep over his short beard. The tips hover over his mustache. I'm like a little girl exploring her father's face for the first time after a long time.

No, Evie.

We are *not* creating a daddy kink.

Crap on a cracker.

I mean, Callum *is* older than me. To be fair, age has never bothered me before. Our family has their share of age gap romances. For a while, when I first started writing, it was one of my favorite tropes.

And with him in front of me, I don't see age. I don't see

older. I see a stoic, grounded man who may have rough edges, but they soften for me. They have begun to . . .

At least, I think they have?

Maybe that's the hopeless romantic in me.

Or the fact I'm the only person he's ever around.

We've gotten *comfortable*.

His head dips, as if too impatient, with the barest hint of restraint. My fingers curl around his jaw before they slip away.

"I need a minute," I whisper.

His eyes turn darker, desperate almost.

Struggling through the next breath, every inch of my body warms. Even this small distance between us is too far. Callum's throat works as he runs a hand through his messy hair, his biceps flexing. The doubt, as if worried he misread the signals, flickers through his eyes.

That ghost of an expression steals the last of my air. It creates an ache between my ribs seeing this steadfast, amazing man crumble in the slightest. I can't take it—

I eliminate the space between us and pull his face to mine. Automatically, his mouth responds. This time, there isn't one sliver of indecision. The self-doubt I usually carry around like a set of Gucci luggage falls away instantly. He's hungry, not gentle. His hands slide under my butt, and I'm hoisted up to his hips. Wrapping my legs around his waist, I let my hands wander through his messed-up, unruly hair.

Nipping my bottom lip, he groans. I open and he plunders his way in, and it makes my head spin. His touch. His body tangled with mine. His taste. Mint and coffee.

Heart slamming in its cage, I push back.

I pant, trying to steady my breaths and my heart rate. His eyes are the darkest blue I've ever seen them. That snaps me from this lust-infused moment. "Callum, we shouldn't."

His forehead presses to my own as his eyes close. "I know."

It's then I feel his hardness beneath me. Hell, my panties are the slickest they've been in forever.

I'm not saying the release wouldn't be worth it. But we have to coexist for months to come. We can't complicate this. Still, his arms hold me firmly to his body. And I realize I don't want to be put down. I don't want him to let go.

Right here, I'm safe. I feel wanted.

Ridiculous as that sounds for a five-minute fling that only consists of one almost kiss and one hot-as-hell, soul-shattering one.

He studies my face. "I'm sorry, I got carried away with your rant and—"

My fire is what got him all riled up?

Interesting . . . and noted.

I chuckle and lean back, face tilting to the sun. His hands rise behind my shoulder blades. Still keeping me safe. Meeting his gaze when my laughter peters out, I suck in a wobbly breath. The things we're learning about each other.

Some of this feels like I'm giving away parts of me I can't get back.

Maybe I don't want them back?

It could be possible.

"You good?" he says, eyes crinkling with amusement and confusion.

Oh crap. Guess my inner monologue got away with me again.

"Yeah, I'm good." Releasing my legs from his waist, my feet hit the warm ground a second later. I dot a peck to his cheek. "Sorry."

Too chicken to stand this close to him any longer, I turn back and head toward the house. When I reach the front door, I can't help myself. I glance back. He stands where I left him, hands hanging by his sides. The look of disbelief flattening his face sends my heart racing again. He's probably regretting what just happened. That look of shock will most likely fade to one of annoyance when his brain reunites with sufficient blood flow.

I putter around the kitchen, and my stomach grumbles. But my head is still lost back somewhere in the very close proximity of Callum. Absentmindedly, I throw together a salad, chopping up last night's left over chicken breast and adding it into the mix. I tug the refrigerator door open and hunt down the Italian dressing.

Movement from outside catches my eye. Muscle-bound arms swing an axe over his bare chest, slamming it into the unsuspecting stump on the block. It shatters into little pieces. The growl he looses drifts through the open window on the ocean's light breeze. The poor stump didn't stand a chance.

Fancy that. A little sass and this man is wound up like a mid-June twister.

I flip the lid on the dressing, still watching Callum as I pour the liquid over the salad leaves. He raises the tool again, turning to the side as he lines up his target. The blade descends at a lightning pace, and the timber cracks right through. He tosses one half from the stump and glances toward the house.

I squeak out a sound.

Something cold and wet splashes my hands.

Shit!

Dressing douses the counter. My salad is drowning in the briny liquid. "Shoot. Ugh."

I flip the lid closed and return the dressing to the fridge. Great, that flavor's going to keep coming back up all afternoon. But with all food accounted for with our trips to the mainland still only every fortnight, I can't waste it. Who knows when Emmett will be back to fix the boat.

I find a fork and sink into a chair at the table. It takes some effort to push it down, but I finish the salad. The door swings open, and Callum strides in, arms loaded with wood.

"Just in case," he says, not looking at me. He marches to the fireplace in the living room.

Great. Now he can't even look at me.

The weather has been nicer. I wonder why he thinks I need a restock? I assume he understands something about the way weather works on the island I haven't learned yet. Why else is he still bringing firewood?

"Going up to the lamp today?" I ask, trying to sidestep the elephant in the room.

As he bends down and starts unloading the wood, I take my plate to the sink to wash up and wait for him to answer. To look at me. For this to not be incredibly weird.

I mean, that kiss was . . .

Straight outta some epic romantasy.

I run the hot water, adding the soap. Distracted, I pour too much into the water, and it bubbles over.

Dammit.

The overwhelming desire to write slides through my veins, infiltrating my mind. My daydreaming whirs to life like a long-suffering diesel engine at the end of the hardest winter.

Good lord, Evie, enough with the analogies.

I roll my eyes at myself and take the dish rag and swirl the suds through the bowl. The heat of the water sends tingles through my hands. My fingers ache with the heat. I make quick work of it, setting the bowl and fork on the rack to drain. After I've wiped down the suds and dried my hands, I spin around and lean on the counter, hands gripping the edge of the sink.

Callum's gone.

Footsteps shuffle upstairs. Pursing my lips, I decide to confront the elephant. Even if I can't say anything in the moment, at least I can get some spicy words in. It occurs to me that the kiss, those fleeting minutes of his hands on my body, on my face, was the best inspiration—or research—I've had in a long time.

Yep, that's what I could put it down to. Research . . .

I find Callum in the bedroom, restocking the woodpile by the smaller fireplace by the bed. Now it's my turn to lean on the doorjamb and stare at him. And I do.

"Needing something?" he grunts out, losing the last log to the pile.

He's sweaty. Which again raises the question of the need for firewood now.

"I have a question. Well, many, but one is whirring out my head more than the others—"

"Spit it out, Evie." He stands and brushes his hands on his jeans. The T-shirt is now stained with sweat, a little dirt, and sawdust. He sets his jaw, and I swear that does something to me, low in my belly.

The thrilling yet unsettling feeling grows wings, flying off with the question I thought of a second ago.

"What did you want to ask?" Callum says, his eyes glancing from me to the bed.

His bed.

The one I am currently occupying as he tries to stay out

of his own house to accommodate me during the day. Sleeping on one half every night—with a literal wall of pillows I insisted on. Guilt weaves a gnarled path through me, and my gaze follows his as it tracks to where I stand. Despite his gruff demeanor, Callum has been looking after me since the second my feet touched this island. In one capacity or the other.

"Can I cook you dinner?" I blurt out. Not the question I originally wanted to ask. But the one that fits now.

He raises an eyebrow and tilts his head.

"I want—I mean, to say thank you and sorry?" I cringe at my own stupid words.

Writer who?

"Eve—"

I hold up a hand. "Please, let me make it up to you for . . ." Unable to look at him as my neck and face heat fast, I whisper, "God, I'm so embarrassed."

He folds his arms over his chest, brows lowering. "Crawling all over me like a cat in heat, you mean?"

His face cracks, the biggest shit-eating grin struggling to stay restrained.

Oh. My. God.

If I wasn't mortified beyond repair, this could be funny.

A laugh rumbles from him, and I can't help but scoff one of my own. I hide my face in my hands. Footsteps pad to where I stand. Warm hands peel my hands from my face.

"You don't need to apologize. I'm a grown man, Evie. If I didn't want it, I would have walked away."

He drops my hands and walks from the room.

I turn, mouth gaping, as he makes the staircase. Reaching it, he turns back, one hand on the railing. He stares at me for a beat as if considering the words he's going to use next. "Dinner sounds nice."

The rumble of a boat engine drifts in on the breeze.

"Emmett's here. Back to work, mo nighean," he says, disappearing down the spiral stairwell like he didn't just chip ice from my heart with something I'm sure is Gaelic.

With hours before the sun starts its descent, I do as I'm told. I write. This time, the chemistry is radiating off the page. Any minute now, my laptop screen is going to melt from the intensity of it, I'm sure. All the while, the phrase Callum used plays over and over in the back of my mind. I would love to google it, but no Wi-Fi means that's not an option.

Finishing up the scene I'm working on, I have an idea. Maybe there is some reference to the phrase in his journal.

Oh, that's right, the one I threw at his feet.

Shit.

The voices of Emmett and Callum tangle up to the lighthouse on the warm afternoon air. They sound like they're knee-deep in boat mechanics. Maybe I could go and see if it's in his hut? A quick flip through those weathered pages wouldn't hurt, surely? It's not like I haven't read it before. And it's not like he doesn't know I've read it . . .

I'm rushing down the stairs like a thief on quiet feet before I can formulate a reason not to. I push through the front door and walk around the house, checking they are in fact at the dock.

Emmett laughs, shaking his head as he sits on the deck of the fishing boat. Callum squats beside him, his face showing no sign of the joy capturing Emmett's. What are they talking about?

Remembering my task, I crunch over the gravel and let myself into the small hut.

Inside is neat, with so few items it hardly looks like anyone lives here. If I didn't know better, I'd think nobody did. But I do, and Callum does. Apart from sleep, that is. I find myself frowning as I take in the bareness around me. The journal is on the small table I guess he eats at when he's not in the house with me.

I can't take it. He'll know it's missing. So, I sit at the table and open the leather tome, willing each page turn to quiet down. Guilt amplifies every tiny sound the book makes until it roars around me.

Heavens, I hate this.

My skin heats, and I swear it crawls its way along my bones.

I hunt for the reference. The words *mo nighean*.

Skimming and scanning as fast as my writerly brain allows, I come up empty-handed.

Those two words are not on these pages. Anywhere.

Another burst of laughter carries from the dock, and I startle.

That's it, I can't do this.

I am no villain. It's evident by my squishy insides that can barely tolerate this small breach of privacy, even after that particular horse has bolted. I close the journal and tiptoe from the hut, like somehow he will hear me in his space.

Chastising myself for the stupidity of my thoughts, I cross the threshold into the house. With a sigh, I pad to the kitchen and start another type of hunt.

The kind that ends with a meal shared by two people.

One edible and within my limited culinary abilities.

It can't be that hard, can it?

firefly

Twelve

CALLUM

"Pass us the wrench, will ya?" Em mumbles, head hidden inside the deck opening, face-first into the engine space. His hand reaches for the tool, and I drop it into his grease-stained palm. Tinkering, he huffs before saying something I don't catch.

"You're gonna have to speak up, bud. Can't hear you over all that hard work."

He jerks up, rocking back onto his heels. The wrench points at me as he says, "Don't start something you can't finish, Cal."

I chuckle at him. It's just too easy.

We've known each other for longer than most friendships will ever last, and I know his mind like it's my own. And this man is so damn easy to rile.

My gaze drops to the wrench as he starts reciting every

task he's done today and some he's yet to get to, before rattling off everything he's missed over the years because of his job. Mainly his family.

I gotta admit, his family life can get a little hectic. But at least he has that.

Iris and I are all that's left of our family. In the States, at any rate. Save one cousin in the city, there's nobody else to speak of.

I'm sure I have uncles and aunts, maybe more cousins, in Scotland. But I've never met them. My parents broke off all ties when they left in the middle of the night after both families forbade their relationship. Ended up here, bought the café, and maintained the lighthouse. They must have been happy, because that's the only way I remember them.

"... You coming?"

"Hey, what?"

Em shakes his head and leans back into the engine bay, disappearing from the shoulder and up again.

"I said"—he sits back up and shuts the small door, securing the latch—"Wednesday night. Iris wants you at the café."

"What for?"

But I already know.

Emmett's birthday.

I don't miss the way he won't look at me as he scrubs a hand behind his neck. He's always been coy around Iris.

Like she makes him nervous or something. I wouldn't put it past her. My little sister is as fiery as a woman comes.

"Yeah, sure, birthday boy." I pack up the tools and leave Em to his humiliation.

He groans and shoves his cap back onto his head. The Coast Guard standard-issue cap has been replaced by his old faithful Yankees cap. God, that thing has seen better days.

"Bringing Eve?"

"I don't know," I say, sighing.

"Fuck. What did you do, McCreary?"

I slide the toolbox back onto his boat and take my time squaring it away. When I turn back, Em stands with his arms crossed over his chest. "I know that damn look. Spill it, Cal."

Words fly up my throat and slam into the stone that formed while I was ignoring the question. My mind flies back to the old Scots words from earlier. The look on Evie's face. Like, on some level, she understood them. The same ones my father used to croon to my mother. The way she always softened with them. If I'm honest, I never thought I'd ever use them. Would never have the *chance* to use them . . .

Em takes a step forward but glances back at the lighthouse. "Not everyone in this place thinks you're a monster." His words are soft, like they're meant to placate an injured animal. Maybe in a way, I am. Was. It took me years to recover from what happened. Even more to look myself in the mirror without loathing every single thing I am.

"I'll take your word for it," I finally breathe out.

"I mean it, Cal. It wasn't your fault. How many times do we have to tell you this? How many years is it going to take for you to let someone else in?"

If only he knew.

We—him and Iris. The rest of this small coastal town wishes she was the one to survive, not me.

For a long time, I wholeheartedly agreed with them. Not that it made them think any better of me. If it wasn't for Iris and Em, I'd be long gone. Besides, this island is the last connection to my parents. Our family. The last thing I have of my father.

"So . . . what happened?" Em prompts.

"We—I—I kissed her." My throat works with the act of saying it out loud.

Em tugs the cap from his head and shoves his hand through his hair, blowing out a low whistle. "I don't know if I'm so happy you finally let someone in or annoyed at you for jeopardizing our last hope to save the lighthouse."

My face falls, and a shit-eating grin splits his face. He thumps a fist into my shoulder.

"Not even a choice. I'm happy for you, man. About damn time," he says with a chuckle.

"Don't get excited, it was a mistake. It won't be happening again."

No matter how desperate she had me with one kiss. Touching her. Holding her close . . .

My gaze is stuck on the house, and all of a sudden, I only want to be there.

"What did she say about it?" Em breaks my daydream.

"What?"

"What does Evie think about this?" Em waves a hand at me, like I'm the goddamn merchandise.

"Very funny." I scoff. "She—actually, you know what, I don't want to talk about it, Em." I clap him on the shoulder and disembark the boat. He follows me.

"You can't stay held up on this island by yourself for your entire life. Iris worries about you. She doesn't want you to end up alone." He's calling out to me now as I make my way back up the dock, heading for the house.

And I'm not alone.

Not anymore.

At least for a little while.

When the Coast Guard boat fires up and the throttles purr as it chugs away, I glance back at my best friend. I know he's right. Until I have no reason to stay, I'll be here. If that ever changes, I might try my luck across the ocean in my homeland. Maybe track down my parents' families . . .

A yearning to visit the fishing hut, to be close to my dad, flares like an old memory. Tomorrow. I'll take off and spend the day there. I could use a day to myself.

Reaching the house, I pull my cap from my head and hesitate. I should knock.

On my own damn front door.

Fuck, Em's right. I've let her in. This feels more like a date than eating my own food in my own house. I resist the urge to drop my forehead on the wooden door. Instead, I take the handle in one hand and press it down, pushing through the door.

It's when I see Evie, flustered and looking as out of her depth as I feel, that I realize things have changed between us. They shouldn't have. I should have been smarter about this.

I'm good at denying myself the things I want, usually.

Usually.

Until this woman.

Until Evie took over my spa—

"Oh hey, almost ready. I think?" she pants.

I offer her a soft smile and wander to the living room. This little dinner is going to have to be two friends enjoying a meal. Nothing more.

We can't be anything more.

Evie is rushing around the small kitchen like it's on fire. Give it a minute and it might be, by the smell of whatever she is trying to cook in the pan. I would step in, but the girl is determined to whip up some sort of apology meal. Who am I to interfere?

The frypan sizzles violently.

She whips back, giving whatever's in there a stir, and spins back around to resume chopping furiously. Pieces of cucumber from the garden fly across the counter. The house looks different. Then I see why. Small jars of flowers are dotted around the place. A few on the windowsills. One placed on top of the fireplace. A handful spaced out on the bookshelf.

The bright colors strike me as too familiar.

They're from the greenhouse.

Stolen flowers for an apology dinner.

I tamp down the chuckle wanting out with that little irony. This girl is all irony. Her being here with me—ironic. For years I have lived with others' collective opinion that no woman should be left in my care. Now, for some godforsaken reason, this one has been dropped on my island. Literally.

The spatula clatters to the floor.

Evie jumps sideways. "Shit."

I wander around, taking in the tiny ways my house has changed since she moved in. The coffee table is turned ninety degrees to run parallel between the two sofas. I think I actually like it more. The bookshelf is . . . organized alphabetically. To that, I raise an eyebrow. I had a fucking system.

Geez, is nothing sacred?

The hats and coats are hung in groups; nothing tossed on the wall any old how.

Grunting, I drop onto the sofa. Three books are stacked in a neat-ass pile in the center of the coffee table.

My books.

I pluck up the first one as Evie wipes her brow with the

back of her forearm. The apron she's wearing is pulled tight around her curves as she stands in my kitchen. The damn sight shouldn't raze me to the ground the way it does. She leans over, reading something on her phone, which I'm guessing is screenshot of a recipe or something. Her cleavage pushes against the deep V of her top, the apron doing nothing to cover her.

Fighting the boner off that's sprung at the sight of her, I force my attention back to the book in my hands. My *just friends* plan is coming along brilliantly.

Fuck me.

"Ow!" A spoon clangs onto the counter.

I'm on my feet and marching for the kitchen before the next heartbeat passes.

"It's okay, I've got it." Her pleading brown eyes find mine. "Please, let me do this for you?"

Christ, this begging is going to be the undoing of me.

I fold a hand over hers and raise it between us. As I turn it over, her eyes drop to my mouth before making it to her burned hand.

What is it with this girl and burning herself?

Ushering her to the sink, I run the cold tap and guide her hand into the cool stream of water. She hisses as the water meets the sensitive area.

"No apology meal is worth this much pain," I say.

Evie huffs a breathy laugh and her body rocks into mine as I hold her hand in the water. She's so close.

Too damn close.

"You make a pretty good book boyfriend for a recluse, Callum McCreary." Her words are no more than a whisper.

I raise both brows, and she takes her hand back, stepping back, her gaze shifting to the stove. Then to the chopped-up ingredients still sitting on a cutting board. Anywhere but at me.

"For the record, I'm a lighthouse keeper, not a recluse. And what the hell is a book boyfriend?"

Crimson flushes her neck and face.

And hell, if that doesn't almost take out the last of my restraint.

She swallows before lifting her gaze to mine. "It's a fictional man, written by a woman, who is the perfect combination of protective, loving, handsome, and—" She spins back to the counter and picks up the knife, re-chopping the already finely chopped vegetables. She clears her throat as her flush deepens.

"And?" I prompt, folding my arms and leaning a hip on the counter.

With a sigh, she drops the knife and imitates my stance. "Sexy. Swoony. A filthy-mouthed man who takes what he wants."

She spits out the words so fast, almost as if she's embarrassed. She grabs her neck with both hands, worrying her bottom lip. She *is* embarrassed.

I chuckle and lean forward. "You think I'm sexy, nighean bhrèagha?"

The old words slip out on their own accord with this woman. Something to analyze later.

"I—" Her look of surprise turns to a pouty glare.

My cock twitches.

It's an effort to restrain the grin wanting out over my face. "Uh huh?"

She huffs, closing the space between us.

Fuck, this is going to be harder than I thought.

"What does it mean? Nighean bheag?" she asks.

I raise a hand, wanting to touch her like I've never wanted anything so badly before. Snagging a rogue lock of dark hair, I tuck it behind her ear and lean down until my lips all but brush the elegant tip of it. "It means . . . I'm hungry, Evie. Let me cook, instead."

She jerks backward. "It does not."

The sweetest scowl twists her face. If a man ever needed reason to bend a woman over a countertop and fuck that look off her face, that would be it. I want to be that man.

Christ's sake, Callum.

Her brows lower further, not that I thought it would have been possible, as she says, "What? Your expression changed . . ."

Nope. No way is that last thought going public.

"I want to help. Please let me help?" I ask.

"Fine. Only because my stomach is eating itself, I'm so craptastically hungry."

I crack up with the words that come out of her pretty fucking mouth. Lord save me.

Just another marker forcing me to recognize the age gap between us. But when she hands me her phone with the recipe on the screen, I get to work starting where she left off.

Twenty minutes later, we have a dinner better than anything we've shared since she arrived.

Evie sets the table as I bring the food over. When she sits down, I wander to the counter and hunt through the bottom cupboards. There's a red in here somewhere. Pushing the whiskey aside, I find an old, dusty bottle of cabernet. I slide it out and find two glasses. No wine glasses here. These short tumblers will have to do. I tug the cork from the top and let a generous portion glug into her glass. Evie looks up at me with the sweetest smile.

Maybe we shouldn't add alcohol to this mix . . .

Hell. You know what they say about best-laid plans.

I return the bottle to the counter and fish out my whiskey. It's been a while since I've had an occasion to bring it out. This seems good enough. I sit at the opposite end of the table. Evie leans over and lights the small cluster of candles in the center of the table I didn't notice before.

"So, Iris invited you and I to Emmett's birthday dinner," I say.

Evie forks a bite into her mouth, not answering.

I shovel some food into my own, and it's not half bad.

"What should I get him?" she finally asks. When my face remains blank, she adds, "You know, a birthday present. What does he like?"

"You want to buy Emmett a birthday present?"

"Isn't that usually what you take to a birthday party? Gifts, wine, etc.?"

"He's forty-four, you can skip the Tonka truck wrapped in Batman paper."

She plucks up a vegetable and tosses it at me.

"Hey, that took me months to seed, tend to, and harvest. Don't you go wasting, lassie."

"Lassie! Well, that's not condescending at all. Woof!" Her face is tight, but then it bursts like . . .

Like a cloud of startled butterflies, breaking into a fit of laughter.

Something low and heavy in my gut turns over, sending warmth to my chest. As if the single sound can wrap my wounded heart up and mend it.

I return the assault with a slice of carrot.

Evie flies out of her chair with a squeal, and I grab up a handful of broccoli, hunting her around the room. Hell, if I catch her, the last thing I'll be thinking about is feeding her her greens.

Run, mo nighean.

She backs away toward the bookshelf, grabbing a title out, wielding it in front of her like a damn shield.

Like that will stop me.

"Please," she rasps. "I'm sorry!"

Cackles have her folding over, the book dropping to the floor. I'm on her in a heartbeat, taking her to the ground. With her underneath me, I grab her wrists, pinning them to the floor above her head. She bucks under me, fits of giggles bursting from those pretty damn lips. I straddle her, my knees by her hips.

"What was that, Evie? I didn't hear you. You say something about wasting the hard-earned food I provide for you?" The words slip through a half smirk, half laugh.

Her giggles peter out when she realizes our position. "I'm sorry I wasted your food, Cal."

Cal.

Not Callum.

Or Ass.

Just *Cal.*

Thirteen

EVIE

The harbor is all waving, glittery water, colorful marina lights, and lit-up buildings as the boat slows, gliding into the slip by the second dock. Cal's been chattering away about this tiny seaside town and all its glory since we left the island. It's not like he needs to sell me on this place. Already, I am dreading the thought of returning to the city.

"Jump out and tie us off," he says, eyes lit up like Bay Shore under tonight's bright moon and shimmering stars. I huff a breath and step over the boat's side, praying my footing sticks.

It does, and I turn back in time to catch the rope flying from his hands. Happiness has his face beaming. The moon's got some competition. He and Iris are surely close if she can pry that particular face from this grump of a man. I wouldn't know. Being an only child, the closest person I have to a sibling is Allie. But I imagine my face looks something like joy when she's with me. I hope it does.

The dock is busy.

People mill about their boats. A few are leaving the marina, hauling the mooring ropes in, and some are returning home. It's friendly and oddly comforting to feel the spirit of comradery echoing all around.

"Eve!" A tall figure jumps onto the dock from the parking lot by the Coast Guard building and closes in.

Emmett.

"Hi!"

"Here goes," Cal grunts from somewhere in the boat cabin.

A giggle bubbles through my lips. Emmett folds me into a hug like I'm his long-lost friend, and I let out a surprised squeak.

"Emmett. Happy birthday."

"Thanks, Miss Eve. You bring the grump or captain this old girl yourself?"

Cal appears, pulling his cap off and tossing it back into the cabin, giving Emmett a dirty look. "As if I would miss the one time a year I can talk shit about you."

"Oh, nice. Thought you'd spare me the humiliation in front of Eve."

"Not a chance, bud."

My brows lower of their own accord. "Never mind him."

I turn to Emmett. "I wouldn't believe a word out of that mouth anyway."

Emmett laughs, hearty, as he slaps a hand to Callum's back. "I think I like her more than you."

"Ha ha. See how that pans out. It's all fun and games until she hears about your senior year jock itch and the way Suzie Hamlin had to ice—"

"The fuck, Cal!" Emmett slides the cap from his head and flings it at his best friend.

I wind my arm through Emmett's, and we turn our backs on Callum, walking along the dock toward the steps to the parking lot. "Since it's your birthday, tell me the worst things you can about Callum."

Emmett's grin stretches his face. "Oh, this is going to be the best birthday yet."

A groan closes in behind us, and I feel Callum right behind me. As Emmett recounts stories of their days spent together years ago, I take in the beauty of this small place. Its quaint size is more than compensated for by the richness it holds. The open, friendly people. Everyone we pass says hi or goodnight to Emmett. Some stop and ask the harbormaster questions, which he dutifully answers, me still hanging from his arm. Some raise an eyebrow, their gazes flicking toward the café half a block away, as if they're confused by my sudden attachment to his arm.

This is the kind of place you find and never leave. The

one spot on this wide, roving world that seekers would claim as their own, should they ever find it.

"Iris is dying to meet you, Eve." Emmett nods to the café as we reach the parking lot.

"She is?" I mean, I've been meaning to thank her for the supplies she sent me when I first arrived. But I've never had the chance. "I can't wait to meet her."

"Don't worry, she's much nicer than her big brother. And much prettier," Emmett says, but his gaze drops to the ground before we cross the street to said café. I swear something like a blush washes over his sun-doused features. I remove my arm from his, and he shoots me a soft smile. I know that look. That's the one the hero has when he is secretly in love with the heroine and something is standing in his way.

Callum moves between us, and I notice a gift in one hand, luggage in the other.

An overnight bag?

Why didn't he tell me we're staying?

"Callum, what on earth?" I poke the bag, hitting him with two raised eyebrows.

"It's nothing. I always carry a bag for evening trips, just in case. No point in getting hung up in a storm because you forgot your toothbrush."

His words die out on the last few syllables.

Okay . . . sounds like a touchy subject.

"We sailors are always prepared, Miss Eve. You'll get used to it."

Will I? I'm only here for a little while . . .

The front of the café is white, trimmed with blue. Elegant font is sprawled above the door on a long wooden sign: *McCreary's Café*.

The lights are on, but the tables inside are empty. The doorbell chimes as Emmett pushes through the door and holds it for us. Callum waves a hand in front of him, and I step up into the café over one broad, whitewashed wooden step.

The inside is so pretty. Whitewashed walls. Silver tables and mismatched, colorful chairs. A long eating counter runs along the side to the left, the ends holding display cases where I assume baked goods and lunchtime treats would be during open hours. Fairy lights are strung across the ceiling in neat rows. Ocean-themed items are dotted around the place. Some sit on the three wide bay windows by the larger tables that are set into them.

And the smell is . . .

Coffee.

Savory.

Sweet.

Delicious tangles of dishes Iris must serve.

"You made it!" A stunning redhead appears through a door behind the counter, her arms wide open in front of her. Her ruby lips are curved up into a smile that would put happiness itself to shame. She tugs an apron over her head to reveal the prettiest green dress. Her long silver earrings dangle and a tinkling fills the room. Emmett stills beside me. I can't resist a glance at his face.

Yep, that confirms my suspicions. He is definitely the hero in love with the forbidden heroine.

Callum grunts before dumping his bag to the floor. "Hey, sis."

Iris ignores him and folds me into a hug as soon as she rounds the counter. "You must be Eve."

Hugging her back, I huff out a laugh. She lets me go, and I give her my best smile. "Please, call me Evie. Oh, and thank you for the supplies. I know it was weeks ago, and I was meaning to thank you ages ago—"

She holds up a hand. "No thanks necessary. If you've managed to keep my ogre of a brother company and lived to tell the tale, that's all the thanks I need."

I can literally hear Callum rolling his eyes.

Iris's gaze snaps to my left and turns to a glare, and I know I was right.

"Hey, Irry," Emmett breathes.

Poor guy's only now taken his first breath since she waltzed through the door.

"Em, happy birthday." Iris steps to where he stands and dots a peck on his cheek. I can feel the heat from his blush to my right, and I swear molars grind to my left.

Maybe it's the romance author in me, but I think I have

this little scenario figured out. Em is head over heels for his best friend's little sister. Said best friend is somewhat aware of this. But is it a one-sided attraction? Lord, this shouldn't excite me as much as it does.

Maybe it's a good thing Callum is held up on the island . . .

Still, if tonight is anything to go on, he could be on Mars and Emmett would still not make his move on Iris. Poor guy. I mean, he has a very rational fear—the McCreary to my left is scary. At first.

And it's in that moment I realize how far Callum and I have come from those first days when he would barely look at me, let alone talk to me. Now—

"You must be starving! Dinner is almost ready," Iris says to me before turning to Callum. "Give me a hand, will you?"

After the McCreary siblings disappear into the kitchen, Emmett beckons me to a shelf. The cheek lining his eyes and smile is ridiculous. "Come here! Look at this while he's gone."

"What?" I cross the diner to where he stands by a bookshelf.

"Bet you've seen that scowl around before." He wriggles his eyebrows, pointing to a photograph of a teenage boy holding a fish on the line with an older man by him.

"Oh my god." I turn and look up at him. "I have. That has to be Callum."

"Yep, and that was his old man." The words lose their amusement as he looks wistfully at the photo.

I pick it up and stare at the boy and the man. The resemblance is strong. He's almost the spitting image of his father. They stand in front of a shack of some sort. "Where's this?"

"Fishing hut. It's on the southern end of the island."

Emmett gives me a confused look, as if I should know.

"Oh, I haven't ventured that far yet."

"Doubt he'll take you there. It was kind of their thing."

"What happened?"

"Which part?"

My mouth gapes a little and I snap it shut, swallowing. "What do you mean?"

"His parents, or his fian—"

"Dinner's ready." Callum's voice is curt. His face is stone. All the warmth from the past few moments fizzles out.

"Yep, coming," Emmett says and walks past Callum to round the counter and into the room behind.

I stare at Callum. His gaze lowers to my hand still holding the photograph. Turning back, I set it down on the shelf carefully.

"Callum." I turn back. "I—"

He's in my space. I look up, and instantly his heady scent infiltrates my senses. My heart winds up speed, settling into a clanging rhythm against my ribs.

He shakes his head. "Dinner."

I rest a hand on his chest and breathe, "Dinner."

His hand closes over mine, and he turns, leading me through the door behind the counter. The space is more than just a kitchen. It opens into a large living room. The dining table sits by the back bay window, now littered with candles. Celebratory decorations in navy and silver. Iris sits by Emmett.

Callum drops my hand and pulls out a chair.

I drop into it, opposite Iris, and heat flushes my cheeks as Emmett winks at me.

Good lord.

Callum drops into his place to my left.

"Right. Before we eat, wine?" Iris says, pulling a bottle of white from an ice-filled bucket.

"Fancy! And yes, please," I say.

I slide my glass toward her, and she fills it up. Emmett uncaps two beers and hands one to Callum.

When he tips it back toward his friend, he says, "Happy birthday, buddy."

"Thanks, Cal."

Iris beams at them both before tracking her attention back to Emmett. "Happy birthday, Em. Get anything good this year?"

She sips her wine, beautiful green eyes looking up at him under long lashes. He chokes on his beer, and Callum takes a long swig of his.

I'm absolutely fascinated.

She's flirting with him on purpose. And I'm not sure if it's because she knows how he feels or because it pisses her brother off. My gut tells me it's the latter.

The dynamic is thrilling.

I truly hope I'm still here when she finally realizes what's right in front of her.

"Nope. Just the usual," Emmett finally says.

"Well, dig in." Iris plucks up a dish and serves everyone before selecting the next dish and loading it onto our plates. Everything smells amazing. The chatter and eating continue until our plates are wiped clean and the wine is gone. The men regale me with stories of each other's most embarrassing moments.

We laugh.

Iris doubles over, leaning on Emmett's shoulder when the Suzie Hamlin story finally slips out. And the adoration lining his eyes with her touch almost floors me.

I'm tucking that little moment away for a scene, most definitely.

As the conversation slows, bellies full and drowsy from the heat of the warmer night and alcohol, Emmett yawns, laying an arm behind Iris's chair. *Smooth.*

She simply lays her head back on his arm and smiles up at him.

Callum grunts at the same time that Emmett's phone pings.

"Shit, sorry, guys." He plucks it from his pocket and taps

the screen. "Damn. Lucky you brought the overnighter, Cal. Front rolling in fast."

What?

"We can't go back?" I ask.

"Sorry, Evie. Mother Nature doesn't consider our plans," Cal says, absentmindedly tracing a finger over the label on his beer bottle.

"Oh. Will the lighthouse be okay? I mean—" Of course it will be, it was built for this. Even the thought seems stupid. But I'm flustered. The heat of slow-blooming anxiety spreads.

Iris leans over the table. "I can give you some things. You'll stay here tonight. I have a guest bedroom. Not the first time this'll happen."

Callum rises, plucking up the dirty plates. Iris shakes her head at him and goes back to chatting with Emmett.

"Let me help." I push up from the chair and grab dishes, following Callum to the kitchen space. He stands at the sink, rinsing the plates and cutlery.

I set the dishes on the counter. "Should I cover these for the refrigerator?"

"Top of the cupboard, left of the fridge," he grunts.

Okay . . . this weather's flipped his mood like the storm clouds it brings, apparently.

I find the plastic wrap in the cupboard and cover each dish in turn before finding a place in the fridge for them. As I close the refrigerator door, a flutter catches my eye.

Blue.

Wings.

A monarch butterfly magnet sits by the handle, only inches from my hand. I try to force myself to see the beauty in it.

I can't.

I rip my hand away like the handle just caught fire.

The searing heat lancing my veins is quick to fade with the sound of the man behind me grunting as he slams ceramic around. I turn back to find Callum stacking the dishwasher like those plates personally offended him.

He shoves another into the bottom rack with a clang, and I touch his forearm, hoping to stave off the assault for a moment. "Are you okay?"

His blue eyes are tightened as they rise to land on mine. "Fine."

"Tell that to the plates." I fold my arms and nod to the dishwasher between us, the open door at our feet, the plates tossed in any old how.

"You're not happy about the storm, about having to stay?" I ask.

He searches my face. Returning the gesture, I wonder what has him so riled in such a short time frame. I thought we moved past this broody, not-getting-close-to-each-other shit.

Maybe he's not comfortable with us being in the same platonic bed here together in his sister's house?

Honestly, I'm lost.

"Emmett said we should stay . . ." I try again.

"We need to." His jaw grinds. "But we shouldn't."

Fourteen

CALLUM

Evie's been in the bathroom for almost half an hour. The tiny guest room above the café is opposite Iris's room. Her light went out ten minutes ago. Down to my briefs and T-shirt, I lie in the full-sized bed that's more like a single. If Iris had a sofa, I'd be on it.

She doesn't, and I'm not.

The kindest move I can make now is to roll over and feign sleep.

May as well tell me to stop fucking breathing.

Just the thought of Evie sliding under this damn sheet in the tiniest bed known to man has me rock hard. I roll over, hoping if she ever comes out of the goddamn bathroom I don't make a fool of myself with a raging hard-on for a woman I won't have.

Can't.

And there is no pillow wall or big king size here.

Light footsteps finally close in on the opposite side of the room and I swear she is muttering something under her breath. She reaches the bed, only to pace to the window. Iris's pajamas on her are baggy, and the sleeve of the wide neckline has slipped off one shoulder already. The T-shirt is more like a tank, and she is tugging it down as she looks out the window and over the harbor.

It's pretty by moonlight. Nothing new to me.

Evie glances over her shoulder. Probably checking to see if I'm asleep. I tamp down a smile and wriggle to get more comfortable on my side. "You gonna sleep standing up?"

My gruff words see her turn back, her bottom lip pulled through her teeth as she worries herself over this whole situation. *You and me both, girl.* I don't take on Mother Nature. Only idiots think they can outrun a storm on the water.

The thought burns brighter than I imagined it would.

"Be there in a bit," she says softly, uncertainty lacing her words.

She turns back to the window and her hair falls over her shoulders, slipping from the rough, messy bun she had it wound up in. One elegant hand trails over her bare shoulder. My molars clench.

Closing my eyes, I think of anything else but the woman by the window.

Muttering something I can't make out, Evie pads to the

bed and climbs in under the covers. She lies still, the only sound in the room is her breathing mixing with the echo of mine. When she clears her throat and rolls over, I open my eyes and stare at the wall. Good. She should get some sleep.

We both should.

Tender fingertips press into my shoulder. "Cal?"

The way my breath hitches at that one syllable should be fucking illegal. "Yeah?" I manage to choke out as my body responds to the tiniest touch from her.

"Thank you for bringing me with you."

This makes me roll over. "You were invited, Evie."

Her eyes are burning as she studies my face. "I know, but . . ." She tucks the sheet around her like she's shielding herself. "This is your family, your friend. I'm only passing through, aren't I?"

Sucking in a breath, I tug at the sheet that's now pressed up to her neck. "Why do you always do that?"

"Do what?" she breathes.

"Make yourself small. Hide. Apologize for existing."

Her gaze turns into a tangle of fear and uncertainty. I fucking hate it. Resisting the craving to strip her bare and show her how incredible she is—that I *know* she is—I close a hand around her hand gripping the sheet.

And to my surprise . . . she releases it.

"Hiding is safe," she whispers.

The hell?

"From what, Evie?" My voice is gravel.

Her eyes snap away, her palm wandering over the sheet between us in random movement. "Life. People."

Christ.

How can I blame her for thinking that? It's a place I've dwelled in for so long.

"It will get better." It's all I can say. Not nearly enough. The undercurrent of grief sucks you down when you least expect it. I know this. She's shaking her head, and silver swells below those beautiful browns.

Hell.

I take her face in my palms. She leans into my hand.

A rock explodes into my throat, pulling every last speck of air from my lungs.

Oh, cailín luachmhor.

"Talk to me, Evie."

"I can't." She sucks in a wobbly breath. "Back home—in the city, there's . . . He—" She squeezes her eyes shut. Her chin quivers between my palms.

What is this all about? If I didn't know better, I'd say she's scared of something. Someone is hurting her?

"Do you feel safe with me?"

She nods, my hands still cupping her cheeks.

"You are safe on the island. I will make sure you are safe. Whatever is haunting you won't take a second breath if it ever steps foot on Fire Island. You hear me?"

"Yes," she rasps.

It's now I notice her chest rising and plummeting

way too quick. Her eyes are dark, her fingers now curled around my own. Her body tipped toward my own. The sheet has slipped down further. Her hard nipples push against the soft T-shirt fabric. Evie's lips part on her next inhale, and her gaze sinks to my mouth.

I sink my hands into her hair and down her neck before reality catches up with me.

My hands fall away as she must have realized the same thing. Shuffling back on the bed, she grips the pillow. A small smile eventually tips her lips upward. "Tell me about Iris and Emmett."

The words sit between us as I try to discern her meaning.

"They've been friends for as long as Emmett and I have been, I guess. Nothing to tell there. He's like her second brother."

Evie frowns, giving me a quizzical look before rolling onto her back, her eyes searching the ceiling. A beat later she turns her head to look at me, her hair falling over the pillow with the movement. Heaviness sinks in my gut. My cock throbs as the last of the blood in my body leaves, heading south.

"Good night," I rasp, hoping those brown eyes will close and save me from myself.

"It was, wasn't it." She flips to face me on her side and props up on her elbow. Leaning over, she dots a kiss to my cheek. "Thank you. It's the best night I've had in a long time."

That was the best night she's had?

Fucking criminal.

I can think of about a hundred different ways I could give her a night to remember. None of them involve other people or damn clothes.

Christ.

"What?" she says with a laugh.

Fuck.

I clear my throat. "Nothing. Go to sleep, Evie."

She frowns and rolls onto her back. "Night, Cal."

Dammit.

This is why us staying overnight was—*is*—a bad idea.

I fold my arms over my chest like it will force the throbbing from my cock to return the blood to my head. Evie's gaze is on my face; I can almost feel it slide over my skin. All warm and needy.

And damn, if that ain't making it almost impossible to lie lifeless beside her.

She pulls the sheet up and it settles around her, sending her vanilla and spice around me. I lie awake until her breathing quiets, and only then do I dare to look at her. She's stunning in the moonlight. Hair framing her face on the pillow, her elegant lines draw me in like a moth to a flame. The curve of her lips, the fine architecture of her cheek bones and arched eyebrows. The soft flesh of her neck that looks like a forbidden fruit. The dip at her collar-bone, the round, plump swell and peaks of her breasts . . .

Something soft pushes back into me, pressing against my cock, and it hardens instantly. I wake to a blurry brown mess in my vision.

Dark hair.

I gently brush it from my face. Evie is on her side, her back to me, her ass pushed into my groin. She's hunting for warmth, if the goosebumps on her skin are anything to go by. I extricate myself from her and pad to the window and pull it down. Plucking a throw from the chair by the door, I lay it over her and slide back into bed.

"So cold," she murmurs, pulling the blanket up to her neck. I wriggle back to the sliver of mattress I was on when I woke. This time I wrap my arm around her and tug her into my warmth before letting my palm rest on the bed. She only wants warmth.

"Thank you," she utters before settling again.

But I'm wide awake.

The ache in my cock is beyond comprehension with her ass pressed against me. My hands tremble with the need to touch her, to tug, grab at any fucking thing I can take.

Inhaling deep, I attempt to douse the fire that's currently blazing its way through my body. It only serves to stoke it higher when I breathe in her vanilla and spice. I groan into her hair, sinking my face into it.

Christ above, this is the hardest thing I've ever done.

Holding Evie without touching her.

Hands down, the hardest.

A little moan slips through her lips, and I almost choke on my last breath.

I slide a hand down to her hip. The tiny shorts barely cover her, but the goosebumps have retreated. That's one thing, at least. She moves, her back arching a little as she mutters, "Too hot."

I peel the blanket off her shoulder. Her skin is flushed now. I can't tell if it's the warmth of the blankets or the proximity that's flipped her body temp so quickly. I brush her hair from her neck, hoping it'll help. Her fine hand wraps around mine.

"Evie?"

"Please." She drags my hand back to her hip.

I take a rough grip and squeeze. Her back arches further.

"E—" Gravel has lined my throat. "Eve . . ."

Just when I think she must be still dreaming or half asleep, her arm reaches back. Her palm cups my jaw, fingertips trembling as they brush over my beard and ghost over my lips.

Fuck me.

"You sure?" I bury my face in her hair and breathe her in.

"Yes," she moans, canting her ass.

"Look at me." The words are sharper than I intend.

But she turns to face me and her hands land on my chest. "I-it's been a long time. And I can't stop thinking about your hands on me. Like last time."

Last time.

The time I caved in to what I wanted. The memory of the decision I made to put space back between us burns.

"It's not a good idea. I'm not—"

Her finger presses over my lips.

"I'm not asking for anything more. Just this."

I study her gaze. Its fire intensifies as her hands travel up my neck. Her fingertips wander the angles of my face.

Hell, it's been a lifetime since anything this tender found me.

I'll break her.

I won't be able to help it.

"How about this, you can have my hands anywhere you want. Even my mouth. But that's all." The last few words are harder to push out than I'd like. Her face falls a little as she nods.

"What do you get?" she whispers against my jaw.

A fleeting moment of her softness against my harsh granite. Her wrapped around me. A moment that'll probably carry me to a place I'm going to have to claw my way out of when she leaves.

But I've been the selfish one too many times before. And if age and experience have taught me anything, it's that selflessness is the only way to minimize the fallout when it happens. It always finds you. No matter how good you think you've made things.

Soft, warm breaths tangle with my own. "*Please*, Cal."

This fucking begging.

I'm hard as concrete.

Her hands are threaded through my hair. I drag them down by the wrists and flip her to her back, nuzzling my face into her neck before stringing kisses up her jaw.

I nudge her legs open with my knees and settle over her, my weight propped up on my hands still around her wrists.

Brown eyes stare up at me, her lips parted just the slightest, as her tongue pokes out to wet them.

My body on hers, holding her down, does something carnal to my mind. I smash my mouth to hers. With a whimper, she responds, opening for me. I dive right in, claiming every inch of her mouth, our tongues tangling. Breathlessness devours the last of my air, and I break from the kiss.

These damn clothes are coming off.

How long have I waited to see this beautiful woman naked before me? Too long.

I tug the shirt down, and the stitching tears at the shoulder. One breast overflows over the fabric.

For a moment I think she's going to struggle free from my grip and tug the shirt back up, but she simply stares at me, waiting for my next move.

"It all goes, Evie. Everything. I want you bare."

Her breath hitches.

I release my grip, and she sits up a little, allowing me to remove the T-shirt.

I slide it over her head and toss it to the floor.

Leaning back, I tug at those tiny shorts. They slip over her hips easily. They join the shirt on the floor, and her pale-blue panties are all that's left between me and her. I glimpse up to find her worrying her bottom lip through her teeth.

"Loose the lip, baby girl. We're not doing that today."

Her lips part and her eyes intensify as she lifts her hips real slow. Keeping my eyes on hers, I slide the panties over her hips. As the lace reaches her feet, I move the panties over one foot and lift the other. With a kiss to her ankle, I remove the last of the lace, and it flies off the bed.

Lowering her foot to the bed, I spread her wide. Her chest pumps with ragged breaths as I sit back on my heels and take her in. Every delicious fucking inch of her.

Her hands fist the sheets.

"Cal . . ." My name is a plea.

Christ, I knew it. She's *fucking perfect*.

Fifteen

EVIE

Spread wide on display for the gruff lighthouse keeper I share an intimate but isolated existence with is *not* how I saw this visit to the mainland going. But things have never panned out the way I've imagined they would in life. And I couldn't resist the man in front of me even if I wanted to.

Blood hurries its way through my body at lightning speed, fueled by my pounding heart, now homed to that one aching spot between my legs.

Callum looks feral.

His blues are so dark they imitate the storm clouds outside. The room lights up from a flash of lightning, the thunder indicating the storm is still too far away to matter, and I sit up and tug his shirt over his head. I'm aching all over for this man—and if I'm honest with myself, I have been for some time.

Weeks.

No, maybe a few months now.

With him bare, I run my hands over what hard work and a simple life grants him. His toned chest is warm. Each muscle is defined and lightly dusted with the dark hair that matches his now messy bed hair. I explore every inch of him.

"I got to move, baby girl. You wanted my hands on you. Now I need to touch you. I'm so fucking desperate for you, Evie."

My breaths stall out.

My mouth hangs slack.

He's still sitting on his heels. I scramble up onto his lap, my mouth finding his in hungry movements.

I've never been so starving.

The fire he stokes in my chest sinks to my core, and the throbbing in my clit is almost unbearable.

Never before has anyone had me this wound up. This desperate for their touch.

No one.

His hands are in my hair, then they grip my jaw as he meets my hunger with his. Two people starved for something they only just realized they have found in the other. After months of being right there.

It's almost poetic.

He's hard underneath me.

I rock back and forth, needing the pressure.

Drowning in it.

It's heaven against my aching center, and his groan turns to a growl, the sound reverberating down my chest and around my heart. My back hits the bed.

I'm pinned down. Nips and licks travel down my neck. Over my collarbones. Teeth close over my nipple.

I cry out, arching instantly.

God above.

The air in my lungs burns.

Too quick.

Not enough.

Too much.

"C-Cal . . ."

My body trembles almost violently. I could come from just his mouth on my breasts.

His hand travels over my belly and he cups my pussy. I whimper.

"Fuck, Evie. You're fucking soaked, baby girl." The heel of his palm rubs my clit. "All this for me?"

Wetness floods my center. Like it wasn't already drenched.

"You have no idea."

"Hands or mouth, Evie?"

My breath hitches as I find his blue eyes. I open my mouth to respond, but nothing comes out.

"Use your words. Or I decide which one you get."

"H-hand is fine."

He raises an eyebrow. "Fine?"

I can only nod.

"We can do better than fine, mo nighean."

I don't know what the phrase means. "What does that mean? I tried to google it, but . . ."

He chuckles but doesn't answer as he shuffles backward. Rough hands part my thighs as he lowers. He's not going to—

His tongue sweeps through my center.

Oh god.

I sink my fingers into his hair. "Hands," I choke out.

"Too bad. You got mouth," he growls.

His tongue swirls around my clit, and I all but buck off the bed. Large, warm palms press my hips to the bed. He suckles my clit, and my insides literally turn to molten lava.

"Callum," I rasp.

"Yeah?"

"Please, I—"

Two fingers slide inside me, and I moan. My fingers, woven into his messy hair, turn to fists. A rough chuckle vibrates over my clit.

The air in my lungs stalls.

He curls his fingers, sliding them in and out in time to his choppy breaths. The heat in his eyes holds me where I am as he watches me fall apart. The most beautiful release unfurls, spiraling outward as it lights up my body from inside out. I curl up off the bed as his lips close around my nipple.

He bites down, and the orgasm explodes like it hasn't already given me the world.

I can't help the cry slipping past my lips. I imagine Iris on the other side of the building. I don't care right now, despite the heat filling my cheeks.

"That's it, baby girl. Milk my fucking fingers. So fucking perfect."

Cal's expression turns painful, as if he's coming undone at the same time as me.

Unable to think of anything else, I'm desperate for a different type of pleasure.

His.

Out of breath, I settle on the bed for a heartbeat. And when his arms push onto the mattress, hands fisted beside my head, I drag his mouth down to mine. He's strung out. Each sweep of his tongue is bruising.

I want to give him what he gave me.

More, if I can.

I tap his shoulder, and he leans back on his heels once again.

"I want to do the same for you." I look up at him.

His head tilts to one side but he steps off the bed. I rise to follow, but he holds up a hand.

"Crawl, baby girl. You want my cock in your mouth, you earn it."

The ego on this grump.

Tamping down a smile, I move to all fours. Maintaining eye contact, I crawl as slowly as possible, ignoring the heat once again flushing my face. My breasts sway with each movement. If I thought his eyes were dark before . . . Now they are the navy hue of the deepest ocean.

His jaw feathers. "Fuck me, Evie."

I reach the edge of the bed and tug his boxers down. I don't wait for permission.

I crawled for this man.

I earned it.

His cock springs free.

All I can do is stare at it.

It's veiny and huge. A pearl of pre-cum beaded at the tip. But . . .

It's been so long, and I don't want him to be disappointed.

Retreating a little, I glance up at him before finally getting the courage to ask, "H-how do you like it?"

His hands slide across my jaw and into my hair. He bunches it up in one fist and tugs me forward. "Rough."

Something explodes low in my belly. My slick pussy hums back to life.

Holy shit.

I grip his hips with both hands and settle on my knees before him.

He removes one hand and moves it to his cock. I fold my fingers around the warm, corded shaft. My mouth waters as I slide the tip onto my tongue. His eyes don't leave my face.

My lips close over him. I slide my mouth back, and his grip on my hair tightens.

"Easy, baby."

"What happened to rough?"

"It's coming."

I take him in as far as I can and suck my way back up. Slowly. Methodically.

"Fu—uck." Callum cups my cheek with his free hand. "More."

I slide down him again, increasing the suction, my grip tightening. My clit throbs at the taste of him. The sounds he makes. His low, soft growls with every upstroke. I could come again just from having him in my mouth.

On the next stroke, his legs start to tremble. He's holding back, his restraint evident.

I look up beneath my lashes and open my mouth wider. I want him rough. I want what he needs to give me.

Interpreting my signal, Cal adjusts his hold in my hair, winding my hair around his fist. His cock slams into my mouth, deep. I gag, eyes watering. His lip curls up on one side.

Feral.

I try my best to accommodate him. Sucking on the upward stroke, trying to relax enough to take all of him. But he's big. My cheeks hollow out on the next stroke as saliva and pre-cum run down my chin.

"Fuck me, baby girl. So damn pretty choking on my cock, aren't you?"

My nails bite into his thighs as he slams into me. Breathing through my nose, I take everything he gives me. Waiting, desperately, for the salty flood of his release.

"Touch yourself, Evie. Show me those pretty little writer's fingers sunk deep into that fucking pussy."

I whimper around him, and his eyes close as his pace slows.

But I do as he says. Trembling fingers sweep over my clit, and I all but fall apart.

"Sink them deep, then give them to me."

I push two digits inside myself. My body convulses as an orgasm swells.

"Fuck, look at you. Come while my cock's in your mouth. Go on."

Pumping my fingers in and out of my pussy, I cry out. His cock pulses as it shoves in deeper than before. My release fades, and I drag my hand from my pussy, dripping wet with my slick need. Cal grabs my wrist. My fingers crawl up his chin and bury inside his mouth. His tongue laps around them.

I can't breathe.

His body shudders. His cock twitches as his pace turns choppy. A low, raw growl cascades around my fingers as he shoots hot ropes of cum over my tongue. I lap it up, swallowing it down.

Every inch of my body tingles. I'm wrung out like a wet rag. Spent and limp, I flop back onto the bed, running a thumb over my bottom lip where I clean up the last drop of his release.

Cal stands, nostrils flaring and eyes burning as I lay on the bed. Bared and still buzzing.

"Ev—" He shakes his head, fisting his cock. "I . . ."

It is the first time I have ever seen Callum McCreary lost for words.

Something snaps in my chest as his face falls the moment he turns and walks from the room into the bathroom.

Iris sure knows how to make a cup of coffee. My steaming mug sits in my hands. Callum sits opposite me at the small café table. The café is bustling with patrons. And Cal has his head stuck in a newspaper, avoiding them all. At least, that's what I think he's doing.

Iris is chatting away, serving customers.

She looks so damn happy.

I had that once. Before the accident. Many contracts ago. I yawn, lifting the cup to my mouth.

"My brother snores, doesn't he?" Iris appears by our table with a smile. Her red hair is twisted up and piled onto her head, an apron wrapped over her T-shirt and jeans, a pot of coffee in one hand.

All but snorting my mouthful of coffee through my nose, I choke it back down. "No, he doesn't snore."

She raises an eyebrow. "You sure? I could hear him growling from my side of the house."

Cal snaps the paper down. "Sure you did, Irry. Don't you have customers to annoy?"

She pulls a face at him before squeezing my shoulder with a happy smile. Moving to the next table, she pours an old man a fresh cup as she turns back. "Oh, Evie, you have mail. It came this morning."

Oh . . . I flinch, not thinking quick enough to stop my reaction.

"Your editor get sick of email not working?" Cal asks, sipping his coffee. His brows lower as I fluster to scrape together a response.

"Probably." I look over my shoulder. "Thanks, Iris. I'll grab it when we leave."

Hopefully it's Livvy. Maybe the renewed contract?

Via snail mail?

It's been an age since I used USPS with anything official. Maybe isolation left them with no choice.

"Can we get to the library before we head home?" I ask Cal.

"Sure. More research?"

Tiny moments from this morning slip into my head. My fingers curl around the ceramic of the mug. I take a sip, hoping the heat on my face looks like it's coming from the beverage in my hand. But I do need to find some resources on a few elements I want to weave into the story.

"Something like that."

firefly

Sixteen

CALLUM

I leave Evie with her mail and head to my little shack to unpack. She was quiet on the trip back. Didn't say a word. My guess is what happened at Iris's sunk in.

We crossed the fucking line.

After last night—well this morning, I guess—I need some time to organize my thoughts. To sort through what happened, and how it happened. I've been with women since my last serious relationship, but Evie was . . .

Fuck. *Christ.*

She pulled something out of me I had long forgotten about.

Something visceral and primal that's been dormant.

It's been years since I've been so messed up about a woman, and the only thing that can help is a little solitude at the fishing hut.

I feel bad running off after we—

Nope.

I rip the zipper on the overnight bag open and toss in some supplies. A few changes of clothes. A book. Flashlight and batteries. The satellite phone I only use for emergencies. Running a hand through my hair, I figure I better tell Evie where I'm going. She should be okay for a few nights by herself. Food is plenty, and we have more than enough stocked in the fridge and pantry.

It occurs to me as I zip up the bag that we haven't spent a day apart since she arrived here.

Space.

This living in each other's orbit is forcing something that shouldn't exist.

That must be it.

I pluck up my cap and grab an extra jacket off the hook by the door before crossing the gravel path to the house. I knock on the door, but it swings open immediately.

"Evie, I—"

She's sitting at the table, her mail in front of her.

Unopened.

I adjust the bag strap on my shoulder, glancing between the woman and the white envelope. "'Fraid it's gonna bite you, baby girl?"

Hell, I have to stop with the pet names. I'm not doing either of us any favors.

"Don't be silly," she huffs, but her throat works, and her

eyes don't leave the envelope. She doesn't want me here when she opens it. Fair enough. I shuffle back to the door and slap the jamb. "I'll be away for a few nights. Things on the south end of the island need a once-over. You be okay here?"

Like she can go anywhere else.

Her head snaps up, gaze piercing the window. "Sure."

When she still doesn't look at me, I nod and leave her to her mail. I can take a hint. Pretty sure the strained look scrawled all over her face is regret.

That's something, at least. Maybe we can find a truce in a threadbare friendship. My gut slips, knowing I'm leaving her like this.

Who am I kidding? I've fucked everything.

I shut the door behind me and head for the forest tree line. It takes a solid thirty minutes of walking through the wild, dense forest before I come across the small but deep freshwater water hole. It's been my place to wash up on these trips many times.

The cooler air under the canopy is a relief. The warmer days sometimes mean afternoon storms, and I'm hoping none roll in in the next few days. I need this.

Evie needs this, whether she realizes it or not.

My stride loosens, and in no time I'm deep into the forest. The quiet is the first thing I soak in. The constant crashing waves near the shore are nice, but sometimes you need silence. From here, they are muted to the point of disappearing. I roll my shoulders, peering up into the canopy as I go. I forgot how much I love this little slice of paradise.

With everything that's been going on—the lighthouse in dire straits and Evie arriving—I've missed this. I'll need this again when she eventually leaves. That seems to be the only recurring pattern in my life. Find something great I want to hold on to. Get attached. Lose said thing. Hide away on my island until the hurt fades.

Some hurts take longer than others.

The only other time I felt anything close to this was twenty years ago. When my life had just started to make sense. Of course, that's when the rug was slipped out from under me, leaving me with the burn of an entire town hating me for how things went down.

I can't blame them.

And I never will.

They deserved better from me.

She deserved better.

I won't make that mistake twice.

So, the forest is where I need to be. Far enough away to think things through without interference. No matter how much I crave her. I won't make a choice that has Evie end up worse for it.

I hear the waves rolling in before the tree line breaks and the old hut comes into view. Steadfast, even on this tiny strip of ocean island. It looks exactly as I left it nine months ago. It's been too long.

The overhang of the roof at the front of the building shelters handmade wooden tables, the one and only place my old man ever worked his fish over. His small collection of knives I haven't touched in decades hangs on wires above it. The windows are opaque, as if blasted by time and sand during the storms. The front door, with its weathered and warped boards, hangs on its hinges. I vaguely remember making a note to bring tools after the last visit.

The door creaks open, revealing a sand-littered floor decked out with one single bunk, a small table, and a lopsided bookshelf lining the space. A wood stove sits on the opposite side. It needs a good sweeping. And the cobwebs hanging like drapes from the corners and tucked away in angles of the furniture have to go.

I set my bag on the table and take in the wear and tear. As my gaze roves the small space, memories flood in. The last day I spent here with my father. Iris complaining the fish guts touched her as he flung them behind him, into the brush. I remember the hearty chuckle that bellowed from his throat as my little sister dry heaved, dramatic as usual. He had shaken his head, getting back to his task at hand. One of the large bass I'd pulled up. My efforts at descaling and gutting already on the pan inside.

The memory of the aroma of frying fish with the potato dish Mom always sent with us hits me low in the gut, hard. Running a hand over my beard, I tug my cap from my head and toss it to the bed.

An hour later, with a sweat well and truly worked up, the little fishing hut looks much more respectable. Cobwebs gone, sand swept out, and some semblance of a small fire smoldering away in the now clean stove for later, I drop onto one of the rickety chairs at the table.

Remembering the kerosene lanterns and candles, I lean over to the bed and reach a hand under it. My fingertips finally land on something wooden, and I hunt for the rope handle. Curling my fingers around it, I slide the box out and flip the heavy lid open. The fumes of kerosene and burnt wicks finds me. Three burners and a hoard of candles of all shapes and sizes sit nestled into the base of the deep box, safe from the elements.

I pull the lanterns out carefully, mindful of the old gas-filled weathered glass bases. Dotting them around the space, I set out the candles next. When the last one is secure, I crack each window for ventilation. Guess all there is to do now is hunt for my food.

That thought splits my face with a grin.

The shallow rock pools along the eastern shoreline are a safe haven for crab and oysters, sometimes smaller fish who find their way in and can't get back. Easy pickings.

I grab up a pot, a less-than-pristine knife from the wire hook, and the wooden spear Iris made our father carve for her when she was nine, just before . . .

The spear's tip is metal. It's been an age since anyone's used this. The tip is not honed to a sharp, lethal point like it once was, but it will still crack a shell well enough. I grab it with my free hand and pull the hut door shut. The sun's warmth tingles my face and neck. It's nice.

But the small swell of clouds closing in from the east catch my attention. They weren't there this morning when I left.

"Hmmm, stay where you are," I tell the clouds, like I'm Zeus and can command the weather. I chuckle at my stupidity. One night without the churn in my gut, worrying about something or someone, is all I want.

Maybe Iris is right. I should relax. Take up meditation like she teases me about any chance she gets.

Like she would ever sit still long enough to meditate. *Fucking hypocrite.*

The sand gives way under my boots as I find the rocky patch to the east. An abundance of crab and small pickings waits for the taking.

This is going to be fun.

With a haul one man could never possibly eat in a single trip, I trudge back to the hut. Those clouds to the east have grown with a ferocity that makes me nervous. It's not that I don't think the hut can withstand it. It's still here after every storm that's rolled through in the last three decades. It's the girl I left alone in the lighthouse that worry is gnawing my insides about.

She knows the drill. But it's not the same when you're by yourself. And I have lived here for almost twenty years. Evie hasn't been here long. I pray she stays inside and hunkers down. She knows where to go if she's scared—the basement, into the generator room, the last resort space. Nothing can break down that robust space. The only downfall is the fumes if the generator is running, which it is at night.

"Dammit."

I slam a hand onto the front door when I reach the hut, dumping my haul before the threshold. I should have stayed.

Nope. Give the girl more credit, asshole. Not like she can't look after herself. She's smart and cautious. Levelheaded. Evie will be fine. She's probably more worried about me in the bundle-of-sticks hut, that the storm will try to huff and puff and blow my house down. I can imagine her saying it, a ridiculous grin on her beautiful face.

That settles it, then. She will be fine.

She will be *fine*.

I take to prepping the spoils of my hunt. With a pot on the stove boiling away, I decide crab will make a decent dinner. Maybe followed by the handful of oysters I managed to scrape from the underside of the salty rocks. And two small fish that flop helplessly in the bucket. Their life force drains as their gaping mouths slow to a still.

Thunder rumbles, its menacing presence moving closer as the light starts to fade. I'm settled in the chair reading by lantern light when the first pitter-patter of rain hits the tin roof. I glance upward, as if greeting it with an eye roll will somehow make it go away. If it rains the entire time I'm here, I may as well have stayed home. But it wouldn't be the first time I've been out here in the weather.

Mud squelches through my clawed fingers. Rain pounds into me. Knees dug into the mushy earth as the air in my lungs burns its way from my body in racking assaults.

How could I let this happen?

The pouring rain drowns out the thundering beat of my heart. And it's the first sliver of relief since I left the hospital three days ago. Left without Ava. Without—

A feral scream rips through my throat. My forehead hits the mud. I claw at the ground.

The blaze consuming my chest doesn't fade.

Nothing helps.

Things were fine. Everything was going to schedule, to plan. When I left, she wasn't far along. Every letter she sent me, there was no reason for me to think she was in trouble. Why didn't she tell me she was in pain all this time?

"Why, Ava?" The words echo off the trees that stand like ever-patient guardians all around me. The rain continues to slam into me. I don't know if it's a comfort or a blunt reminder I'm alive.

And my Ava is not.

I shake the memory from my mind and readjust my focus on the page. Twenty years, and it still burns like yesterday. Still chokes me up like it damn well should.

I should have been with her when she needed me.

She should have told me.

I stretch, glancing at the time on the satellite phone.

21:50

Hell, I must have fallen asleep.

Hunting and sunshine will do that to a man. The wind howls outside and the lanterns flicker wildly. I rise and shut the windows, all but the one on the western side. The howls turn desperate, rattling the little wooden hut where it's planted in the sandy earth.

I swear I hear my name.

But it can't be. It's just memories tormenting me, like they've done since that day.

I ignore them and decide to rest my body on the bunk.

When the screaming wind doesn't let up, I slide an arm over my face.

The mind plays tricks on a man when he's down. With my head all messed up over Evie and the memories this old hut brings, I try to ignore the way the wind sounds like the last moments of Ava's life. The vision that's played through my head since the first inkling of feeling something deep for Evie, where my mind puts her in Ava's place.

And I lose them both.

Seventeen

EVIE

My hands tremble around the note. The obliterated remains of a blue monarch butterfly litter the table. It's been hours, and only now have I drummed up the courage to open the letter.

I wish I hadn't done that.

Panic has me strung out. With clammy hands, I pluck up the mug of water on the table and try to ease my parched throat before replacing it to the table beside the letter.

Words bleed together on the page as I try to force air into my lungs.

If I close my eyes, maybe it will morph into a publishing contract, or maybe a letter from Livvy . . .

I slam my eyes shut.

One.

Breathe in.

Two.

Breathe out.

Three.

Breathe in.

Four.

Breathe out.

I snap my eyes open.

The violent scrawl across the page stares back at me. Whimpering, I drop the page and back away from the table, hand covering my mouth.

Bile rises and burns, but I force myself to read the letter out loud. So my mind can't misinterpret the words, can't placate the meaning. Can't alter the message on the page . . .

Hello Butterfly,
You thought you could disappear?
Not a chance, precious heart.
What kind of man lets the best thing in his
possession slip through his fingers?
Not this one. You want to know why?
So many questions, I know.
But I have one answer for you, too.
Remember the time you tried to marry some other
guy? Jake?
No, that's right, his name was Joshua.
At least, that's who you were calling for from the
back of the ambulance that night. That little
incident cost me a few hundred to fix the bulbar of
my cousin's truck. Very naughty of you to take
things so far. I'm sure you can make it up to me.
In fact, I look forward to it.
Things didn't have to end the way they did.
You pushed me—not responding to my
correspondence repeatedly.
Your fiancé, no you husband, died.
Repenting will be something for you to look
forward to. I will help you through that. It won't
be long now, Butterfly.
Love you, precious heart.
        T xxx

Legs trembling, I sway, hitting the table. The mug topples over and water spills over the page, encasing it in a watery veneer. I bolt up the stairs and stumble into the bathroom. Hands gripping the seat, I lose my stomach to the toilet.

Sobs chug upward as the bile renews its burn. "Fuck . . ."

I scream into my hands, crumpling onto the tile in a shaking mess of limbs. He killed Joshua.

It's all my fault.

It's. All. My. Fault.

The fiery grip of fear, anxiety, and disgust wind through me inch by inch. Keening, rocking back and forth with fingers tangled in my hair, I scream into the tile.

"No . . ." I slam a fist into the floor. Something cracks, and pain lances through my knuckles and wrist.

Heat and the agony of fresh grief slam into me. I try to rise but fall to my knees again. The only thing I can think of is hiding in the solace of the arms of the man who's made my days bearable for the last five months.

I stagger to my feet, gripping the doorway to the bathroom. Something bright flashes outside. The gnarly grip of terror renders me still for a moment. Then the rumble follows. The wind howls. How did I not hear it before? The roar of the blood rushing through my ears must have drowned out the storm brewing outside.

I make it to the kitchen to sweep the curtain to one side. Lightning scrawls across the sky. The crash of waves on the rock of the western shore roars alongside the continuous thunder. The tree line of the forest sways violently. Something knocks against the window, and I jump with a start, a yelp spewing from my lips.

My heart is racing, keeping its chaotic, manic rhythm in time to the tremor in my hands.

"I'm not staying here by myself," I whisper, as if Cal can hear me.

Like somehow, even though we're at opposite ends of this island, we're still connected.

The front door jostles under the force of the storm. Logically, I know this old house will keep me safe. But if T, or whatever he signs off as, knows where I am . . .

Am I really safe here, alone?

Fresh fear closes my throat around a new stone set on not nudging. I'll take my chances with Mother Nature. Man has never turned out to be a safe option. The paper on the table that's now moving as if by some invisible puppeteer's strings as a draft finds its way inside is evidence of that.

How hard can it be? Callum said it only takes an hour to walk there. If I run . . .

In the dark.

In a storm.

Something clatters to the ground outside. I freeze, holding my breath.

I swipe up my useless phone just in case and grab one of Callum's caps from the hook before shrugging my coat over my shoulders.

A shadow moves past the window and I barely manage to tamp back the scream that flies up.

"Out. I need to get out," I whimper, shoving my boots onto my feet. My hand trembles on the doorknob.

"You can do this, Evie. Go on!"

I pull the door open and cross the threshold, and it all but tugs from my hand, slamming shut behind me. Battered by the wind, I make a beeline for the trees, holding the cap on my head with one hand. When I reach the trees, I break into a run, heading south. I hope. The rush of the wind is less in here. But the canopy swirls above me. Twigs crack underfoot as I push my legs faster.

A groan sounds from behind me.

From what, or who, I can't tell.

Tears swell, blurring my vision. "Dammit, not now."

I swipe low branches away as I plow through the forest. My heartbeat hammers through my ears, clanging my brain in my skull.

My heavy, heaving breaths burn, and I slow. Only a little.

I look over my shoulder. Everything's a blur.

My foot stubs into something hard, and I fly face-first into the soaked forest floor.

"Ah, fuck," I sob.

Rolling over, I lay on my back and let despair wash through me. Let it wring my exhausted body out until the remnants of the fire I've found these last few months is all that's left. The world seems to slow as I lie here, mesmerized by the chaotic canopy above me. For the first time in hours, I take a long, deep lungful of air.

I let my eyes flutter shut, curling my fingers into the soft, mossy ground underneath me with both hands.

Both hands.

My phone.

"Fuck," I groan.

Now, even if it worked, I have no way of reaching anyone. I must have dropped it in my hysterics.

God, you idiot, Evie. My exhales echo in the air above me. I listen to each one against the storm's grumble. It's almost soft. Poetic, for sure.

A twig snaps mere feet away.

Whimpering, I hesitate before I scurry to my feet and get my bearings. Something hits the tree to my left and I scream, sprinting south. I think.

Fuck. Fuck. Fuck, fuck . . .

No . . .

I don't know how long I've been running when my aching legs start to tremble. Lightning flashes, the thunder roaring a split second later.

I glance back, knowing it's a risk.

Trees move. Something moves between the great timbers.

The smell of wood-burning smoke drifts on the wild air around me.

Callum.

"Callum!"

I push faster. Heat prickles its way down my spine when I reach a small clearing to find a waterhole. But no fishing hut.

Nobody.

"Shit!" I take off again. Sweat trickles down my chest, and I wrangle the coat from my shoulders and lose it to the ground, going as fast as I can.

"Callum!"

Tears burn my eyes again, and every breath is laced with a choppy sob.

I can't stop.

I don't know what's behind me.

I run.

And *run*.

When I can't catch my breath any longer, I stagger to a stop, propped against a tree. Trying to steady my breath, I strain to listen to the forest around me. Trying desperately to separate the sounds of the storm from everything else.

A moment passes, and I regain an inkling of stability in my legs, so I push off the tree. Taking off at a jog, I pray the wind carries my pleas to the fishing hut. Or by some miracle of nature, or whatever universal force is responsible for human connection, Callum hears me.

Please hear me.

"Callum!"

My hand hits a tree as I fly past, over the now slippery

forest floor. An ache works its way through my knuckles, and my fingertips tingle. A shiver racks my body. With the jacket gone and the misty air rolling, my body temperature has dropped. I lose my footing as I weave through the trees. The rain presses down, sending fat drops cascading from the canopy. They splash onto my hair and face, rolling over my skin.

The tremble that held my body captive for the past forty minutes morphs into shaking.

Each breath now curls into a suspended cloud in front of my face.

The burn between my ribs is most likely setting the air in my lungs to smoke.

The lightning has faded, and now the forest is dark.

I push through the forest, steadying myself against the trees as I go. But cold, exhausted, and close to giving up, I sink to my knees.

Staring through the forest, I have no idea how far I have left to go.

"Callum!" I huff out a cry, losing my conviction. "Where are you?"

Hanging my head, I let the sadness roll through me.

Joshua.

The scream of tires pushing sideways tears through my mind. Bright lights and scared eyes holding mine as they fall closed.

Never to open again.

I slump over, curling up on the cold, wet ground, and hug my knees to my body.

Maybe if I just lie here, life will forget about me. I will be gone. Pay penance for my poor choices. Leave another good man to a life without drama.

Thunder rumbles in the distance. I shake violently against the temporary parcel of cold air from the storm. Soaked to the bone, I wait for numbness to set in.

Maybe I can convince it to stay . . .

Maybe if I just lie here.

I'll be found. And either way, I can stop being so lost.

T.

Callum.

Either way.

Fat, round spheres fall from above when the canopy moves. They explode on impact as I stare, unseeing. The storm rumbles past, leaving its cold trail as it goes. If only I could whisk away with it.

Then regret folds in around me at the thought of running from this island.

This island is the first place I have been able to relax. To breathe.

I wouldn't leave—

Crashing blunders toward me through the forest undergrowth. I'm so turned around, I can't tell which direction it's coming from.

I should get up.

I should run.

Put distance between me and whoever it is.

After a moment of hesitation, I push off the ground to sit up. My back meets the rough bark of a tree. My body aches. My lungs are only capable of short bursts.

Leaning my head back on the tree, I let my eyes fall closed and accept my fate.

Footsteps close in, slowing as they crunch on the ground near me.

A huffy breath is followed by warmth moving in, right in front of me.

I hold my breath, swallowing down a sob. Wringing my hands, I don't dare to open my eyes. I don't want to know who found me.

I can't bear it.

firefly

Eighteen

CALLUM

I jolt off the bunk.

The echo of a scream reverberates through the hut.

"Fuck!"

I'm off the bunk and out the door before my head can catch up.

Another scream.

I take off at a run toward the sound. The brush is whipping around in the wind. The ground is too damn slippery. My feet are bare.

Dammit.

Thundering through the trees, I'm a man possessed. The only other person on this island is Evie. If those are screams, they're hers.

The storm releases its fury on my little island like it has fucking permission. I pick up my pace.

Another scream. This time, it fades out. Like she's giving up.

Christ, mo nighean.

I slide to a halt, breathing hard as I brace against a tree. Water courses down the bark, washing over my hand. The canopy looses its watery load onto me. Its icy fingers slide down my neck, soaking into my collar before running down my back and chest.

The faint sound of something moving toward me comes from not too far away.

She almost made it.

I take off toward the rustle, hoping to find her unharmed.

Why the hell is she out here in the fucking storm?

What would possibly drive her from the safety of the lighthouse in this shit show?

I round an oversized trunk and slow my stride as I see her lying on the ground. The tons of weight that hit my heart at the sight of her steal the hot air from my lungs. I stand, hands hanging, taking her in. Her desperate face, pained and twisted as she sobs, lying on the forest floor.

With gentle movements, I eliminate the space between us and squat as she sits up, eyes still closed. Her shoulders heave. Her hands wring. Her throat works. Her body shakes.

She's terrified.

Oh, my girl. What the hell?

I burn to touch her. To take away the fear. Pull the pained look from her face.

My calloused fingers sweep over her jaw. She jerks backward. Her chin wobbles as she struggles to take her next breath.

I swallow past the boulder in my throat before cupping her face with both hands.

"Evie . . ." I choke.

She's shaking something fierce. Her skin is pale, cold, and awash in goosebumps.

I fold my arms around her and pull her away from the tree.

Her ragged inhale tells me all I need to know. "You're okay, baby girl, I got you."

I stand, bending down to sweep her up off the forest floor and into my arms. Pressed against my chest, my arms holding her, she opens her eyes.

I almost lose my composure at the torment lining them.

"Fuck, baby. Let's get you dry and warm."

"Callum?" She sobs, fingers curled around the opening of my shirt.

I grind my jaw shut, tamping back the emotion that wants out badly, and adjust my focus on tracking back to the hut.

When the faint lights of the hut finally poke through the rows of trees, I look down to Evie.

She's out cold.

What has she been through since I left? What the hell was in that envelope? What happened at the house?

I push through the hut's door and am thankful the wood stove is still burning. Depositing her on the bunk, I bundle up as many blankets as I can find. Which is four in total, since no one but me has stayed here for years. I arrange them in front of the stove and add two more logs to the burner, leaving the door open. It's more like a small fireplace now. Evie sits on the bunk, staring at the floor, shaking.

"We need to get those wet clothes off," I say softly, coming to stand in front of her.

Wide brown eyes look up at me as she nods slowly.

I reach for her shirt, and she raises her arms. I tug the wet shirt from her and lay it over a chair to dry. Her shivers intensify. Her white lace bra is also soaked.

"This too," I rasp.

Her teeth chatter as she studies my face. "Y-ou d-do i-it."

I lean over, sliding my palms over her back for warmth before I unclasp the hook of the bra. The wet lingerie slips away, and I tug it over her arms and toss it over the chair.

With trembling hands, she pulls her long hair to one side and squeezes the water from it. It hits the floor, splashing my feet. It's fucking cold.

Christ, I need to get her warm. And quick.

I pull her to her feet and unbutton her shorts. As I get

them to her boots, I undo the laces and slip the boots off before taking her shorts and panties as well. I turn back to lay her clothes over the chair. Her chattering teeth fill the small space, urging me to hurry up. A reminder of what I'm doing.

Tell that to my throbbing, rock-hard cock. To the shallow cycles of air barely gracing my lungs. And when I turn back to face Evie, she's shaking, hugging her arms around her body, eyes trained on the fire.

My girl needs warming up. And that's what I'm going to do.

I sweep her off her feet again and carry her to the blankets. I lie her down on them, but she sits up, crossing her legs. She shuffles closer to the fire. So I drape one blanket over her shoulders and sit behind her, wrapping my body around hers.

I want to ask her what happened, but my curiosity can wait. After a while, she places her head back on my shoulder. I can't resist nuzzling her neck. She's warmer now. I rub my hands over her belly as we sit on the floor in front of the fire without words. Her hands move to cover mine. Her fingers are warm now, too. Not icy like when I found her.

Good.

"It was my fault . . ." she whispers.

I look up at her, my lips still hovering by her neck. "What was, baby?"

"Joshua." The word is rote. Emotionless. Like a shock victim.

I should have thought of shock.

Fuck me.

"What'd you mean?" I ask.

"That he died. It's my fault he died."

"Hell, Evie. Don't say that."

Those words will bury their way into her soul and eat it from the inside out.

"I should have known. I should have put a stop to it the first time. But I'm just a coward, and now a good man is dead." Her voice is too soft, but it drops an octave as she says, "And it's all my fault."

Grabbing her shoulders with both hands, I tug her around to face me. She relents and turns on her seat, brown eyes finding mine. I tilt her chin up when she tries to break eye contact.

"Hey, you listen to me. It was an *accident*. By definition, that's no one's fault. Least of all yours."

She's shaking her head. My fingers slip away.

"It wasn't. I know now."

"What are you talking about?"

"I made the wrong choice."

She lies on the blankets and curls up on her side.

Christ.

I'm no more the wiser than I was back in the forest where this is concerned. But I won't push her. Not now.

Evie falls asleep in front of the fire, and I lay beside her, studying the old tin roof like I'll be able to find the answers to the mystery of this girl who has burrowed her way into my heart.

When none present themselves and my back aches from the hard floor, I fold another blanket around Evie and pad to the bunk. I don't want to wake her, so I take the only pillow from the bunk and gently slide it under her head. She moans the sweetest sound but doesn't wake.

Back on the bunk, I lie on my back with my hands under my head. Exhausted from a day in the sun and crashing around the forest mid-storm, I close my eyes. My body sinks into the old thin mattress and I let sleep take me under.

I wake with a start. The early rays of morning stream through the opaque windows. Evie is sound asleep on the floor, the fire long gone out. But it's much warmer now, the remnants of the storm's cold trail a distant memory. I sit up and run a hand over her clothes. They're mostly dry.

"Please tell me there's coffee in this shack of yours," Evie drawls softly.

I roll off the bunk and set up a small pot with instant coffee from my bag and water from the rainwater tank, setting it on the burner of the stove. Evie hugs the blanket around herself, watching me. She looks paler than usual.

"How you feeling?" I ask.

"Fine, I'm okay." Her eyes snap to the front door, as if she can avoid me by not looking at me.

"What the hell were you doing out in the storm?" I try to rein in my worry, but my words still sound harsher than intended.

Her knees slide up to her chest, her chin settling on top of them as she worries that goddamn bottom lip through her teeth. "I got scared, that's all."

I squat and brush the hair at her temple back over her ear. "What scared you?"

She looks up, hesitating, as if wordlessly saying *what do you mean?*

Her brows lower, and I thumb her bottom lip, ignoring my stirring cock as she subtly leans into my touch. "What scared you, Evie?"

A small breath hitches inward, and she shakes her head. "I don't want to talk about it. But thank you for finding me," she whispers.

I push to my feet. "Okay, coffee's ready." I pull the pot from the stove as steam billows from the small spout and set it on the table while I find two enamel mugs. No cream or sugar in this old hut. Pouring two cups, I drop into a seat. Evie turns to watch me, eyeing the steaming mugs.

"One's yours when you're ready," I say, not letting her gaze escape mine.

She stands and pads to the other chair, sinking into it, the blanket still wrapped around her naked body.

"Did my clothes dry?" she asks, taking a sip with one hand, the other clutched around the blanket.

"Mostly."

"Are you staying out here another night?"

"Are you?"

She looks around the fishing hut, taking in the rustic minimalism. "It's very similar to your other man-shack at the house."

I chuckle. My man-shack. Nice.

"'Spose it is. You didn't answer my question."

"I don't want to intrude. You came out here for something. And I doubt it included me." Her eyes are glued to the tabletop, as if it's fascinating.

Always putting other people's needs first. "This sweet, nice girl shit is getting on my damn nerves, mo nighean."

"Mo nighean? What does that mean?"

"You're the queen of words, you tell me."

Her cheeks flush. She knows what it means, alright. Smart little thing figured it out. Of course she did.

"My girl," she whispers, her eyes staring at the floor by the wonky bookshelf.

"Do you want me to stop saying it?"

She swallows, her mug resting on the table. After a beat,

her eyes meet mine as she sets her shoulders back and says, "I don't know yet."

I drain my mug and pluck her clothes from the chair and slide them across the table. "If you're staying, you help hunt."

"Hunt?" Worry and anticipation mingle through her brown eyes, her lips parted.

"For food, Jane."

She chuckles and fists her clothes, sliding them closer. "Okay, Tarzan."

"You won't catch a thing wearing a blanket, baby."

"I won't?"

The look in her eyes transforms. It's darker, like the color I saw in them a day ago. Instead of asking for or taking what she wants, she simply stares at me.

I'm hard at just the storm in her eyes. Her hand falls away from the center of her chest, letting the blanket slip away.

Christ.

I'm supposed to be clearing my head.

Making smart decisions about this.

Doing what's in her best interest.

Not entertaining the urge to bend her over the table and slam into her so fucking hard she screams my name and milks me dry.

But those are the very images that commandeer my brain as every last drop of blood sinks to my aching cock.

"I—" she starts as color fills her neck and face, her fine fingers grappling to pull the blanket back up.

I snatch up her hand and move between her legs. "Don't. Don't do that."

"We don't have to . . ."

I grip her chin with my other hand. "No, we don't. But you wanted something, or you wouldn't have dropped the blanket. Wouldn't have braved a storm to find me."

Her breaths have turned choppy. Her nipples are hard points. My mouth waters, desperate to draw them in. To suck them between my teeth and bite at the soft flesh surrounding them.

Fuck. I have no control around this woman.

No one has pushed me to this point, to the point where I barely have a semblance of say in how I respond.

Ever.

"Show me how much you want it. Convince me, baby girl."

Her hands brush over her face before fisting at her hips. Wriggling in her seat a little, her gaze darts around the room as if what she needs is anywhere but with the man in front of her.

She's flustered.

I hate how much I love seeing her needy. Besides, she started this, and I'm going to make sure she damn well finishes it.

"I want to see the woman, Evie. Not the little girl who's too afraid to take what she wants."

She huffs a breath. With a swallow, she closes her eyes and pushes to her feet. The chair scrapes backward, and she moves until mere inches separate us. We're chest to chest, but I don't move.

Her eyes open, and she moves one elegant hand to her breast.

With one finger, she circles a pert nipple, drawing my attention to the display. "Here is where I want it . . . You."

I raise a brow.

That fucking bottom lip slips between her teeth. I tilt my head in warning.

"Not convinced," I rumble.

Liar.

I'm a goddamn liar. A liar with a rock-hard cock that throbs with an ache that's going to take me down any second. But this isn't about me.

"What do you want, then?" she whispers.

"It's what you want, remember?"

"This feels like begging."

I smirk at her. "That would work."

Her face hardens and she slides a hand down her belly. I can't pull my gaze from her fingers as they disappear into her pussy. Her lips part, her breathing ratcheting up a notch. Her face slackens for a heartbeat until she pulls her fingers out.

My lungs cave in with each heavy breath as she raises her hand and . . . slips her fingers between my lips.

Fuuck.

I grab her hips and throw her up on the table on her ass. A sweet little squeak turns to a whimper as I sink onto the chair, push her thighs wider than is polite, and tug her hips to the edge of the table. Propped up on her hands, her hair hangs behind her back, brushing across the tabletop. Her perfect fucking pussy glistens with her slick need.

Christ almighty.

I thumb her sweet little clit, and she squirms on the table, eyes snapping up. Desperate to savor her, I sweep two fingers through her center and study her reaction.

Her mouth opens on a long moan, and I exchange my fingers for my tongue. She tastes so goddamn incredible. I sweep through her, her soaked entrance covering my tongue. God, I could blow from the taste of her.

"Callum," she rasps.

"More, baby girl?"

"More."

I lick her clit, sinking two fingers inside her, and she tightens around me. Lapping and suckling her clit, I pump my fingers in a steady rhythm, curling them forward as she bucks, setting the rickety old table wobbling under her weight.

What I wouldn't do to be balls-deep inside this woman.

The way she riles me up, with just the bare minimum.

It's too fast.

Too much.

The fact that I'm falling for the little twentysomething who showed up at the marina and turned my life upside down . . . It's—

I—

Fuck.

Hands slide into my hair, and I realize I've stilled.

"Hey, what is it?" The softest brown eyes find mine.

"We—I—nothing, it's nothing." I dip my head to continue.

Her hands capture my jaw, tilting my head up. "No, it's not nothing. Tell me. Whatever it is, we'll work it out. We don't have t—"

I push to my feet, and her hands fall from my face.

It's more than too much.

Not only is she the softest place I've ever wanted to fall, even the slightest touch from her sets me on fire.

An impossibility.

She's almost half my age.

She's not staying.

I'm the world's biggest idiot. This can only end badly. I don't get this type of relationship. Life would never allow it.

"Get dressed, mo nighean. We need to hunt."

Now the hurt in her eyes is not her own. It's for me.

Another reason this is a fucked-up idea. Because it doesn't feel like fooling around anymore.

Not to me, at least.

Nineteen

EVIE

From everything to nothing in a heartbeat. Hot to frigid cold. That's what Callum and I are like. He's not saying it, but something is holding him back. Something has him all up in his head about this. Us. If there is such a thing as 'us.' I don't know what happens at the end of my time here, but I want to spend my days with him while I can.

I tug my shirt over my head and pull on my shorts. Slipping my boots on, I push through the door of the hut. Wandering toward the sound of waves, I find him on the beach, sitting on a large dark granite rock, tossing pebbles into the angry waves. The ocean breeze whips my hair around my face, and I scramble to tame it back as I reach him.

Sitting beside him, I stare into the stretch of water as if

searching for the same thing he seems to be looking for. His gaze doesn't break from the waves as I nudge his shoulder with my own. "Need to talk about it?" I ask, feeding his own words back to him.

After a long moment, he tilts his head and looks at me. "You ever make a decision thinking it's the best one, only for it to implode your world in ways you could never have imagined?"

Heavens, that's deep.

The more I think it over, the more it sounds like the words T wrote. Accusing me of making choices that led to Joshua's death. For a brief slip of time, I believed it. Running through the darkened forest amid the storm, I believed it. Laying down, wanting to give up, I believed it. But when I woke up this morning, warm and safe in the company of one of the best men I have ever had the blessing to spend time with, I realized protecting myself was not a choice.

T is wrong.

In so many ways.

"You sure it's the choice that was the cause? Maybe there's more to it than you think. More complicated than we like to think," I offer, staring at the ocean as the words spill over my tongue. They're far too wise for my age, but I earned them. In every moment of grief, every day I survived after the accident. Every time I held those threatening letters in my hands and decided not to give them life.

"Evie—" His hand slides underneath mine, resting on my thigh.

"Callum?"

He huffs a strained breath before sucking in his next inhale like it's the last parcel of oxygen left for humankind. "Never mind. We should hunt."

I can't take my eyes off his face.

The burn of whatever he left unsaid sends a swell of emotion into my chest. "Sure," I finally whisper. "Show me your hunt, Tarzan."

He chuckles and presses a kiss to the back of my hand. He's off the rock a second later, pulling me down with him. We gather buckets, two very blunt-looking knives, and something I think is supposed to be a spear. Walking in a comfortable silence, we work our way around the rock pools, filling our buckets with tiny morsels the ocean offers up.

A school of small fish darts through one of the larger pools.

"Stab a couple, will you? Breakfast." Callum nods to them.

"I'm not doing that."

"Yes, you are. No help, no eat."

Caveman.

No help, no eat, I say as pompously in my head as possible, giggling as I adjust the stick in my hand. He glances at me, his hands working an oyster loose from the rock as his eyebrows quirk up.

I must look like a madwoman. Spear in hand, cackling as I line up my next unwilling sacrifice.

Mwah ha ha ha.

Now I lose it, doubling over, and the spear clatters to the rocks.

"Care to share with the rest of the class?" Cal says with a chuckle.

"I—" Laughter steals the words forming in my mind. I clutch at my side. My belly aches before I can suck in a fresh lungful.

Callum darts from the rock and rushes me, sweeping me off my feet, spinning me around. My head falling back over his arm, the clouds spin above me. Happiness slices through every vein, every inch of me. The rumble of his laughter murmurs against my ribs, and I shift my gaze to his face. The happiness captured there—a grin so wide it stretches his features and blue eyes lit like neon flame—is stunning.

My laughter peters out.

My world stops spinning.

My feet touch the ground and hands cup my face.

The warmth of his forehead presses against mine. A rough chuckle slips past his lips as I palm his jaw, working the soft bristly beard under my fingertips. I'm mesmerized as it moves under my touch. Running a thumb over his bottom lip, my breath hitches as his lip drags under my touch. Flutters are set in flight in my belly, giving way to a delicious warmth as I huff out, "Huh."

"Evie, fuck . . ." His face turns pained.

I swallow hard.

"Fish," I whisper.

"Fish." His jaw feathers, and his hold softens.

Slipping from his embrace, I walk back to the rock pool in a daze. I swipe up the spear and try to focus on the task at hand. My mind loops on the tiny slice of happiness we found. The bridge of my nose prickles, and tears bloom behind my eyes. This man—this island—has brought me back to life. I thought grey would only ever be the lens I looked through. Now, color is weaving back in.

Something moves below me, and I remember the spear in my hand.

I throw it at the movement.

Miss.

Hunt. Eat.

So very *Eat, Pray, Love.*

The Fire Island version . . . *Hunt, Eat, Happiness.* My stomach grumbles. Leaning down, I swipe up the spear and double down on my efforts. I squat down and still, poised and waiting for an unsuspecting slip of a fish. We're going to need a few.

I stab the quick fish that dares to dart by. The sharp barb pins him to the rocky wall of the pool.

"Shit! Oh god. I'm so sorry, buddy." I cringe as it flops helplessly.

A warm hand slides behind my neck as Callum moves into my side. "You did good."

"Ah, not sure I'm the hunt them, eat them type."

"Own it, baby girl. Take life by the balls. Lest you want it to find yours?"

"Ugh, fine. But for the record, I hate this."

He dots a kiss to my temple before tugging the spear up and plucking the fish off and tossing it into the bucket. "Next one." He hands me back the spear.

With a sigh and a hunger that's now burning a hole right through my belly, I narrow my focus to the quick little fish. I line up another, making sure to stay as still as possible. That seems to help.

I snag one, tossing it into the bucket myself. This Jane doesn't need Tarzan's help.

My heroines never need assistance. Why should I?

I decide right there and then to channel my inner heroine from this day forward. When another oyster hits the bucket, I glance over to see Cal wink at me. I chuckle and shake my head at him.

"Winking? Really, old man?"

The joy leaches from his face, and he pushes to stand. Marching to where I am perched on the side of the rock pool, he grabs my waist and hauls me up onto his. His teeth nip at my breasts through my T-shirt. I lean back, a soft moan slipping past my lips. The delicious assault pauses, and I look back down.

"Who you calling old, brat?"

I'm dropped to my feet as he swats my ass and returns to his oyster hunt.

I've never been so turned on in my life from such a short interaction.

I like this version of me. The way this feels, being here. Being squared away on this island with Callum.

But this isn't my life—it's a temporary solace to ensure my productivity is restored. And it is. I'm grateful.

But I can't help thinking, now that I've found all this . . .

How will I ever go back to the city? To a world Callum's not a part of.

So many *buts*.

With a full belly and a fire blazing in the small wood stove, I sit on the blankets, Callum beside me, drinking the only drop of alcohol he brought. It's whiskey, and it's harsh. It warms me from the inside as it slides down, and my body tingles. I look around the hut, wondering why he came out here. There is even less here than back at the house in his little shack. And at least that has running water in its tiny sink.

His attention is lost to the flickering amber flames.

"Penny?" I ask.

He drops his head and huffs out a breath. "You don't want my thoughts, baby girl."

I can't help but smile at the pet name. Cal looks up at me, and my smile melts with the sadness reflecting in his blues, so I offer, "Maybe two, then, because it looks like the thought oughta come out."

He nods, a shallow movement. "Possibly."

I wind my arms around my knees and rest my head on his shoulder. "We have all night . . ."

The words are no better than a whisper. The hint of permanent longing flickers to life when I think of all the ways we could spend an entire night. The heat from the fire is suddenly overwhelming. But I don't move from his shoulder. I don't want to.

I don't want to move from here.

"Was thinking about the last time I was here." His voice is rough.

"With your family?" I ask softly.

"No, after that."

What does *that* mean?

"Oh?" I lift my head, tilting it, desperate to get a glance of what's written on his face. But he continues, and I drop my gaze to the fire.

"It was after Ava. I was in a bad place. This hut's always been a kind of solace for me. Like the only place I want to be when life implodes on me, you know?"

My thoughts drag their knuckles back to the accident. The whir of sounds, the heartache barely dimmed by time. "Yeah, I think I do."

"Nobody—" He clears his throat. "The town, they didn't like the idea of me and Ava. She was the golden girl, the mayor's only daughter. Adored by every single person." He shifts on his seat with a strained swallow, and I sit up and slide my arm through his as he continues. "I was a bad influence after I lost my parents. Went off the rails. Iris almost disowned me, I'm sure of it. Then Ava walked into my life and it was like something just clicked. We were inseparable. So many folks tried to talk her out of dating me. We were young. She was seventeen. I was twenty-two. Didn't help that I rode an Indian." He huffs a strained noise that sounds like amusement.

Excuse me?

"An Indian?" I ask, an eyebrow raised.

"An Indian motorcycle. A '99 Chief. Black, leather. She was a beauty."

"You don't have it anymore, I guess . . ."

"Actually, it's sitting in the shed. Hasn't run for years."

"Oh." So that's what the big bulky item was in the chained-up shed.

He runs a hand through his hair, focus drifting back to the fire.

"Keep going," I whisper.

Calloused fingers tangle with mine. "We got pregnant. That sealed the deal for the town. They hated me even more for stealing her future from her. Least that's what Iris relayed to me. By the time Ava told me, I was away. God, I loved her, and all I wanted was to make sure they were nothing but taken care of. With nobody willing to give me a job locally, I'd enlisted."

"Oh, Callum." Breath lodges in my airway at the heartbreak lacing his words, and I know where this is leading.

"She wrote me every week. And I her. We missed each other something fierce. I asked her to marry me in the last letter I sent. Shipped the ring I'd bought to her. Things were going well with the pregnancy. The ba—" His hand slips away as he slams his palms into his eyes with a groan. "I never got to say goodbye. They both died. She was barely six months along."

Tears course down my cheeks with his grief. I snuggle into his side, taking one of his hands back between my two. "You couldn't have known. You sorted your life out for her, sacrificed to take care of her. If the town can't or won't see that, that's on them." Heat courses through my veins like the flames in front of us as my anger rises. How could they be so narrow-minded? So cold? He and Iris lost their parents.

So much for small towns taking care of their own.

"So you moved to an island?" I whisper.

"Ava's parents had the funeral without me, then moved clean across the country. The second I landed back here, no one would look at me." He sighs, shaking his head. "It's easier this way. I still have Iris and Em, but I don't have to deal with the town."

If I could undo the years of hurt this man's been put through, I would. In a heartbeat. Nobody should be punished for choices they made eons ago, let alone be judged for their past mistakes when they work so hard to better their life.

"You have me, too. For a little longer."

He moves, eyes studying my face. I can't help myself when my hands brush over his beard. The wounded young man in those eyes, I know now, is what I have mistaken for broody old guy all this time. The overwhelming urge to make Callum feel better catches me in its intoxicating grip.

His warm hands curl around my wrists. "Eve—"

I shake my head. "Tell me something."

He tilts his head, a mix of wonder and confusion dancing in those blues.

"Where would you go if you could be anywhere?"

His brows furrow, his gaze dropping to the spot between us that's shrinking by the second as he hesitates. "This island. With you."

God above, my heart's completely melted. Its puddly remnants drip through my rib cage. I open my mouth. I should respond, but nothing forms. Callum rises to his knees, capturing my face, pulling my mouth to his. He devours me like I'm the last good thing left in his life. Like at any moment, I too could slip away.

I tear at his old work shirt, feral to touch him. Heat blazing through my core, I scramble to my knees before climbing into his lap. Rough hands slap onto my ass, gripping tight. The tender mewl that breathes through my lips detonates his hunger.

"Fuck, Evie. Fuck, nighean bhrèagha."

I'm flipped onto my back on the pile of blankets a heartbeat later. I'm caged in by Callum hovering over me, propped up on all fours, before I recover the breath that huffed from my lungs. I trace a finger over his jaw, then his lips. He nudges my hand with his face, planting a kiss to my palm before closing his eyes.

"Where would you be, baby girl, if you could be anywhere in this world?"

His eyes open when the question lands.

Blue, the depths of the deep ocean, now searching for an answer.

firefly

Twenty

CALLUM

"**R**ight here," Evie breathes.

The tight leash I've had on my impulses around her since she woke up this morning snaps. Every last thought of putting distance between her, of trying to stay away for her sake, vanishes like the morning fog on a sultry day. Curling out of existence like it was never there.

"Is that you asking me to stay, Callum?" Her words are threadbare.

My heart flings wildly in its ribbed cage.

Yes. No?

Christ.

I can't ask such a thing of this woman. She's too incredible to be wasting her life away on an isolated island with just me for damn company. I can already see how it would end. Her hurt, me cemented into this life like the immovable, intolerable bastard I am.

Her face reddens when I can't respond.

"Sorry, I didn't mean . . ." She tilts her head, gaze fixing on some random point in the hut.

I take her face in one hand, sliding the other under her shoulders. Leaning back on my heels, I haul her up to me. That option, her staying and this thing having a real chance, will never make daylight. I'll never let it.

She can't want that.

This is her empathy talking. The sweet woman, with the big brown doe eyes and even bigger heart. It's her way of trying to fix what she didn't break. "You have a big, wonderful life to live, and this island ain't where that's going to happen."

Evie studies my face. Her mouth works like she wants to say something, but she can't find the right words.

I cup her face and dot a kiss on her lips. "Hey, don't feel sorry for me. I won't have that shit. You're going to write your book, have an amazing career. Then one day, you'll think back to the old guy on the island you spent nine months with. That's all, baby girl."

Releasing a huffy breath, emotion tightens her face.

"That okay?" I ask, hating myself right now.

She nods, and I tamp out my disappointment. I can barely get the next stupid fucking word out. "Good."

"Good," she echoes, and her chest rises and falls in quick

succession. Her brown eyes are so damn dark, they appear black in the muted firelight.

"What do you want right now, Evie? Tell me, or I'm taking."

Her arms move, lifting her shirt over her head. She shakes her head, and her long brown locks spill over her shoulders, tickling the top of her perfect tits. I tug at the bra straps and plant kisses to her shoulders, over her collarbones. Impatience finds me, and I rip the lacy garment from her body. The most tender squeak puffs from her as she startles and settles on my lap.

"Fucking *mine*," I growl.

My mouth closes around her soft, fleshy breast. Her moan sinks somewhere central to my soul. Cock throbbing, I work my way to her dusky hard peak. As my teeth close over her nipple, she leans back on both hands, flat on the floor, offering up a feast for this desperate man.

Mouth watering, I devour one peak and then the other. She wriggles on my lap, whimpering with every long, hard stroke I send over her nipples. The sight of her writhing on my lap almost takes me under.

I may not be able to give her everything, but I can give her this.

She's so fucking beautiful like this, half dressed, lapping up every little movement my tongue, my teeth, my mouth make. Old wounds split right open against her skin on mine. My self-deprecating thoughts are tossed around my mind like rusted, blunt javelins. I don't deserve happiness.

She's not mine to have.

She deserves better.

She . . .

She—

"Fuck," I choke out. "Eve, we shouldn't."

Her head snaps back up, confusion and lust warring for dominance in her eyes. She pants, "Why not?"

"I—You—" I lift her from my lap and scramble to my feet, making for the door.

Darkness swallows me as the sound of waves crashing floods in. I drag in a long, agonizing breath. It's been a lifetime since I've wanted someone this way.

As much as I adored Ava, we never had this torturous chemistry. Where not touching her, not claiming her torches me, burning me to cinders. I could disintegrate to ash without her. It's too much.

It's dangerous.

It's—

I groan.

Fucked. I'm fucked, that's what I am.

I'm incapable of putting distance between us, if I have a choice.

I haul my ass toward the beach, praying Evie stays put in the hut. I drop onto a cluster of rocks, tilting my face up to the moon. Maybe this is my penance for everything that went down when I was younger. Finding the woman my soul talks to, only to be too old, too broken.

Evie is sunlight. She's vibrant and bursting with life, even if she hides it away from the rest of the world most of the time. I see it when she thinks nobody is around. When she thinks nobody notices, I do.

To have her wrapped around me, to take what I want would be my own undoing. We've already gone too far. Haven't we?

The waves roll in, keeping time with my bruised heart. Hell, even now the thought of Evie leaving cracks me wide open. Another curveball life thought was a great idea to toss at me. Timing's never been my strong suit. I kill another hour on the rocks trying to figure out a life where we all get what we want. Coming round full circle to no solution for the third time, I push off the rock and trudge through the sand. Walking along the beach, I let the breeze cool my frazzled nerves.

I came to the hut to put distance between us.

Because it's the right thing to do.

Never before has the right thing felt so fucking wrong.

The moon is high in the sky when I turn back, heading for the hut. The door is ajar when I make it back. I find Evie sleeping on the bunk on her side, room for me beside her. Dappled moonlight spills in through the window and illuminates her elegant face. She's in her T-shirt and panties. A blanket covers her legs, but they have tangled their way into a mess.

Tugging my shirt off, I lie beside her. Turning onto my side, I brush a stray piece of hair behind her ear, and she murmurs in her sleep. Her pretty pink lips curve as she moans. She rolls away from me, and I slide an arm over her belly and tug her into my body. Her head turns, back arching as if on autopilot with my touch.

As if her soul heard mine, even in her sleep.

I breathe her in, tucking this moment away as a memory I will treasure for the rest of my life.

"Cal?" she moans.

"Yeah, baby girl."

"Where'd you go?"

"Nowhere, mo nighean. Go back to sleep."

She hums, her body pressing in a little more.

Fuck me.

A moment later, her breathing settles, and she's sound asleep again. My forehead tilts to press into her hair, and I close my eyes. Happiness is a man wrapped around the woman he loves.

The—

Jaw feathering, I tamp down the groan that's painfully filling any cavity it can find.

I swallow hard, trying my best to dislodge the stone that grew in my throat with that last thought. I know, this time round, it's going to hurt. More than I've had to endure before. Because despite our short time together, this woman has cracked open my seized-up heart, revived it, and sent it to bloom. With her elegant ways, her fiery streak, her tenderness. Something my hard old heart needed more than I will ever admit.

I needed her.

I need Evie.

But more than that, I need her to be happy.

Whatever that means for me.

The house comes into view, and for the first time in my life, I wish it wouldn't. I wish the last few days, lost to the wilderness and just the two of us, could have lasted forever.

Squash that stupid damn thought, buddy.

Switch it off.

Stomp it down.

Ain't happening.

Watching her hips sway in front of me for the last hour, those long legs, short fucking shorts . . . Hell, I've been hard for thirty minutes.

"God, look at that beautiful thing," Evie says, a grin wrapping around her gorgeous face. Her clothes are dirty, her hair is a mess, but her stride is busting at the seams as she all but runs back to the lighthouse. Everything looks in place, no visible damage from the storm. The lamp is still on and oscillating.

By the time we reach the front door, I have a million things I want to say to her. None of them leave my mouth. She pushes through the front door and stops just over the threshold, arms out, head back, and eyes closed. "Did you miss me?"

I chuckle, stepping inside. "Shower, Evie baby."

"God yes. You want to go first?"

I raise an eyebrow at her. "Why waste water?"

"Okay? But I thought we weren't—"

I dump my bag to the floor and grab her onto my waist. She giggles, sliding her arms around my neck. "Fine. Water conservation it is."

I scale the spiral stairs with her legs tight around my waist and her arms draped over my shoulders, and I feel like the luckiest man alive. We bypass the bed and head straight for the bathroom.

"Down, please." Her lips roll and she glances at the vanity.

"You have one minute. Or I'm starting without you."

"I'd watch that." Cheekiness lights up her face.

Christ.

I slap her ass and step toward the shower, peeling off my clothes as I go. She plucks her toothbrush and toothpaste. Of course.

I hold my hand out to her as I lean over to turn on the faucets. My toothbrush drops into my hand, with paste in a long, neat line on the bristles. The hot water bursts to life, and I adjust the cold tap until it's perfect and steam starts to curl into the space. Stepping in, I brush my teeth as days' worth of fishing, hunting, and exploring the forest are washed away.

I can always appreciate the first shower after making it back from the hut, but this is the first time I've had someone with me. As if on cue, one elegant foot slips past the curtain. A heartbeat later, Evie stands with her hands by her sides just out of the water spray, her eyes set on mine. Her gaze falls to my mouth. Toothbrush still working my teeth clean, I lean out to the basin and spit. With the toothbrush forgotten, I move back into the water and open my mouth to rinse the paste from it.

Evie's eyes track over my face, my body. Her breaths are coming in little pants, and I can't help but reach for her.

God, we are both fucked.

Hands on her shoulders, I maneuver her into the water. She simply watches me as I grab up her soap and wash her body before squirting a generous amount of shampoo into my palm. Her long locks take a while to lather and rinse out. I repeat the process with conditioner before her arms tangle around my neck, her brown eyes searching. "Your turn," she whispers.

She sinks sudsy, shampoo-lathered hands into my hair,

and my eyes shutter closed. Fine fingers work my messy hair clean. While the shampoo sits, she takes to my limbs, one by one, with her bar of soap. Running it over each muscle, each part of my body in turn.

Every sweep of her hand with the soap sends me higher. I'm hard as stone within seconds of her hands on me. A blush fills her face as she lets her hands wander, not stopping as she finishes her task.

Christ, I need more than I want her to give me.

I want to take it all. And by the way she studies my face as I struggle with this, she knows what's going on in my head.

I rest my forehead to hers. "I can't be gentle with you, Evie. You're too much for me."

"I know. I don't want gentle, Cal. I want you." The words are pleading. Lifting my gaze to meet hers, I find her desperate.

So. Fucking. Beautiful.

We made it three days in the forest without crossing this line. Now, back home, it's impossible to control. She must feel it, too. This impossible, improbable thing between us.

"Promise me one thing." I grip her hips with too much force.

"Anything."

"Leave when your nine months is up."

Her breath hitches and her hands splay over my chest,

one covering my heart. Her face bunches before she schools it back and nods.

"Good girl."

Her eyes flutter shut, hands tracking up my neck, fingers curling over my jaw. "Please, fear milis."

My throat closes over. The words she found, the ones no one has ever said to me before, splinter my heart.

I slam her into the tiled wall, my grip turning feral. Tilting her head back, she opens for me. I sink into her, claiming her mouth. She's pliable, soft flesh and warmth.

She's *mine*.

Twenty-One

EVIE

anting someone has never hurt like this. The ache growing for this man is sending me to the brink. His fingers curl in my hair, one hand collaring my throat. It's all I can do to drag his mouth back to mine when he goes up for air. The throb between my legs has long since turned my insides to lava. My heartbeat thunders, turning every breath into fiery nothingness.

"Callum," I rasp.

His grip around my neck fades and knuckles graze over my stomach, heading to the ache at my center. Mouth agape, I whimper when his fingers sweep over my clit. He holds his eyes to my own as my face twists with pleasure. His lip curls at one side, like he can feel it, too. Like each jolt he sends through me buries itself inside him, too.

"Evie, this is mine. This wet-as-fuck pussy—all mine."

I pant as he runs two fingers through my center. I fight the need to close my eyes and sink against the wall at my back. I don't want to miss a moment of this. Every look he gives me, every face he pulls—I want to capture them all and commit them to memory.

For . . . when I leave.

I hate that sentence more than any other that has ever existed.

The fact that my time here with this man is limited burns. A hole, right through me. Teeth find my nipple and the thought bursts and disintegrates. Writhing against the wall, I want him everywhere.

It seems all I ever do with this man is beg.

"Fuck, look at you, baby girl. So damn needy for it."

He sinks two fingers inside me, and I arch off the wall with a whimper. His thumb circles my clit as he pumps his fingers deep, curling them forward. My body is vibrating, my footing getting sloppier by the second. A hand grips my hip, steadying me in the slippery tub. The water turns cold, and Cal groans, pulling his fingers from my core.

"No," I choke.

A sly smile curls over his lips as he slides them into his mouth. He growls around his digits, tasting my need dripping down his palm. When he's done with his hand, he turns and shuts off the water, shoving the curtain back. I step toward the edge of the tub, and he grabs me up, settling me on his hips.

I slam my mouth over his before he has a chance to take a step. Fire consumes my body, and the only cure is him.

Inside me.

The bed meets my back a moment later, and I'm caged in, his knees nudging my legs wide apart. Cal crawls backward, nipping my flesh as he goes. Finally, his mouth hovers over my needy point. I struggle to catch a full breath, sinking my hands into his hair. His tongue circles gently over my clit. I look down at Mr. I-Can't-Be-Gentle.

He bites down, sending me off the bed with a cry. It's heaven, the lancing pleasure of the sting doused by the most agonizingly beautiful sensation when he sucks the bite away. The explosive heat of an orgasm builds fast.

God above, please do that again.

"More," I beg.

Always begging.

I can't even say I hate it. That would be a lie.

Two fingers sink into me as he laps at my clit. My too-short breaths turn into choppy pants.

I—

I can't breathe.

His teeth find my clit again. My cry echoes off the rounded house walls. Whimpers follow as he sucks down hard. I come around his fingers, waves racking my body with such force, my whimper cracking to a sob.

Fuck.

Blue eyes burn. His face looks as wrecked as I feel.

I lay on the bed, propped up, looking down at him. His knees biting into the wood, he clenches his jaw.

"Keep your promise, baby girl. You leave, you hear me?"

"I—" I whimper.

I can't say it.

"Leave, Evie. You staying isn't going to be how this ends."

"I'll leave. But not without this first."

He has his conditions; I have one nonnegotiable. I like the feeling of some sort of control. It feels good to ask for—no, demand—what I want. The thrill of it rises like warmth.

He pushes to his feet, hooking his hands under my knees. When I'm over the edge of the bed, he closes in, the tip of his cock nudging my entrance. "Good girl."

He slams into me, hard and fast. My leg is over his shoulder a second later. His face is desolate as he thunders into me. The stretch of him is delicious. There's none of the usual self-consciousness I have at being this close. This exposed.

Every last thread that makes up my existence can feel it. The rightness, the bloom that unfurls with his touch. With every rough, selfless move he makes.

Head tilted back, bliss takes me under. Eyes faltering shut, I grip the blanket as pressure finds my clit. The warm pad of his thumb caresses me into a desperate state. I'm falling away from existence, teetering on the line between nothingness and everything.

As if reading my mind, he leans over, his hand sliding up my belly and between my breasts before clasping down hard on my throat. "Don't you go wandering off on me."

I open my eyes, finding his tortured gaze.

He releases me as he rises and grips my right side, flipping me over without breaking contact. I huff a needy breath as he crowds me on the bed from behind. Calloused fingers sweep my hair over my back to hang down my right arm. I turn back, my mouth hunting for his. Not tasting him now would be an agony I doubt I'd survive.

"Cal," I utter as his lips find mine.

His hands cover my own, our fingers lacing, he moves deeper inside me. I cant my hips, taking him further still.

"So fucking tight, baby girl. Made for me." He bites down on my shoulder again, and I buck underneath him. The feral growl ripping through him sends a new wave of wetness to my core. His fist twists through my hair as he picks up the pace. Each long, deep stroke builds something exquisite deep inside.

Like nothing I've ever felt.

I widen my thighs for him, wanting him deeper. Wanting more of what only he can give me.

"Look at me, mo nighean." He tugs my head to one side. "Good girl."

His body is rigid, every muscle tensed to satiate me. He quickens. Rough thrusts slam into me, and I whimper when he finds a place so deep, my breath forgets to cycle back into my lungs. A low, raw rumble claws its way up his throat, and he grips my hip with his free hand. Leaning over, his other hand skirts my ribs until fingers find my nipple. He pinches it, rolling it between his fingertips, and pulls out so slowly.

I let out a sob.

"You like that, Evie baby?" His voice is gravel.

I can't respond. His hand on my hip finds my mouth and his thumb slides between my lips, tugging my bottom lip down. I suck him into my mouth and am rewarded with another slow, agonizing stroke. I'm needy for it. Drowning in the scraps he gives me while dreaming about the entire meal.

Leave.

His word from earlier burns.

It's cruel. To find something so ethereal, only for it to never be mine.

His.

Ours.

"Come for me," Cal rasps before picking up the pace, his hand finding my clit. "I want you to milk my cock. I want to know what that feels like. Just once."

My back arches instantly, his words sending me closer and closer to the precipice. I don't want this to be over. I don't want that moment to arrive. The one where he's not sunk deep inside me, where our two souls are no longer retrievable without one ending up with a little of the other.

That loss seems too great.

"Please, *cailín luachmhor*." His voice is raw and all begging.

Too painfully, we are viscerally affected by the other. Warm kisses track up my spine, and the first explosive spiral of my oblivion releases.

"Good girl," he whispers against my back. His strokes stay steady and long, his fingers now circling my clit, drawing out each blissful wave. Whimpers turn to ragged cries as I detonate around him. I need every inch of him as I clamp down.

I'll never have this with anyone else. I know this the second it starts. God, he's perfect.

"Callum, plea—"

He works me over, the rough man who couldn't rein in his need temporarily lost. The soft comfort of his breath is on my neck as he slows and pulls me up into his chest. I tilt my head back, knees digging into the mattress as I plant open-mouthed kisses to his neck. Jaw. Teeth tugging at his bottom lip.

Satiated, but still hunting for more.

Unfolding from around me, he spins me on the bed only to tug me to his hips. I don't care about anything but claiming the gorgeous face in front of me. Palms cupping his face, I smash my mouth to his.

He moves, taking me with him. We're by the desk. My

laptop flies onto the bed. He leans down and sweeps the rest of the items to the floor in one swift motion.

My ass meets the cool wooden surface, and his palms push my thighs wide. Two fingers sweep through my center. They drip with my release when he raises them to my lips. I take the offering, sucking them clean. He pushes his fat tip against my pussy, notching at the entrance. Still now, my breath hitches at the stretch of that delicious part of him opening me.

I grapple at his neck and face, wanting his kiss. He shoves me down, one hand on my collarbone as he slams into me. His face is so goddamn feral as my breasts bounce with every hard, punishing thrust he sends deep.

"This pretty little cunt has been mine since the second you stepped foot on this damn island. When you leave, it will still belong to me."

I can't breathe.

He thunders into me. Harder still. The desk hits the wall under the window. My head meets the glass pane. The window rattles with every stroke. Fingers pinch down on my clit, and I snap up off the desk, legs wrapping around his hips. The restriction sends him wild. He scoops me up, and the wall crashes into my spine a heartbeat later. Hands slide under my ass, and I open wide for him. Thighs aching, I widen further still. Mouth open and hunting for his.

Heat coils low in my belly again, and when I open my mouth to ask for more, his head drops automatically, lips closing around my nipple. He sucks hard, and I cry out through another soul-shattering orgasm. My hands slap to the wall behind me.

"Callum! Fuck, ple—"

Oh god . . .

His face twists as he locks eyes with me, his movements turning sloppy. "Please . . . you have to leave."

Only now falling back down to earth after he shattered me apart, it's all I can do to nod.

One hand hits the wall, his palm slapping by my head. He growls through his release, sending heated ropes deep into me. I cup his face, watching him fall apart further with each stroke.

His forehead drops to my breastbone, and I wrap around him. As if that will hold the rest of the world at bay. As if it will cease to exist and we can stay suspended in this little life we have been wandering through for the last six months.

For the first time in my life, I wish tomorrow could simply be a repeat of today.

If I could, I would strike the word *leave* from existence.

Firefly

Twenty-Two

CALLUM

Nothing burns like getting a taste of something you've hungered for just for it to be so obviously not yours to keep. Moonlight streaks through the house window, its soft beams illuminating the gorgeous dark locks spread out on the pillow beside me. On my side of this old bed, Evie lies, sound asleep.

Figures. After that many orgasms, she oughta sleep for a week. Once wasn't enough. We recovered. Then we couldn't keep our hands off each other.

We showered again.

She climbed me like a tree.

At least, those were her words for it.

I tamp down a chuckle at the sweet little memory. Already, it's a memory. That grounds me like nothing else. Because all this woman will ever be to me is a handful of memories that will sustain me for the rest of my days. It's all she can ever be. I swallow down that indignant thought and roll out of the bed. Padding down the staircase, I head for the kitchen. I take out a mug and fill it with water.

Em's coming out tomorrow. Or today, I guess. The last of the boat parts arrived this week. Might make a trip to the mainland. I'm sure Evie will want to see civilization. Maybe Iris could take her shopping. Me, I'll be hanging by the docks. I'd rather avoid town if I can.

I chug the water and place the mug in the sink.

Not wanting to wake the sweet woman in my bed, I drop onto the sofa, shoving my head into my hands. Regret eats at me the second I have a moment to mull over the last day or so. So much for keeping my distance. So much for keeping my hands off her. A piece of paper under the table catches my eye. I move to the table, squat down, and pick it up.

A letter.

Something blue and dusty covers the smudged writing. Most of it is unreadable. As if it got wet.

The powdery residue is like pollen, or maybe—

Pieces of blue butterfly littering the floor shine in the moon's disappearing rays.

I sweep up a small piece and rub the blue-silver dust between my fingers.

What the hell? Blue belongs to those big, beautiful monarchs. They're not on this island. I try to make out the words that aren't smudged. But not much makes sense. The water damage means I can't put the meaning together. Is this Evie's?

I drop it to the table and make a mental note to ask her about it when she wakes up.

Falling with weary limbs to the sofa, I rest my head back. Never mind Evie being too young for me; I'm too old for her. Exhaling, I turn over the last few weeks in my head, the parts I had no control over. The parts I did, but I gave in anyway. I should go back to bed . . .

As the drowsy pull of sleep tugs at the edges of my concentration, I lay along the sofa and drag the throw blanket over myself haphazardly.

Something soft presses against my lips. Everything is dark. The bed dips. The glorious aroma of coffee winds its way into my senses, and I blink my eyes open. Happiness radiates from brown eyes framed by mussed hair. The coffee mug in her hand steams. She sits on the sofa at my hip.

Sofa, not bed.

Fuck, I fell asleep here.

"Morning, sleepyhead." She offers the mug, her sweet smile the backdrop to her gesture. "Emmett's outside."

I sit up with a groan. This is no place for a worn-out old

man to rest. I rub my neck with one hand, taking the coffee from her with the other. "He been here long?" I sip the scalding coffee, and when I manage a swallow I say, "Thanks."

"About twenty minutes, but he was at the boat for a bit."

"Probably fixed the damn thing already."

"Probably. You need a moment to"—she waves a hand, gesturing to my general head and neck area—"make it look like you didn't spend all night—"

I grab her neck and drag her mouth to mine. With a chaste kiss, I put space between us. "Nope."

"Okay then. I have words to write. Twelve weeks left until deadline. You be here for lunch later?"

Twelve weeks until she is gone from my life.

"Sure," I mutter. "Em can eat with us."

"Sounds great."

I watch the sway of her hips with a whole new appreciation this morning. And the crashing weight of a man with an expiry date lands hard.

What does anyone with limited time do? They make the most of it.

As those long legs disappear up the spiral metal stairs, I make a promise to myself to make each day count. From this one on.

Wrapping the blanket around my waist, I follow her upstairs a moment later. I make a beeline for the bathroom and pull on fresh clothes. Cleaning up, I run a hand through my hair and brush my teeth before making it out of the bathroom.

Evie's fingers fly over the keyboard, something upbeat floating from her headphones, words pouring out onto the white screen like string confetti. I wander up behind her and dot a kiss to the crown of her head. Her hands briefly curl around my wrist as I cup her head with my hands. But she returns to her focus a second later.

My cue to leave.

I find Em in the kitchen when I peel off the last stair. Making himself at home, he stirs his coffee. Probably his fourth for the morning, knowing him. "Finally. Need some extra rest this morning, sleeping beauty?" Em winks at me.

Asshole.

He absolutely figured out why I'm in the house this morning and not in the hut.

"Lucky you'll never need to worry about being kept up all night, bud."

His face flattens under a lingering stare.

Fuck. Now I'm the asshole.

"I did—"

He holds up a hand. "Forget it. Please. My nonexistent love life is not what I came all the way out here for."

"Sure. How's the boat?"

"Fixed. Good as new."

I scoff out a laugh. "The fuck it is."

"See for yourself. You haven't been off this rock for

weeks. Not that I could blame you." He glances at the stairs, absolutely implying Evie is the reason I haven't seen the mainland in almost a month.

I rip the fridge open like it's personally offended me and hunt for something that tastes half-decent cold. I settle on cold chicken and roast veggies from before we left. *On second thought, maybe only the veggies.* Dumping the tinfoil-wrapped parcel onto the counter, I pry a cold root veggie from the mix. It tastes like it sounds. Soggy and cold.

But it beats continuing this conversation.

No way in hell am I getting into why or why not Evie and me are a good idea with Mr. Positivity here. He only ever sees the pros. Cons don't exist in this golden retriever's world. Poor sap. Lucky Iris pulls his head out of the clouds on a regular basis. We all need a reality check every so often.

Mine just happened to come crashing in in the wee hours of this morning.

A little too late.

Bitter about the whole situation, I rip another frigid carrot in half with my teeth.

"You have no idea how glad I am to not be a vegetable in your garden right now. What's got you surly as a bear with a sore head?" Em says. Now concern narrows his eyes. He's been my best friend for decades. There's no hiding anything from him.

I'll be damned if I'm gonna pour my heart out. Be sticking to hard truths.

"Show me the boat, and then we can talk."

As if I'm doing him a favor. God, this shit has me all fucked up. Emmett simply obliges, walking out the front door and sliding his cap on. We walk in silence to the dock, and his gaze swings to me every few steps.

"What?" I grunt out. I can't stop myself, and apparently, it's written all over my goddamn face.

"You know, you keep bottling this shit up, its gonna kill you, man. Almost did before . . ." His words fade out as we reach the boats.

It almost did. After Ava.

Out here on the island by myself, I thought about ending it all more than once. Every time. And every single damn time, I couldn't do that to my little sister. I'm the only family she has left.

I have no doubt this time will drag me under the roiling current like it did last time. This time, however, unlike the whirlwind of Ava's adoration that fueled my last significant relationship, my feelings grow from somewhere much deeper. From a selfless place. The man I am this time around understands with a profound soundness the gravity of spending my days without Evie. By choice.

"Jesus, Cal, you look like someone died."

I swallow, grinding my jaw shut.

"You can't work it out?" Pain is in his eyes, and I can't tell if it's a mirror of what is surely lacing mine or solely empathy.

"Nothing to work out, Em."

He rubs a hand behind his neck and huffs a breath as he drops his focus to the wooden jetty. "You don't have to stay here, if you want to go somewhere else."

"I'm not doing that to my sister. She'd have no one left. Besides, that's not—"

"Irry would have me. Not like I'm ever leaving."

I stare at him.

He's always protected her like a brother. I guess he's right. Emmett will always be around to make sure she's okay. But I can't. Fire Island is who I am.

That's about right. I'm a fucking island.

Figures.

"Well, if you change your mind . . ." Emmett steps onto Firefly. The engine turns over a beat later. She purrs like she never missed a day. "You can leave. Just saying."

I board the boat and check the gauges. Everything looks good. No pungent electrical fire smell, so that's a bonus. "You staying for lunch? I could use a hand in the old shed."

Emmett looks up from his inspection. "You sure?"

"Yeah, it's time I threw half that old crap out."

"Righto, I can load up a fair bit on the big boat and toss it into the marina dumpster."

"Thanks."

An hour and a test run out on the open water later, I'm satisfied the old girl is fit as a fiddle. We head back to the house for a bite of lunch. The lamp is overdue for a clean, and I'm sure I could use the solace of the lantern room. Em sits at the table as Evie comes down the stairs.

"How's the boat?" she says, dropping into the chair by Emmett.

He pulls off his cap and grips it between his hands. "Running good. You'd be ready for a trip to the mainland by now?"

"I guess." She couldn't look less excited about getting off the island if she tried. Something like hope tumbles around my gut, sparking against the cast-iron walls I've built over the years. Her eyes connect with mine as I assemble the sandwiches and she asks, "Need a hand in the garden later?"

"If you have time. How's the words coming along?"

"Two thousand for this morning. So I'm all yours."

Her face changes as her own words register, and she clamps that bottom lip between her teeth.

I plate up the food and carry it to the table. Emmett takes a plate from my hand and slides it to Evie. She says a quiet thank you before taking a tentative bite. Those small moments where she shrinks into herself have become fewer. Watching her uncertainty around Emmett takes me back to those early weeks.

"Well," Em starts, swallowing before he continues. "If you two have plans, I'll make myself scarce."

"No, you don't have to—" Evie starts.

"No, bud—" I say at the same time.

The easy connection Evie and I had last night and this morning is strained.

Emmett stands. "I really should be getting back. Errol will have my balls for wasting half a day already."

I roll my eyes. "Fuck Errol."

Em laughs. "Only you can get away with saying that, McCreary."

Only because Errol's respect for me is nonexistent. Em plucks up his cap and slides it onto his head. It matches his Coast Guard uniform. Less the grease from his side hustle of marine mechanic, that is.

"Bye, Emmett," Evie pipes up with a small wave.

"See you round, Miss Evie." His gaze alternates between us for a moment before it lingers on me and he's out the door.

I finish my food as Evie takes small bites of hers. Her attention is stuck on the front door.

Good. She should be thinking about leaving.

Sweeping the crumbs on my plate to one side and contemplating life, I change my mind. "I have to head up to the lantern room for a bit. We can get out to the garden in a couple of hours."

"Okay. Can I help with the lamp?" Hopeful browns glide to me.

"I got it. You do your research or whatever you need to."

She huffs a small breath, and her cheeks turn pink. "Yeah, I still have to get to that."

I raise an eyebrow, but she doesn't elaborate. I take her plate and my own, placing them by the sink before heading up the stairs. Glancing into the bedroom as I pad by, I take the treads two at a time to the lantern room. As clean as the bright space is, today it feels dirty. Most likely it's all in my head. I tug open the small door to the cleaning and polishing gear and get to work. I make a start on the louvered outer glass first.

When that shines, letting the midday sun's rays pierce my vision, I turn back and select the polishing cloth for the Fresnel itself. The huge light catches dust and tiny particles in its awkward angles. I spend extra time and care on the heart of my home. My entire reason for being here. Without this old lamp, this overgrown light bulb, my purpose here is null and void.

With the navigational technology on modern boats, lighthouses are an outdated coastal feature. Maybe I am, too. This whole Evie situation has me all up in my head. The woe-is-me is riding my ass hard.

Snap the fuck out of it.

My life will simply return to what it was before her.

A man and his island.

Nothing more, nothing less.

$$Twenty-Three$$

EVIE

Research is what I'm doing . . . so why is my body lit on fire, my breaths so quick I can barely draw a proper lungful? I flip the page on the book I borrowed from the library. The way my face burst into flaming heat when the librarian scanned this one to check it out still sears over my skin like a surly ghost.

The pile of books sits to my left as I hunt through the pages for different ways to up the chemistry and deepen the main characters' connection. I've been here, tucked away on this sofa, for hours. The book in my hand, *The Joy of Sex*, is packed with illustrations. Images I am sure will be burned into my brain for the rest of my days.

My panties are slick, nipples pert, and I all but pant as I turn the page.

The things an author has to do to get a scene right on the page . . .

I drift a hand over my chest, my fingers slipping past my lips as I take in a man bending a woman almost in half as he—

A throat clears somewhere nearby.

With a start, I slam the book shut, eyes darting to the sound.

Cal stands in the door frame.

Of course he does.

The pile of sex books may as well burst into lurid red flames as I fumble the pile, trying to hide them under a cushion.

"What'ya reading?" he drawls. The smirk over his face tells me his question is redundant.

Oh, good lord.

"Um, just those research books I grabbed. Nothing interesting." The words are far too breathy. And by the way his brow snaps up and he closes the distance, he notices.

He stands over me, head tilted.

"Research gets you all hot and bothered, does it, baby girl? That's your thing?"

"Ah! I—" I sink back into the sofa.

Leaning down, he swipes the cushions away.

"Heavy stuff." He picks up the pile of books.

I pray the sofa will do me a solid and suck me into its velvet maw, never to let me see the light of day again.

Sliding through the books, one after the other, he glances at me. "*Your Pleasure Map.*" He slides it from the top and drops it onto the cushions. "*Fabulous Foreplay.*" A half smile pops over his cheeky damn face as it lands on top of the last one. "*Couples' Kama Sutra . . .*" The rest of the pile topples to the sofa as he moves between my legs. "This is what your book boyfriends do?"

"Well—they—I . . ." I close my eyes, his scent fencing me in, and I swallow. Hard. "In the scene I'm working on, the female main character is captured by the enemy. Tied to a chair and . . . but she gets herself free. I wanted an intimate scene for them, but everything feels so vanilla? Not really them."

Cal's face turns to stone, his eyes darkening. "So she is like a warrior of some sort?"

"She's a fae pirate, actually. Admiral's daughter, so she has rank. Fights, leads, all that heroine stuff, you know?"

"Mhmmm," he rumbles.

Walking to the table, he plucks up a chair and brings it over. "She was tied to something like this?"

"Yes," I breathe as he drops it in front of me and walks back to the kitchen. He rummages through a drawer before returning.

With rope in his hands.

"What's that for?" I ask tentatively.

"On the chair, baby girl."

"I—we . . ."

A rough hand reaches under my arm, tugging me to my feet, spinning me round, and depositing me on the chair. Cal steps around, and his mouth dips to my ear. "You don't need a book to help you write this. You have me."

Electricity skitters over my skin. I lay my head back on his shoulder. He slides my glasses from my face, placing them on the sofa.

"Is this the first time they've been close?" he rasps.

"Uh-huh," I say with a rapid nod.

"And he just found her in a room where she'd been tied up?"

"Yes." The word is thin against my parched lips.

A growl vibrates through his chest as he ties my wrists to the slatted chair back. Every breath heaves. His fingers brush over my skin, and I tamp back a whimper.

Damn sex books. I'm a writhing mess, and I still have my clothes on.

"Your book boyfriend is in love with your heroine, I assume?"

I nod, my eyes burning into the man in front of me.

He leans over, forehead pressing to mine. "Does she feel the same way about him?"

I want to pull his mouth to my own. To drown in him.

But my wrists are secured tight to the chair. I pull at them, and my movement jostles the chair.

Cal nips my bottom lip. "Does she?"

"Yes, she does."

I don't think I'm answering for my heroine anymore.

Deft fingers travel down my neck, slipping behind my button-down shirt. They dip behind the lace of my bra, ghosting over my hard nipple. I arch against the chair, mouth agape.

Cal's mouth finds mine. It's all I can do to open and let him plunder what he wants.

Panting, we break apart.

"Your book boyfriends take what they want, that's what you told me."

I nod.

Before the next heartbeat falls, his hands grip my shirt, ripping it apart. I gasp as buttons fling over the floor, and my shirt hangs open. Cal drops to his knees, kissing his way down my belly.

Short burning parcels of air wash through my chest. My clit throbs, achingly so. The cutoff shorts I wear tighten around my thighs as they fall apart. Tugging at the button, he rips the zipper open and pulls the shorts over my ass. A moment later, they hit the floor, leaving only lacy panties behind.

"After all that rescuing, you think a book boyfriend would want to just flee with his girl . . . I doubt it, any man worth his salt would take his fucking time." His finger slips behind the fabric covering my soaked pussy. It brushes over my entrance before swirling over my needy, throbbing apex.

"Cal," I whimper.

The panties join the shorts on the floor. Large warm hands spread my thighs wide.

I wriggle on the chair. "What are you doing?"

I mean, I know what he is doing. But he's supposed to be ....

"Taking what I want." His tongue plummets through my soaked center.

I tremble on the cool wooden surface.

Wrists bound, I arch on the chair. His hand presses down on my belly, holding me where he wants me. His tongue darts inside me and I can't breathe.

A low, raw growl vibrates over my entrance when he sweeps his perfect damn tongue over me.

"This is what I want, baby girl. You writhing on the fucking chair."

He bites down then sucks hard. It's too much, and I feel too empty.

"Hands," I rasp.

He stops, lifting his head with one brow raised. "Is that a trait of a book girlfriend, asking for what she wants?"

His finger flicks my clit.

"Of course . . . I-it is," I splutter.

Another flick over the too-sensitive bud, and I jerk on the chair.

"Noted." He dips his head, returning his mouth to my center. This time, two fingers sink inside me.

God, and the need to touch him, to wrap myself around his warm, muscular body is driving me insane.

Fingers curling forward, he pumps them, suckling and nipping my throbbing apex. Whimpers and mewls fall from my lips like a damn background instrumental song, ratcheting up in tone and intensity as he works my body, sending it high and higher.

With one long, blissful suckle, he sends me toppling over that edge.

"Oh! Go—Callum . . ."

I convulse around his fingers, pussy grinding over his bearded face. He growls and the orgasm splinters me into two, doubling down. Another bite and suckle, and I can't help the cry echoing through the lighthouse.

As the bliss fades and I drop my attention to the man between my legs, my breath hitches.

Dark blue eyes look up at me. Something like satisfaction beams through them. Dropping my gaze further, I find the tented strain at the front of his jeans.

What I wouldn't do to tie *him* down now.

Cal pushes to his feet, dotting a kiss to my lips, then my forehead. "Get cleaned up. I have something for you."

"But—what?"

He nods toward the front door. "It's outside, come on."

"You were supposed to take what you wanted."

He smiles at me, adjusting himself in his jeans as my gaze glues to that one spot. He leans down and nuzzles my neck. "I just did."

Releasing the rope from my wrists, he walks from the house.

I sit on the chair, naked, swollen, and intoxicated. Every inch of my body thrums. His name morphed into the word *god*. I'm never going to live it down. Doubt he'll ever let me forget that little moment.

Regaining my composure, I grab up my clothes and head upstairs. Wearing a fresh outfit, I pull my hair into a ponytail and push my glasses up my nose. Grabbing my hat on the way out, I find Cal waiting by the greenhouse.

"You wanted to help with the garden, so I made you one of your own."

I stop in my tracks. "Wait, what?" A grin splits my face. First, the orgasm of my life, now, my very own garden. This man is—

"Cal!" I jump onto his waist, hugging him before hunting for his mouth with my own. He kisses me hard but sets me back to my feet.

"You can seed, tend, and harvest this season's tomatoes."

My mouth gapes. "Really?"

He chuckles. "Absolutely."

I squeak out a sound I'm sure any mouse would recognize as he grabs my hand and leads me into the greenhouse. A new bed, soiled and raked level, waits. A packet of tomato seeds, a trowel, and a pink watering can all sit on the ground by it.

"They're easy enough to grow, and you get the best bang for your buck with tomatoes." He squats down, passing the packet of seeds up to me. "Dig three-inch-deep furrows and scatter the seeds sparsely through each. Fill the furrows in and level it out. Water each day," he says as he rises to his feet, "making sure they're always moist, and you should see some green poke through in a few weeks. Then, in around ten more weeks, you have a harvest. Think you can oversee all that?"

"Of course!"

I bend down and pick up the trowel, eyeing the bed as I make a plan. The handheld radio at Cal's hip squawks.

"Trinity to Fire Island Lighthouse, do you copy?"

Cal plucks the radio up in one hand. "Fire Island Lighthouse, read you loud and clear. Over."

"Trinity to lighthouse, we are in need of assistance. Our nav system's gone down. Over."

"Lighthouse to Trinity, what's your position? Over."

"Ten miles due east. Over."

Cal looks to me. "I gotta go, baby girl. You be alright here with your gardening?"

I lay a hand on his chest and push up on my toes, dotting a kiss on his lips. "I sure will. Thank you for the garden."

"Gotta earn your keep somehow," he says with a

chuckle, slapping my ass as he walks away. "Be back before sunset. Keep the house radio turned up."

"Okay, I will. Be careful!" I call out to his retreating back.

His hand waves over his head as if in salute to the sentiment between us.

Twenty-Four

EVIE

My hands tremble. Cal's are tight around my wrists. His blue eyes pin me to the spot like a butterfly on a square of cork. Unlike the very alive yellow insect in my palms, flapping its vibrant presence all over my fingers. Yellow dust brushes over my skin, sticking.

I breathe through the panic burning up my chest.

It's just a bug.

It's just a flappy, sweet, tiny bug . . .

Tell that to my insides. My thundering heart.

"He won't hurt you, baby girl. I promise."

For a moment, I believe him. That this time, with Cal, T won't stand a chance.

The bug flaps about, teetering on the edge of my pointer finger, and Cal guides it back to the center.

Apparently my obvious objection to butterflies has been noticed. Since we spend hours tending the greenhouse plants each day, me flinching every time one passes is getting old. Callum doesn't know the significance of the butterfly for me.

I've had over six years to attach this negative association of mine to the tiny insect.

As a girl growing up, I loved butterflies. I'm sure I did.

Now, they are a constant living reminder of the choices I made, the situations I could never control, and the lurking threat that no doubt will rear its ugly head the instant I'm back in the city.

Callum closes around me, enveloping me as another butterfly lands on my palm. The tiny dot of nectar he planted there to reel them in works. As bile rises in my throat, I wish it didn't.

"I can't." My hands tremble as the second set of minuscule feet touch down, barely detectable against the lifeline of my palm.

"You already are," Cal whispers, his lips brushing the shell of my ear.

My eyes shutter closed, and the tiny feet on my palm are forgotten. Was that his plan, seduce my fear away? Replace the terror the winged miracles bring with something better? Him, around me.

A wing flutters against my ring finger and I jerk, eyes snapping open.

Teeth bite down on my neck, gently. My body automatically surrenders to his. My fear melting back into submission.

"Cal . . ."

I rest my head back on his shoulder, and he grazes my neck with lips and teeth. "I could fucking eat you, Evie."

"I would let you," I breathe.

Hell, I'm a gooey puddle of slick need and fire right now. My hand finds his hair as I reach back, the butterflies long forgotten. I spin in his hold, and he grabs me, tugging my body to his. In the warm greenhouse, we are already sweating. The humidity of the enclosed space makes everything bound faster than it should.

"Maybe I should start growing my own food." Emmett chuckles through the garden.

We startle, jerking apart, sending gravel scattering from our feet.

Shit.

My cheeks heat. I worry my lip through my teeth, hand covering my mouth. Callum throws his friend a dirty look before dotting a kiss to my forehead and stalking from the greenhouse.

Oh my god.

Since when was Emmett coming out today? He was just here yesterday. I fix my still-orderly clothes and clear my throat before heading back into the house.

Writing. I should be writing.

I glance toward the dock and see the men wandering toward Firefly, Emmett pointing at something as Cal tilts his head, rubbing his jaw. Okay . . .

I all but run up the center spiral stairs and flop into the desk chair like I'm about to miss a deadline. Laughable, since that's the reason I ended up here.

It's not like Emmett to turn up unannounced. The mind boggles with that one. I guess Cal will tell me if it's important.

Opening the laptop, I click on the manuscript. I'm at the eighty percent mark, just about to let the heroine take the fall before she ultimately saves herself in the final hour. Because of course she does. *Hero who?*

It wouldn't be a great romantasy without a heroine with an arc that could be seen from space. From zero to hero. In her case, from zeroine to heroine.

God, that's corny. I snort a laugh, but it fades.

Without her arc continuing, there is no more series.

A quandary for sure.

I push out of the chair and pace the room. I'm on book two of this six-book series. But . . .

Something feels right about the change of plot. The authentic and organic way it unravels to come to a close at the end of this novel.

Four books short of what I was supposed to write.

My contract is for this book only, though. Does that mean they will only consider the next four if this one does well? How long am I going to be locked into writing something my heart just isn't in? Not one hundred percent, anyway.

"Okay, I'm the author. It's your story, Eve. What do you really want to do? What plot fits Syra the best?"

I half expect Cal to swing around the doorjamb and call me out for talking to myself. I wish he would. Then I could put off deciding on my fate. Or Syra's.

Moving to the window, I lean against the wall. The waves roll in, fading into the sandy beach like it's their final destination. So sure. Not a doubt. No hesitation, they simply keep rolling in. What would it be like to have that amount of certainty in life?

Maybe the waves simply decided one day and held to it?

Maybe.

I slide back to the seat. Opening the notes application, I tap out the ending in bullet points, making sure to give Syra her well-deserved finale. Her fears replaced by her actions, her kingdom saved and rebuilt, her hero by her side because she wants him there and not because she needs him there. The crown is hers. The ending she deserves, after thousands of words of trial and torment.

Scanning the notes, I add small details in parentheses as I go. Fleshing it out best I can in the spur of the moment. Something hangs back in my mind. Another story I want to tell. One that has my whole heart.

One I can't ignore any longer.

"Evie?" Callum calls from downstairs. I save my notes and shut the laptop.

"Coming!" I jog down the stairs to find Cal and Emmett in the kitchen. The embarrassment from earlier edges its way back in. I try to push it back down as I breathe, "Hi, Emmett."

"Hey, Miss Evie." His smile is genuine, but it slips a little as I reach the counter and lean on it, my eyes meeting Cal's.

"Em is out doing an inspection. Some boats in the marina were tampered with. One went missing, and they found it floundering ten miles north."

"Oh? What did you find?" I turn to Emmett.

"Nothing concrete. But I wanted to come out here, make sure you guys are okay."

"Thanks, we're okay," I reply.

Emmett's grin eats his face. "I can see that."

I sink my gaze to the floor.

Something thuds.

"Ow! What the hell, McCreary?"

I look up to find Emmett rubbing his shoulder, and Cal's darkened eyes holding him where he stands.

"Watch out, Evie, this one's vicious." Emmett points to Callum, who hasn't shifted an inch.

"He takes a while to warm up. You should know that, Em," I say way too fast and decide now is as good a time as any to scurry back up the stairs and hide out until the burning embarrassment I'm trying so hard to flatten fades.

"Em. I like it. See, she likes me, Cal."

The groan that follows is nothing short of hilarious. Those two are adorable. Cal in his overbearing, protective, grumbly way. And Emmett, the sweet, funny one. How Iris hasn't caught on to that, I'll never know. Maybe she has? Maybe her brother is the only thing stopping her . . .

I make it to the desk chair before the smile on my face blooms. Head shoved into my hands, I stifle a happy squeal, kicking my feet. Happiness rolls through me, and I lift my head, leaning back to peer at the ceiling above me. A new type of butterfly takes flight, low in my belly.

The kind that has a more concrete meaning than those small yellow flutterbys from the greenhouse.

Flutterbys. Maybe new branding will bring a new association with them.

Can't hurt to try, right?

With that thought, I open a fresh document and tap out a daydream. A story that has my heart exploding, sends fire through my veins, and makes emotion swell in my throat.

The romance I have wanted to tell since the day I first let my waking dreams hit the page.

With the meet-cute jotted down, I find my fingers sail over the keys, my new heroine's life blooming across the screen like the flutterbys, a rebranded type of romance.

My kind of romance.

Cal is writing in his journal when I pull the towel from my head and wrap it around my body. He hasn't written anything since before I arrived, going by the entries I saw before I threw it at his feet. Freshly showered and bare-chested, he sits in bed penning down the page.

Running a hand through his damp hair, he pauses. When he starts writing again, I lean on the doorframe, arms crossed, eyes homed in on him, intrigued.

"What'ya writing?" I ask softly.

He glances up from the page. "A few things Em told me today. Thought they're noteworthy."

"Sure. You think it's odd someone tampered with the boats then left one floating in the middle of the ocean? I mean, does that sort of thing happen often?"

What I really mean is . . . Could it be connected to me?

Is it a warning?

Surely, the letter at the café was a stretch. Maybe T thought in a small town where everyone knows everyone, the letter would find me eventually. Could he know the connection Iris has to Cal, and Cal to me?

That thought burns.

Iris in danger because of me—

Cal in danger because of me.

Fuck.

The air in my lungs burns out. Heat prickles up my spine, setting my eyes on fire with unshed tears.

Rolling off the doorframe, I pad back into the bathroom. I close the door behind me before leaning on the vanity. The towel slips, hitting the floor as I turn the cold tap on and splash my overheating face with the cool water. Pressing a hand into my chest above my heart, I will my choppy breaths to slow. To not burn so badly.

A soft knock rattles the door. "You okay?"

No.

"Yes, be out soon." The words are too wobbly. Hardly believable.

I splash my face one more time and turn off the faucet. Swiping the towel from the floor, I dry my face and neck. Now, I lean on the vanity, catching my reflection. I search my face for signs of the lie, only now noting the sun-kissed blush my cheeks have, my slightly darker skin from the hours outside. In the garden. The beach. The forest. With Cal.

"Nighean bheag."

Something thuds against the door.

I imagine his forehead hitting the wood.

The knob turns, and I suck in a breath, schooling my face to neutrality. As the door opens, I drop the towel at the last second. I can't tell him. I can't let him become a part of this nightmare. So I go with distraction.

Blue eyes darken and meet mine, and I know my decoy worked.

His heart is safe for now.

My own will weather the storm, like it's done for the last six years.

I will leave this man safe on his island, taking my problems far away from his peaceful existence.

"How many days have we spent together, Evie?"

His question catches me off guard.

"I—" I huff a breath as I brush my hand over his jaw. "Not nearly enough."

"They will have to be enough when your book's done. You keep that promise, you hear?"

I can't respond. The air filling my lungs barely a second ago is nowhere to be found.

Rough hands find my hips, sliding beneath me. My skin hits cool porcelain next as he deposits me on the vanity. I draw him in, thighs parting wide, and I pull his mouth to mine.

Mine.

For now.

And I am going to take a lifetime's worth in whatever time I have left, since this is all we get.

firefly

Twenty-Five

CALLUM

The look on her face tells me all I need to know. Evie's not telling me something. A big something. Going by the gut feeling that rose with the look flickering in her eyes as I closed the space between us, it's nowhere near good. But fuck. I can't think straight with her like this.

Bare.

Stunning.

Spread wide for me.

Perfect fucking tits heaving with every breath, she's the flame, and I'm her entranced night butterfly. With the knowledge I will be burned to ash the day she steps off this little island jetty and doesn't look back.

I can't think of anything but savoring this thing between us for as long as I can.

"Eve," I rasp.

Brown eyes flick up to mine. Her breaths shatter out, a small sob slipping through the sweetest damn lips I've ever felt. My cock aches at the thought of them wrapped around me. Those sun-kissed, flushed cheeks hollowed out. My hand fisted in her damn hair.

"Knees," I growl.

Her lips part. The deep cycling of her chest turns even more ragged. Wriggling off the vanity, she drops to her knees for me.

Good fucking girl.

My aching length strains against my boxers. Her fingers sweep over the tented material, almost snapping my last thread of restraint. They wander up my hard stomach and slide behind the band of the shorts. I send my hands through her hair. "You're going to choke on my cock, baby girl. Then that pretty pussy of yours is going to be wrapped around me till you're screaming my name and yours is long forgotten."

Big brown eyes look up at me. Her face is a desperate mix of need and anticipation. If I could capture one image of her stunning face, it would be this one.

I commit her to memory—on her knees, eyes burning, hair mussed and damp, my fingers tangled through it.

"Please, Callum."

I nod, and she tugs the boxers down. My cock, rock-hard, springs free. Pre-cum pearls at the engorged tip. Evie's throat works. I hook a thumb on her lower lip, dragging her mouth open. The tiniest of whimpers slips out as her eyes flutter shut and her head rolls into my palm.

Christ, baby girl.

Fuck me.

Warmth floods my chest, emotion spilling over my senses.

I grind my jaw shut, shoving my hard length onto her tongue. Elegant fingers curl around my thighs, nails biting into muscle. She closes around me, eyes opening. Brown eyes, darkened and laced with heat, flicker up to me.

"That's it. On your knees, taking every fucking inch."

Her shoulders heave as she pulls up.

I brace myself against the sink. Bliss swallows my cock, spreading through my body inch by beautiful inch. My grip in her hair tightens. A whimper rattles her as she takes me in again. This time, she pulls up ever so slowly, sucking so fucking hard I see stars. Brown eyes hold me to the spot, pleasure lacing through them as if this gives her as much as it does me.

"Evie baby. Fuck, that fucking mouth of yours . . ."

She releases me with a pop, her hand gripping the base of me as she catches her breath. "You taste like . . . you *feel* like home."

My jaw feathers. *Christ, girl, start saying that shit and I'm not going to be able to survive the next few months.* I can't take this anymore. This not having her. I haul her to her feet, sweeping her onto my hips. Her wet pussy rubs against my stomach, and she wraps around me automatically, like being tangled up with me is exactly where she's meant to be.

With a growl, I toss her to the bed. A little squeak escapes her as I come down on her. Predator stalking over his prey. She rises up off the bed, reaching for me. I slap her hands down and pin her to the bed. "The only way either of us is going to survive this is to put every feeling we have aside. I can't be your home. You can't be mine. Got it?"

I fucking hate myself.

Never before have words burned so hot on my tongue as they rolled off like truth.

I'm a goddamn liar. A selfish asshole.

I'm taking what I want while telling her she's not allowed to feel.

A hypocrite with a raging hard-on for the woman beneath me. If I'm honest, I've fallen so fucking hard that not a bone in my body hasn't shattered with the impact.

I'll keep the sappy fucking thought for my journal. No need to complicate something that should simply be a no-strings arrangement.

"Fine," she breathes. But she swallows, her face tightening as if the thought is as repellent to her as it is to me.

"Good girl," I choke out, crawling backward, not letting our eyes meet.

The kisses I dot on her turn to sand in my mouth with the lies I've just spun. With each press of my lips to her skin, she trembles, her fingers wrapping around mine. I retract my hands, letting them push into the mattress on either side of her slim waist.

With a nip to her hip, I spread her thighs, finding her soaked and glistening pussy.

Christ. I've made it to heaven only to realize it will be taken from me.

"Cal . . ."

"Yeah, baby girl?"

"Tongue, mouth, teeth, fingers."

She's telling me what she wants. No wobble in her voice like there once was when asking for the smallest of things. Now, with me, she asks for what she wants.

And I will always give her what she wants.

Except for one thing.

I run my tongue through her soaked center and swirl it around her sweet little nub. Her back arches off the bed instantly.

"Oh, fuck." Her sweet little syllables tumble softly through her open mouth. Head tilted back, her slender neck is all cream and elegant angles, her beauty never more grounding than it is now.

I nip and suckle away the sting that would have lanced through her. Her hands find my hair. I love them there. I love my mouth here.

Fuck.

No.

Sliding two fingers into her center, I suck hard on her clit, knowing it will bring her close. Make her pussy swollen and tight, bring her more pleasure when I finally slam into her. She shoots up off the bed. I plunder each sensitive part of her over and over until she is crying out my name. Hands gripping tight in my hair, she comes, grinding against my mouth. I take everything she gives up.

"Need more, Evie baby?"

"Yes . . . Please, Cal."

I rise from the floor and sit, leaning back on the headboard. "Come sink your pretty pussy on my lap."

She rolls over, pushing up onto her knees. Walking on her knees, she straddles my lap.

"No. Turn around. I want to see that tight ass of yours bounce on my cock."

Evie huffs a shy laugh but does as I ask. And when she sits over me and looks back, those brown eyes almost take me under. I grab her hips, lining up my tip with her slick entrance. She pulls her hair to the side, exposing her spine, and lets it rest over her right shoulder.

Fucking perfect.

I slam her down onto my hard length, and she cries out, rolling her hips.

"Fuck, baby girl. So. Fucking. Tight."

Her fingers wrap around mine on her hips, and she rises.

Slowly. Too slowly. And I almost come with the sweet agony of it.

"Bounce," I growl.

She turns back, her face turned serious. "It feels too good. I don't wan—"

"Now."

She rises and plummets, taking up a quick rhythm, still watching me. Her tits bounce with every single drop of her body. My mouth waters at the sight of those pert, dusky nipples pointing at nothing, the curve of her under breast tantalizing me with every stroke. Fuck, I need them between my lips. But the sight of her sweet little ass bouncing on my cock is too good.

I grip her hips, slowing her movements.

She rolls forward with the next stroke, tugging my tip deeper inside her. I drop my head back, groaning through the bliss her movement brings.

"You like that?" she breathes.

"Baby, there isn't a thing I don't like about you."

A sweet giggle leaves her lips, but it fades as she whispers, "Good."

That's the undoing of me. The telltale heat in my lower spine spreads as my balls tighten. Evie lowers, her hands gripping mine, which are still on her hips, tighter. Her face breaks as she tightens around my cock.

"Cal," she cries on one breathy, ragged syllable.

"Fuck, baby girl. Ride it out."

She picks up the pace, hips rolling as she strangles my goddamn cock. Each beautiful wave she works through milks another hot, ropey shot deep inside her. Pressing my forehead to her spine, I growl through my release.

Her whimpers turn to breathy whispers.

She settles, and I wrap my arms around her waist. She leans back, her face turning to nuzzle into my neck. The definition of cruel is giving a lonely man this kind of heaven, this woman, only to steal her away for some bigger, more noble purpose.

"Don't let go yet," she whispers.

The stone forming in my throat may as well be a boulder. Unable to reply, I tighten my hold on her. The second I can draw air again, I kiss her neck, her jaw, brushing my nose over the shell of her ear.

"How are you so tender under that rough exterior, Callum McCreary?"

I huff a strained chuckle.

Only for her.

Only with the pure desperation I have from needing her.

With a nip to her earlobe, I utter, "You do that to me."

She shifts on my lap, turning back until she is facing me but sitting sideways in my lap. Draping her arms around my neck, she drops her forehead to meet mine. "Say that again."

"You do that to me, Evie."

She smiles. "I like that."

Yeah, baby girl. Me too.

Cupping her jaw with rough hands, I draw her mouth in, crashing her lips against mine in an open kiss. A sailor drowning for a taste of his siren.

Who am I kidding? I'm done for with this woman.

I have no idea how I'm going to say goodbye to her.

Twenty-Six

EVIE

Plump, ripe red tomatoes stare up at me from the bushy plant. The warm spring air sends the distinct tang of plant life through the greenhouse. Pride ripples through me, and I bite on my bottom lip to tamp down the squeal of delight wanting out. I jump—just a little—on the spot. *I did it!*

I really grew the season's worth of tomatoes.

I pluck the fattest one I can find and bite into its crimson flesh. Tomato juice spills past my lips, running down my chin.

Oh. My. God.

It's incredible.

I tug another from the bush and sprint into the house. Callum sits on the sofa, radio in his hands, jotting down something in a notebook that looks like a record of some sort.

Coming to a halt in front of him, I all but wriggle out of my skin waiting for him to look up at me. Never before have I felt as much like a child waiting for a parent's attention as I do now.

I let a little squeak slip, and his blue eyes glance up at me.

His face breaks with a chuckle as he slides the book to the sofa with the radio, and I drop into his lap.

"Close your eyes," I breathe.

"Okay . . . why?"

"Just do it."

I give him my best stern look. He shakes his head but closes his eyes as instructed. "What you got there, Evie baby?"

"Open your mouth."

One eyebrow raises, but he opens up.

I shove the tomato in his mouth like a pig with an apple stuffed in its snout. Cal's eyes fly open as he tries to talk around the large tomato. He looks ridiculous. I crack up, my hands palming his jaw as he tries to bite down. His face pulls in all directions. I slap a hand to my mouth, laughter spilling from me in hysterical waves.

He finally bites the fruit in two, and one half falls to his lap. "Mmmm." He chews, swallowing before he picks up the last half. "Your turn, baby girl."

"Ah!" The tomato is stuffed between my teeth as I go to object.

Rough hands find my waist, tugging me closer. "I like you with your mouth full."

My chest caves. I swallow the bites down, making small hums as he tugs down my shirt. His lips close over my hard peak.

"Cal," I rasp, thumbing the overspill of juice from my bottom lip back into my mouth.

His head snaps back up. "Sorry, baby, we have plans this afternoon. You done writing?"

"Uh huh. Did you like the tomato?"

"It was delicious. Good girl."

"It was my first season crop!" I shift on his lap as a thought crashes in. "My last, too."

My first and my last. That sinks in as my gaze burns into his blues.

Something dark invades his eyes, and he shifts his focus to somewhere behind me. We sit in silence, our breathing too heavy as the words bury and take root. The sentiment stings.

"Maybe I could pot some in the living room of my apartment?" I say feebly.

His throat works, and I wish he would look at me.

But his focus clears, and he slaps my ass with a hand. "Up. We're going to Iris's."

"We are?"

"Yep, she wants to talk about the house, repairs, costs, options, etc. Just in case the restoration society can't be convinced. Which they probably won't be."

"Oh, sure. It's been forever since I've seen Em."

Cal rolls his eyes at me, and I pull a face. I like seeing him this way.

"Wear something nice. The festival is tonight. We're going after dinner."

Excitement burst in my veins. "Are you serious? Yes! I could use a night out."

"Don't get too excited. Bay Shore isn't known for extravagance. Only low-key celebrations. Sometimes, if the budget allows, fireworks."

"Don't care. It's going to be great. Are Iris and Em coming?"

"Of course, whose idea did you think it was?"

Iris, I love you!

I rush the stairs and am up in the bedroom tossing clothes on the bed before Callum can object. Not that he would. The only thing he loves more than this falling-down old lighthouse is his little sister. I toss jeans, too many tops, some flats, and a pair of boots onto the bed. No, too warm for jeans and boots. Maybe a dress and boots? Maybe a dress and flats? Ugh, I hate trying to pick clothes.

"I have nothing . . ." I whine to nobody.

After an hour and a half of trying on every possible combination of clothing I brought with me, I settle on a robin's-egg blue summer dress with ruffle sleeves and a V-neck, its hem ending just above my knees. I decide to go with short boots and pick out a yellow cardigan to layer up just in case. It's pretty, cool enough, and the extra layer will work well if I need it.

Using the few hours I have before late afternoon, I add to my word count. I hit the ninety percent mark following my new outline. Happy with the new direction, the words flow effortlessly. It feels right. When the knock on the bedroom door finally comes, I save my work and close the laptop.

"I'm going to have a quick shower and check the boat while you get ready, okay?" Cal says.

His expression is soft as his gaze studies my face.

"Yeah, sure."

He rolls off the doorframe. I swear, that's his favorite place to hover. As the bathroom door closes and the water turns on, I stare out the window, trying to warm up to the idea of going back to the city. It's only a matter of days now. Just over three weeks until I have to have this book done and submitted.

Waves roll in, flattening on the beach side of the island with such effortless ease, it makes me wish I could stay here and learn their secret.

"All done. Your turn, smelly."

A kiss dots to my temple when the man wrapped in a

towel drips water onto my arm with his wet hair, taking me by surprise.

He's stunning. All muscular and bearded. Blue eyes for days.

I swallow past my anticipated loss, at the thought of him being here alone again. "Won't be long," I manage.

I have a quick shower and blow dry my hair. After applying a light smatter of foundation, blush, and a little mascara, I finish with my berry-tinted lip gloss from my makeup bag. I haven't used it since I arrived. It's almost strange to get done up now.

My reflection makes me smile. With a small sigh, I slip my clothes and underwear on before fluffing out my hair over the shoulders of the dress and slipping my boots on. Downstairs, I find Cal at the kitchen counter, dressed in Levi's and a navy button-down shirt, the sleeves rolled up.

"Oh," I utter as I take him in. *Really* in.

He looks up from the apple he's cutting. "Christ, baby girl."

Heat flushes my cheeks, as if it's the first time he's laid eyes on me. "You look nice," I say.

Cal grunts, shoving a slice into his mouth. He snaps it in half with his teeth as he studies me, eyes darkening by the second. God, with that look, we will never make it off this floating rock. Not that I'd be complaining—this man is incredible—but it's been so long since I've done anything for fun.

"Ready?" I prompt.

Swallowing, he slides the rest of the apple slices into a ziplock bag and seals it. "Yup."

He grabs his coat off the hook by the door, and I grab my bag, tossing my purse and new phone in for good measure. We walk in silence down to the dock. His gaze burns into the side of my face the whole way. I dip my head and will the tug-of-war in my heart to fade out of existence.

I'm leaving.

He asked me to leave.

My time here will forever be a marker of what I want. In a man. In my life, period.

Cal boards the boat and turns to me, extending a hand. I take it and step aboard. How far we have come hits me with a sucker punch.

I clear my throat and find a seat in the cabin as he casts off and pulls the fenders over the side. When the engine roars to life, I remember the overnight bag he had last time. "Bag?"

"Under the dashboard, baby. Extra toothbrush this time."

I huff a soft, half-amused sound.

But my stomach is a tangle of knots and butterflies, and I don't know which will win the battle for control. We cruise away from the jetty, and I stare at the open water, lost in thought.

Iris's smile stretches her face. "Hello, come in!"

Cal holds the door for me, and his sister raises a brow at him. I try to hide the amusement on my face by wandering around the café. Much the same as last time I was here, it's such a lovely spot. Quaint, homey, and inviting. An accurate reflection of Iris.

"Hey, Irry." Cal messes up her gorgeous red hair with a rogue hand. She bats him away.

"Have a seat at the window table, I'll grab the papers."

I wander to the shelf with the photos. Now the fishing hut in the picture of Callum and his father is familiar. And I remember Em's words. *Doubt he'll take you there.*

He didn't, not exactly, but we did live wild in that small hut for days. He let me in. To his fishing hut, to his last connection to his dad, to his past with Ava, and to his strained relationship with this town. That was where whatever changed between us grew roots. Found its foundation. I'm sure of it.

A foundation I'm going to obliterate in three weeks' time.

"Come sit, Evie." Iris pulls out a chair. "I've been meaning to ask you something."

This could be interesting.

I walk over and drop into the seat she pulled out at the head of the table. Her and Cal sit on either side of the weathered rectangular wooden table. A pile of papers and something that looks like an old-fashioned accounting ledger sit in the middle.

Cal slides the book over and flips the cover open, thumbing through pages until he comes to the one he wants.

"So just how famous are you, Miss Eve?" Iris asks.

The question takes me aback. "What do you mean?" I try to smile. But the knot of hope-infused butterflies from earlier petrifies and sinks.

"A fan of yours was in here this morning asking about you. He was so excited I knew you. He left this for you." Iris glances at her brother before returning her gaze to me as she slides a cream envelope across the table.

My throat closes over. My fingers close around the fabric of the skirt of my dress. "Not famous," I choke out. I'm shaking my head, but I can't move my body.

"Evie?" Cal says. It echoes through my senses before fading away.

"I have to go." I shoot up off the chair and it topples over, clattering to the floor. I'm out the front door, its chimes tinkling behind me as the heels of my boots snap down the sidewalk. Trying to haul air into my lungs as the night's darkness folds in around me.

Not my best idea.

Out on the deserted street, alone.

Everyone must be at the festival.

I run my hand through my hair, pacing back and forth in front of the hardware store a few doors down from the café. The streetlight's glow doesn't make it this far and when I look up, my eyes pointing toward the glittering marina, I realize how dark it is.

Panic claws through my veins, sending sickening heat through my spine.

T.

He's here.

He's fucking *here*.

I should be anywhere but alone in the dark. I try to smooth over my hair and pat down my dress. Dragging in a large lungful of air, I head back to the café. I find Cal leaning on the doorframe outside the small diner.

Of course he is.

I was probably never even out of his sight.

"You're going to tell me about that. Right now." He pushes off the frame.

I stop, wrapping my arms around my body.

I should tell him.

I should tell the world and take away T's power.

Then every self-deprecating thought I have ever held about having a stalker floods in. How could you not notice? Why didn't you say something the first time? He hasn't done

anything bad, really . . . He hasn't done anything real, only
letters and vague threats.

Until the last letter, that is.

He killed Joshua.

Because I *ignored* him.

I stare into the serious blues now holding me to the
spot. "No."

"No?" He closes the space between us, eyebrows raising.
A seriousness I've never seen on his face turns it stone. I dip
my head, not wanting to see the reprimand in his eyes. A
finger curls under my chin, lifting so I have no choice but to
meet his gaze. "Now, baby girl. All of it."

My chin wobbles as tears burn the back of my eyes. I
shake my head.

"You either have some sort of phobia about mail, or it's
the contents you're afraid of."

I swallow hard.

Heaven knows what's in the letter. After the last one, I can't
bear to open another. Will it be a death bell tolling for Cal this
time? I'm not naive enough to think T wouldn't orchestrate
another accident. How many ways can a lighthouse keeper die?

Oh god.

I slap a shaking hand over my mouth.

"I need some space," I say, pushing past him.

"Evie," he growls.

Walking back inside, I make a beeline for the bathroom

in Iris's little apartment behind the café. Running the cold water, I splash it over my face. The second it hits my skin, cold and wet, I remember my makeup.

Shit.

I dry off the best I can with the hand towel, trying not to ruin my mascara. Maybe I should leave early? Finish the last of my novel back at my apartment. Get as far away from Cal as I can. I can't be here if T is this close to us.

A soft knock on the door pulls me from the dark thoughts.

"Evie?" Iris's voice is worried.

Sorrow for a life I've lost before it even began sinks, burning into my chest. I wish I could stay. I wish Cal wanted me to. I wish Iris and Em were part of my world.

Oh god, Allie. I'm the worst friend; we haven't talked in weeks.

"Be out in a sec."

"Okay, dinner is ready."

"Thank you," I say, too quiet, as my forehead hits the door. I close my eyes. Three more weeks, and I go home. Cal will be safe, tucked away on his island. Pushing through the door, I wander into the dining area. Cal and Iris sit at the table with the papers pushed to one end. A large casserole dish sits in the center, and three bowls sit at our places, steaming. The fragrant scent of savory and herbs reaches me.

"Eat. You'll feel better. Then we'll go see some fireworks, hey?" Iris squeezes my hand.

"Sure." I look to Cal. He sits slouched to one side, the fork in his hands flipping through his fingers. As if he's not happy with his sister's quiet ways.

"This looks wonderful, thank you." I give Iris a small smile. It's straining my face, but it's genuine.

"Don't mention it. Let's eat."

We eat while the siblings talk numbers. By the time I finish my bowl, Cal's frown has dropped lower and lower. It's not looking good. The numbers don't add up. The only solution would be to receive funding from the Restoration Society who, by the sound of it, are not interested in outdated relics like Fire Island Lighthouse. Or to come up with around twenty grand in repairs and upgrades.

That island, that lighthouse, is Cal's whole life.

My heart breaks for him.

As echoes of laughter and music drift in from down the street, Iris stands and sweeps up the empty bowls. "Misery aside, let's go have some fun, even if it's just for tonight."

Cal grumbles something I can't make out.

"Sounds like a plan." I stand and glance behind me to watch Iris disappear into the back before I dot a kiss to Cal's cheek and whisper, "Take me somewhere good."

He smiles. It's the first slip of light I've seen on his face since the letter appeared on the table earlier. Iris returns with her jacket and something blue draped over one hand.

"Here, you'll need something extra, the wind is nippy tonight." She hands me a blue ombré scarf. It's silken between my fingers and a perfect match for my dress. "Thank you, this is beautiful. I didn't think to bring one."

I wrap it around my neck, and she adjusts it a little before turning my collar up on my jacket for a snug fit.

"Gorgeous. Ah, look at those stunning brown eyes against that blue." Iris shakes her head with a smile. She's like the older sister I never had. I can practically feel my heart getting attached. Iris locks up and we make our way down Main Street, heading for the festivities.

firefly

Twenty-Seven

CALLUM

Main Street is lit up under strings of rainbow lights. Stalls line the sidewalk, and we meander down the center of the closed-off street. Townsfolk mill about, chatting, purchasing from stalls, eating, and laughing. Live music drifts through the space like the ocean breeze it mixes with. Em finds us before we even make it a block.

"There you guys are. Geez, it's crazy out tonight." He beams a smile at me before turning to the two women at my side. "Iris. Evie."

My little sister scrunches up her nose, smiling as she takes him in. She leans in, saying something to Em as Evie gives him a little wave and a hello.

They part, and a suspicious glint lines my sister's green eyes. But when Em's brows lower, I glance at Evie. She's wandered away, looking over a stall of candles and knick-knacks. She leans down, hands holding her hair back as she smells a large three-wicked candle. I can't drag my eyes from her. The way the warm night's breeze plays with her hair, how the soft amber light highlights the angles of her face and neck.

Iris joins her, and I break my gaze and shift on my feet before crossing my arms over my chest.

"You guys staying for the fireworks?" Em asks.

"Don't see why not."

"Good. Iris misses you."

I raise an eyebrow. Since when do Em and Iris talk feelings?

"She has friends. And I get here as much as I can."

"It's not the same as—" He clamps his jaw shut, his gaze swinging to the ground as he shoves both hands in his back pockets.

"Evening, Emmett." A gruff voice breaks through the tense air thickening between us.

Em turns. "Oh hey, Errol."

Great.

"Errol." I don't look at the old man, hoping he will think better of this conversation and keep moving through the crowd.

He doesn't.

"Figured you'd ruin a nice night for the folks, did ya,

McCreary?" Errol's rumble catches the attention of the people around us.

For fuck's sake. How long is he going to carry this shit for?

"Something like that, old man." I pay him a passing glance.

"Sounds about right. If it wasn't for that little woman"—he nods toward Evie—"I'd have you marched right back to the dock you slithered into."

Christ.

Em shifts on his feet. "Calm down, Errol. Festival's for everyone."

Errol wobbles toward me, and it's now that I smell the alcohol on his breath. "Don't cause any more trouble." His gnarly finger stabs my chest.

Annoyance turns to daggers in my eyes, and I stare him down. "Get fu—"

"Okay." Em guides Errol away and back through the crowd. He talks calmly to the old man.

But my mood is ruined.

"What was that all about?" Evie asks, worry lining her eyes, her words tender.

"Just the status quo. Forget it. Let's grab some food."

"Sure, let me tell Iris where we're going."

She wanders to the stall my sister stands by chatting to one of the women from the small business association. Evie leans in, and when Iris nods and she returns to me, my stalled-out breath flies free.

"Oh, hi Eve!" A woman's shrill voice calls out before Evie reaches me.

Evie spins back. "Sherry, hi."

"My goodness, I haven't seen you at the library for weeks. Too busy writing, hey?"

"Mostly, yeah," Evie says with a chuckle.

"Did you come across by yourself?" Sherry is looking past Evie, searching until her gaze finds me. The pleasant look on her face fades to something more like a toddler sucking a lemon. "Oh, I forgot . . ."

"Forgot what?" Evie says, her tone changing.

"Never mind. I guess . . . You have a good night. I might see you later." She feigns a smile and shakes a feeble wave before disappearing through the crowd.

Evie closes the space between us. When big, confused brown eyes meet mine, she tilts her head. "What was that?"

"Status quo. Told you."

"Are you serious? I thought you were being dramatic. Or pensive or something, not . . ." She glances back over her shoulder at the crowd of Bay Shore folks. "This."

"We can leave if you want to. Iris won't care too much."

"Do *you* want to leave?"

"The fireworks have always been my favorite." I smile, but it's sad.

"Then we're staying. Come on, let's find some dessert."

She walks through the crowd like a woman on a mission. The sway of her pretty dress, the lilt of her hips as she goes, captivates me. Hard-pressed to drag my eyes from her ass, I clear my throat and catch up. She stops at an ice cream truck and waits as I file in beside her, and we scan the menu to the side of the large serving window.

"Hi, can I grab a vanilla cone with chocolate syrup?" Evie asks. The woman in the truck swings her stare between Evie and me. The woman hesitates, and Evie steps forward. "Can I order, please?"

"That it?" the woman snaps loudly. People turn and stare.

Evie flinches as she notices the eyes on us. But she simply turns back, brown eyes imploring my own.

"No, actually. Cal, what would you like?"

The woman, who I vaguely recognize as one of the cashiers down at the convenience store, sets her jaw.

"I'll have the same," I finally reply. Heat lances my veins as I'm annoyed for the second time tonight.

"Great," Evie says with a smile. "Two, please."

The woman taps the screen on her device and holds it out for payment. I tug my wallet from my pocket and slip a card out. The woman sets her shoulders back, moving the small payment system out of reach as I hold the card out.

"Oh, for heaven's sake," Evie murmurs, the first glare I've seen on her face in a long while settling on the woman.

The woman relents, lowering the device the slightest bit, and I tap my card.

That wasn't humiliating at all . . .

Evie takes the cones when they slide over the counter toward us in a cardboard tray. A second later, she's stalking her way toward the large grassy area by the town's center-piece, a three-tiered fountain currently lit up by lights the colors of the rainbow over the cresting water. Couples and families are set up, dotted over the lawn.

We find a space and I take the food from Evie as she drops to the ground, sitting with her legs crossed. She reaches for her ice cream, and I sink down beside her.

"How do you live with these people?" she finally whispers. Her voice wobbles like she is upset.

I release a strained chuckle. "I don't."

"The island feels like a much better option in this moment."

"Welcome to my world, baby girl," I say, leaning in.

She turns her head, her eyes catching mine. They're pained, and I know that's the closest to pity I'm getting from this little woman. I don't care for it. I'm a grown man, and unlike Errol, my ability to hold a grudge doesn't span decades. So I stay out of their way. They usually leave me alone. Bar Errol, I suppose.

"What time are the fireworks?" Evie asks, licking choco-late syrup from the top of her cone.

"Around nine. Errol's apprentice is doing them this year.

Him and Errol alternate. Lucky for us, the drunkest sailor at the festival will not be handling explosives tonight."

She chuckles.

I smile, watching amusement light up her face.

Much better than fucking fireworks.

The music gets louder as the night wears on, and the young families take their babies home. Some of the older folks call it a night. Before I know it, the first fizz and streak of color shoots into the sky above us. Evie shuffles closer, her head resting on my shoulder as colorful streaks paint the sky before exploding into crackling sparkles.

The smallest gasp slips through her lips as a bright red explosion booms overhead. I dip my head, my gaze stuck on her beautiful upturned face. I press a kiss to her temple. Fine fingers weave through my own and I squeeze them as her scent tangles through my senses. The whisper of her hair against my cheek sends electricity through me.

My body hums with hers pressed against me. And I have to adjust myself to hide the boner she gave me simply by snuggling close. I search the crowd for Iris and find her sitting by Em twenty feet away. They are sharing food, like Evie and I are. Em leans back on his hands, looking up at the sky, and Iris drops her head to his shoulder. Her mouth moves as she says something, looking up at him.

Em sits up, wrapping an arm around her, tugging her into his side. She must be cold.

He's good to her. Always looking out for her. I like that

she has him when I'm not around. Like having a second big brother.

Evie sighs and pushes up. "Which way to the restrooms?"

"By the library. Half a block down. You want me to walk you?"

"No, I'm good. Enjoy the serenity." Giving me a sweet smile, she stands and wanders toward the library.

I lay back on the grass and stare at the stars shimmering above me. With the fireworks over, the tang of gun powder fills the air. The smoky remnants hang like a cloud slowly skimming by.

People start packing up, gravitating toward the music and stalls. A few couples are left on the grass, lying back, probably stargazing like I am. I fold my hands under my head and close my eyes. Content, I let the cool earth underneath my back soothe the harsh words and sideways looks the townsfolk still harbor for me.

Drowsy, I startle as footsteps fall in. I crack one eye to find Em standing over me. "Where's Evie?"

"Restroom."

Iris files in on the other side, brows lowered and face pulled into a frown. "I was just there. She wasn't."

"Fuck." I sit up and glance at my phone. It's almost ten. I must have fallen asleep. "Where the hell did she go?"

"She's probably back at the stalls," Em offers. "Call her."

"I—I don't have her cell number." Panic claws through

my veins. Why didn't I get her new number? Not that we've ever had the need to use a cell on the island.

"I have it," Iris says, pulling out her phone. She taps the screen a few times and lifts it to her ear. When she frowns and drops it away from her face, something heavy sinks in my gut. "She's not answering."

"I'll check the stalls and then down by the dock." Em takes off at a jog.

"Call me if you find her!" I yell at his back.

"I'll check the ladies' again," Iris adds, marching back that way.

I weave my way through the remaining crowd, the revelers now gripping cups in one hand, moving to the beat of the music. I push through sweaty, moving bodies, head swiveling as I scan the crowd for Evie. This doesn't exactly feel like her kind of thing, but I'm checking regardless.

Having scoured the crowd twice and coming up empty, I pull out my phone.

A text from Iris.

"Nothing. She's not here but there's a light on at the library. Heading that way now."

I push from the crowd and break into a run toward the library.

My phone buzzes.

Em.

"She's not down at the dock, that I can see. But someone's been on your boat, Cal. You should come see this."

Fuck.

Fuck me.

Not now. Evie comes first. If some motherfucker wants to screw with my boat, I'll deal with them later.

For fuck's sake, people. Build a bridge and get the fuck over it.

I round the library's eastern side and slide to a halt as I come up on Iris too fast. "Shit, Irry."

She smiles, grabbing my arm and turning me to face the library's lit-up foyer. Inside, a small table is set up. Evie sits behind it, head down, scribbling in a book. She's signing it?

"Told you she was famous," Iris says, her smile stretching her face.

I run a hand over my jaw.

Well, shit.

Evie looks up, handing the book back to the teenage girl in front of the table, who promptly squeals and jumps on the spot before snapping a selfie with Evie in the background. Evie's smile fades at that, and I brush Iris's grip off and walk into the library. I bypass the long line of folks waiting to see their favorite author. Gaze glued to my girl, I don't notice the shoulder until I run right into it.

A skinny guy, around thirty, with a cap pulled down over his face waits in the line, standing a little to one side, his stare burning into Evie. In his arms is a stack of what I assume are Evie's books, something blue poking out of the top of one. His stare breaks briefly as he gives me an annoyed look. I reach the table, and Evie's face blooms under a tired smile.

Fuck, she's been here since the restroom? How long was I fucking asleep?

"Baby, you gotta tell a person when you disappear to go be famous," I whisper into her ear as I lean into her side.

A tentative chuckle turns to a yawn as she stands briefly for a hug. Her hands are cold and her eyes are weary. She didn't look tired on the ride to the mainland. I guess wandering Bay Shore for an hour and trinket shopping with Iris will do that to a person.

"You don't have to stay here for every one of these people. We can go home." I release her as she drops back to the chair.

"A few minutes more. Then we can go."

I spy Sherry from earlier behind the library loans desk. My guess is she cornered Evie in the restroom and talked her into this. Or dragged her here.

Most likely the latter.

Evie signs a few more books and then stands. "I'm sorry, you guys. But I can come back Monday?" she says, glancing at me.

I nod and give her a smile. "Sure, Monday works."

"Thank you so much for waiting for me." She says to the dwindled line and grabs her belongings.

"What if we won't be here Monday?" the skinny guy in

the cap says, and I swear something like annoyance lines his words.

I step forward. "Then you miss out, buddy."

Evie huffs a strained breath.

He stares at me, his pasty skin and thin lips making him look like some kind of nerd villain. After he's taken his time sizing me up, he turns on his heels and marches from the library.

Sherry slithers up by Evie's side. "Thank you so much for doing this for us, Eve."

"It's no trouble. I didn't realize you had so many copies of my books here."

"Actually, we got a surprise donation a few weeks ago. We don't have shelving space for an entire carton, so we decided to sell the extras, just a little bonus for the library."

"Hold up, doesn't Evie get a cut of those sales?" I grind out.

"Um, usually. But we—"

Evie holds up a hand. "It's fine. Keep it. Maybe we can arrange a commission next time."

"Thanks, sure," Sherry chokes.

She had no intention of doing any such thing. Fucking hell.

Evie yawns again as she leans into my side and glances up. "I think home is next on the book tour."

Sherry waves us off as I guide Evie from the library. Iris waits outside, her hands clasped together.

"You scared us, sweetheart. But I'm so excited to see you in action!"

Evie chuckles. "Sorry, I should have texted. Sherry was relentless."

"I bet," Iris says, beaming. "Take her home, Cal."

"Aye aye." I wrap an arm around Evie's shoulders, and she rests her head on mine. We wander back to the marina where Em waits for us, his face pulled into a frown. The boat is ransacked, cupboards open, the radio pulled out, everything floating in the water.

"Oh no!" Evie gasps.

Fuck. "She still seaworthy, Em?"

He passes me a handheld radio. "Yeah, starts and runs fine. Probably just some kids pranking the first boat they found. I'll check the security cameras tomorrow. But you're good to go."

I board and wait for Eve to follow. After checking she's safe and sound in the cabin, I fire up the old girl and we head home under the clear, star-riddled night sky.

Twenty-Eight

EVIE

I wake up to Callum wrapped around me. And in this moment, I'm content. Happy. If the world stopped turning right now, things frozen in time, I would be good right here. I run my hand over his roped forearm, sliding my fingers through his where they're draped over my stomach.

Rolling over, I trace the angles of his face and the brush of his beard and wait for his blue eyes to open and find me looking, longing.

Maybe we shouldn't have let things go this far?

How could this be wrong? I mean, I almost have a full manuscript done. I've written more words in the last nine months than I have in six whole years. Deciding that Callum can only be a good thing, I press a kiss to his jaw. A low, raw noise rumbles from his chest as I rise to all fours, planting kiss after kiss over his face and down his neck as my lips meander over his shoulder.

This man is *perfect*.

With only the sheet lying over the lower half of his body, he puts even the most incredible book boyfriend to shame.

I straddle his waist, pressing my palms into the pillow on either side of his head. Nudging his jaw with my nose, I whisper, "Wake up, sweet man."

A rough grip finds my rib cage. He moves—so fast. My back hits the mattress.

Now, blue eyes burn into mine. A lazy smile grows over his face. "I am anything but sweet, baby girl," he growls. Calloused hands pin my palms above my head.

"You keep thinking that." I smile around the words.

"Guess I'll have to show you."

"How?" I breathe.

His eyes darken as my wrists are released. Hovering over me, he plucks up my hard nipple between his teeth. Heat and wetness sink to my center. He sucks on the peak, hard. My back arches from the bed, and the air in my lungs expels on a breathy huff.

Cal growls, low and soft. His gaze flickers over my bare body. Only my soaked panties cover me. Teeth skate over my ribs before hot, wet, messy kisses drop onto my skin. He moves back even further, his hands gripping my hips in a bruising hold. I wriggle in his grasp.

I didn't think this through.

Shou—

One hand slides down, ripping at my panties.

Shouldn't hav—

The flimsy fabric tears.

"Don't cover up what's mine." The words are almost a snarl.

Fuck.

Shouldn't have poked the bear. The very burly, grumpy, gorgeous bear . . .

My body burns with every feral move he makes, every grunt and growl leaving this intoxicating man. My panties give way with a final tug and crumple to the mattress by his side. Deft fingers spread my thighs wide. One finger sweeps through my wet center.

It's all I can do to stare at him, my breaths burning my lungs.

"This pretty little cunt, dripping fucking wet, is all mine."

A strangled whimper slips past my lips.

"Say it, Eve."

Eve.

Not Evie.

No baby girl.

No Scottish endearments anywhere to be found.

"I—my . . ."

"Say it," he growls, his thumb brushing my clit.

I cry out, gripping the sheet with both fists.

"I'm yours."

"Which part?"

What?

My face twists, and I gasp around my indignation.

He sweeps another digit through my center. The part of me that wants him badly overrides any thread of self-respect or dignity left in this oxygen-starved brain of mine.

"My pussy is yours," I finally grind out.

My need flares hotter.

"Not enough. Keep going."

My mouth parts. I grapple for air.

"My *body* is yours."

"More."

"M-my mind, yours."

Every inch of me trembles.

His face turns pained. "Still not enough." His chest heaves, its manic rhythm matching my own.

"Hear—" I choke around a sob as tears burn behind my eyes. "My heart, it's not my own."

"Whose is it, mo ghràdh?"

Ghràdh. I know that one . . .

Love.

Mo ghràdh . . . *My love.*

The air in my lungs stalls out.

Cal's grip around my hips turns harsh, and I whisper. "Yours."

His jaw feathers, and I swear he stops breathing.

The overwhelming urge to scramble to my knees and wrap my body around his blooms in an ache so deep. But his hold doesn't waiver.

I try to move, and he shakes his head.

That line we weren't supposed to cross is so far in our rearview mirror I can barely see it. It may as well be invisible. Nonexistent.

Poof.

Gone.

"Cal," I utter.

He makes a low, raw noise before clearing his throat. I brush my fingers over his knuckles, almost white over my hip now.

He looks like he needs a restart.

It's like his heart was just defibrillated. Brought back to life. And he doesn't know what to do with it. Like it sits, beating messily in his palm.

I want to take it, carefully, with gentle hands to stow it away somewhere safe. I want to make sure that look, the one that says he can't believe someone could love him back, never crosses his gorgeous face ever again. Ever.

He looks like he needs someone to throw him a life preserver. So, to save him, I whisper, "Not sweet, remember."

The look of shock fades a little and his eyes clear before they darken. With a single sweep of his fingers, he reclaims control. I tremble, desperate for his touch. His fingers. His mouth. Lips. Teeth.

All of him.

In a swift movement, he hauls my hips up to his waist. I slip off the pillow, hair dragging behind me. My breasts bounce, sending his gaze feral. He rocks back on his heels, his hands sliding under my ass. My eyes flutter shut the second his warm mouth finds my clit.

If this is his not sweet, I'll take his sour any day.

Maybe even the bitter parts.

His tongue works over my apex. Every strong, purposeful stroke has me climbing higher and higher. My head tilts back, lips parted. I arch from the bed, lost in this ecstasy he brings me.

And this man thinks he's not sweet . . .

He's fire.

He's a force of nature.

He's *everything*.

My legs tremble uncontrollably, and I try and fail to tighten them around his waist. His tongue runs through my wet center. I whimper, so close to falling apart.

The contact breaks.

The hell?

I snap my eyes open, pinning them on his with a burning gaze topped with a confused frown.

"Still think I'm sweet, baby girl?"

"Please . . . don't stop."

His face scrunches with something I can't place. "You want more. I want to take it *all*."

I know he's not talking about this. Just him and me on this bed. For a fleeting moment, I can envision a life here. Days spent in the sun. Tangled in these sheets. Wrapped, safe and warm, in the arms that have held me for months, knowing all too well their hold was temporary.

"We can't. I promised . . ." The words fade.

He tenses.

"Good."

Good? How is letting this fade out of existence good?

His teeth find my clit. I jolt at the sudden contact, struggling between my never-ending need for him and the back-and-forth of our conversation. The promise I made conflicts with the position I've put my own damn heart in.

Ours in.

Could I be happy here for the long haul?

Without my family. Without Allie. The life I've built in the city . . .

Warmth tugs on my aching center, and I arch from the bed. Sweat trickles between my breasts, my shoulders digging into the mattress.

I'm burning up. Under the touch of Callum, under the heaviness of my impending departure.

I'm leaving.

He will stay here. Alone.

My chest caves in on itself.

A hand lands on my elevated ass. The sting burns. I stifle a whimper, moving my gaze to meet blue eyes.

Those darkened blues have me wriggling under their scrutiny.

"Back here," Cal growls.

I must have checked out, lost in my thoughts.

"Do that again, baby girl, and I'll force your attention to where I want it."

I swallow, whispering, "Okay."

He raises an eyebrow before diving back down. His tongue plunges inside me, hands spreading me so wide, the pounding ache in my clit ratchets to insanity. Driving me senseless.

"Oh god, please. Cal . . ."

He runs his tongue through my center before suckling, licking, and tugging at my throbbing center with his teeth.

Fire spirals low in my belly. The telltale feeling of splintering light ascending into my soul starts. I roll my hips, wanting him closer.

Two fingers slide into me.

I can't breathe.

Bucking against him as he licks, sucks, and pumps into me, edging me closer and closer to oblivion.

"Cal," I pant. "Don't stop."

The tight grip on my hip fades, and with one long, slow suck on my clit he does exactly that.

He stops.

"No . . . please." The begging falls out of me so easily. "Cal, please."

My need glistens on his face. His beard is painted with it. On all fours, he crawls over me. As his gaze levels me, his mouth claims me.

I taste my need for him. It's almost torture, driving me past my breaking point. I break the kiss and bite down on his lip. Hard.

Copper slides over my tongue.

"Fuck," he rasps. He swipes at his mouth, and a crimson streak covers the back of his hand. "Vicious little thing. Not getting what you want does this to you?"

"Only with you."

A low grunt slips through a smirk as he brushes his knuckles over my cheek and across my jaw. "Mine, remember?"

A rough hand closes over my throat. The heartbeat in my clit blooms back to life. I buck on the bed, my need like gasoline tossed onto a fire. I grapple for purchase on his face. Before I can get a hold, he flips me over, pushing my shoulders into the bed. One hand tugs my ass toward him as he fists my hair with the other.

Warm breath tickles my ear. "There is nothing sweet about me when it comes to you. I would tear the fucking world apart for you, Evie."

His legs nudge my thighs wide.

I swallow around the emotion that's claimed my airway. His tip grazes my entrance. I cant my hips upward. So needy. So desperate for us to be one. For his body to claim mine. Taking what he wants, giving what I need.

A hand slides over my ribs, a thumb caressing the underside of my breast. My head is tugged back when that hand makes its way up to my cheek and his thumb snags on the side of my mouth. I turn my head, sucking it.

He slams into me. When he's seated fully, he hesitates.

I turn my head, looking back. His finger falls from my mouth as it opens.

"Take me, then," I hiss.

I'm so wound up, every inch he takes, every thrust I am sure will tip me over the edge. Rolling my hips, I try to take him deeper. To move. Something.

With a sharp tug on my hair and a hand under one arm, I'm pulled to my knees. "So needy, baby girl."

My head falls back onto his shoulder, and his hand in my hair loosens.

"You make me that way."

With a feral groan, he thunders into me.

Slick need coats my inner thighs, running down my skin. Each powerful thrust is perfect. Delicious.

I move a hand, letting my fingers fall over my clit.

The bed rocks, creaking as it shunts over the floor, the headboard hitting the wall. The slightest brush of my fingers over that sensitive nub between my legs, and I'm trembling.

"No," Cal growls, his hands finding mine. He raises them over my head, holding my wrists with one hand, the other returning to my hip.

He thunders into me. His hot breath hits my neck. Every inch of me is a lit fuse. Sweat trickles down my stomach, rolling down my spine. A hot tongue licks the bead from my neck, and I shudder. The flicker of something sublime explodes in my center and I whimper. Breathlessly, I cry out.

"Don't you dare, Evie."

I lean back into him and his movements slow.

With a brief kiss to my neck, he whispers something I don't understand.

"*Beannachd leat, a nighean milis.*"

He's turning me around before the next heartbeat. I fall back onto the bed. Gripping his cock, he pumps his release over my stomach. The low rumble seeping through his parted lips as his eyes burn right through me takes the tentative breath from my lungs.

Something is off. A tiny crack in our happiness facade. The one we have carefully curated, despite the unspoken rule we wouldn't be something meaningful to the other. Ships in the night that even the Fresnel above us couldn't find.

"No, Cal . . ."

His face curls with something painful and involuntary. He's off the bed a second later.

I lie, watching him walk to the bathroom and fail to draw a useful lungful.

Never have I ever been so desperate or so floored by a silent plea. It screams volumes.

He's already pulling away.

And it's my fault.

firefly

Twenty-Nine

CALLUM

The little pout on Evie's face as she chops ingredients for dinner tonight pushes a smile up on mine. I jot down the metrics from the weather for this week, scanning the pattern that cycles through the spring and summer seasons.

She's been pissy at me all day.

I know why.

Arrogance personified is a man who thinks he understands the workings of a woman's mind. But I'd hedge a bet it's because I left her teetering on the precipice of oblivion and left her there to fend for herself while I took what I wanted. Well, almost.

Or it could be the fact she's finally realized this shouldn't have happened. We shouldn't have got this far.

Even making her promise me she'll leave and have a

big, beautiful life doesn't seem like enough. I won't believe I've done the right thing by her until she leaves and doesn't come back. I know how it sounds—McCreary, the martyr.

Perhaps it makes me that.

Or it allows her to not have to choose something she will regret down the line. It's not like I'll ever leave this floating rock. Another life for me wasn't available when the fates were assigned. Sometimes I think about it, leaving. Traveling to the motherland. Finding my family. Seeing the world.

The promise I made her give me is my gift to her.

Freedom.

You know what they say about love something, set it free and all that damn bullshit. I see the merit in it now. And am acutely aware that I do.

Love her, that is.

I shouldn't.

I don't want to.

I don't want her to carry that burden.

There is a sliver of selfishness that wishes she would stay. Where Evie decides the rest of the world isn't worth the hassle and stays put here with me.

I'm hopeless when it comes to the quiet little woman who showed up at my slip, carry-on in hand, confusion written all over her beautiful fucking face.

I tried to stay away. Truly, I did.

Slamming the book closed, I run my hands through my hair.

The knife that's been chopping furiously stops. I swing my gaze to the kitchen to find her chewing that damn bottom lip like she already holds all the worries of the world.

Another reminder she should be living her life, happy and free. Her best life is not on this island. I push out of the sofa and toss the book to the coffee table. "Going to the lantern room."

I tread the stairs, needing to be anywhere but looking at her pretty face, wanting to envelop her in my hold if only to erase the worry that's gnawing at her lush bottom lip.

By the time I reach the top of the house, I'm goddamn hard.

It's too much.

She's too much.

I fling the maintenance cupboard open and pull out the polishing cloths and the glass cleaner and get to work. The soft cloth works the glass panes over, not leaving any streaks. I let the rhythmic, methodical pattern of the polishing take me out of my head.

The sun is lowering as I give the lantern room a third round of arm-aching, completely unnecessary finishing touches.

A knock taps on the door to the room.

I suck in a breath before letting out a sigh. "Yeah?"

Without a word, Evie pushes through the door. She's in her sundress, her once pale skin is now sun-kissed, her cheeks blushing with color. She's stunning.

The way she looks at me . . .

A tangle of desperation and determination.

Nothing like the meek girl who stepped onto my boat almost nine months ago.

Up here, she glows. The sun lights up her dark hair, giving it a golden halo as deep browns study my face. The Fresnel's got nothing on my Evie.

My heart explodes inside my rib cage, its ragged pieces splattered against the cavity.

God, I need her so bad the ache could kill me.

I am well aware it absolutely will, the day she leaves.

Evie isn't like Ava. This isn't like last time. Last time was friends, then lust, to lovers.

Not this.

This is soul-achingly, heartbreakingly deep. When her hands cup my jaw and heat swells in my chest, my lungs burn.

"Breathe, Cal. Please."

I choke through a raw sound. "Fuck, Evie."

"Why did you make me make that *stupid* promise?"

"You'll figure it out one day, baby girl."

"What if I break it?" The words are so gentle.

"Don't, please? That would . . ."

Make me a whole man again. Make me the happiest man alive.

Me.

Me.

Me.

Fucking hell.

I'm not that man anymore. Haven't been for years.

"Just don't," I repeat.

"Okay," she says, scrunching her face. "But." She studies my eyes, like there is something she needs to know that I'm not saying. "Give me one last time. P-pl-lease?" The word breaks, and the tears welling in her eyes with the last phrase spill over. She forces a smile, her hands on my face trembling.

I stand, shoulders heaving. Heart breaking. I grab her face and smash my mouth to hers, and I'm intoxicated within less than a second of touching her. She whimpers with the groan I loose into her mouth, as if this is hurting her as much as it is me. I manhandle her to my hips. Spinning around, I plant her on the edge of the lamp's platform.

Fine hands tug at my work shirt, the buttons pop, and my T-shirt underneath is all I have on a heartbeat later. I pull at her clothes, hauling the cotton dress down at the sweetheart neckline until one full, perfect-as-fuck breast spills over.

No bra.

Maybe . . .

I run a hand up her thigh and when I don't find material, I can't restrain the growl ripping past my lips. "Fucking hell, baby girl."

"The last pair are in shreds. I can't lose any more." The prettiest smile blooms over her face.

"Christ, Evie. You don't make this easy for me."

She spreads her legs. "Easy is the idea, Cal."

My forehead hits hers as I struggle to catch my next breath. I slip two fingers inside her. She's absolutely soaked and so damn tight.

"How long have you been downstairs thinking about this?" I ask, curling my digits forward.

Her back arches, head falling back onto the Fresnel.

"A while . . ." The syllables are breathy.

I clasp my lips around one delicious damn nipple, and she opens further for me.

"Good girl. I want to see you come on my face, on my fingers, and on my cock. If this is our last time, it's going to be fucking perfect."

"Fuc—per—oh . . . god."

She comes, hard. Gripping waves quiver over my fingers. I pump in a rough rhythm, watching her beautiful face wreck right in front of me.

On a pant, her pretty pink tongue pokes out as she wets her bottom lip. That gorgeous thing will be in my dreams for years, I've never been so sure of anything in my life.

She grabs my face as she straightens and moves off the

lamp, her mouth finding mine. My little woman is so wound up.

I didn't stand a damn chance.

Her tongue slides inside my mouth and I battle for control. Who am I kidding? When it comes to Eve Holland, I have none.

Fingers traveling the contours of her collarbones, neck and jaw, I draw her attention. As she breaks at the kiss, I pull her onto my hips. Cycling through ragged breaths, she stares at me like I could disappear at any second and she is dreading the moment. With one foot, I turn over the wooden crate housing a few spare rags and brushes. They clatter to the floor as the upturned crate settles.

I sit on the crate and deposit her on my lap. "Here do, baby girl?" My words are soft.

They take her by surprise. She's used to rough Cal. Grumpy lighthouse keeper.

Not this time.

There's no place for anything but me loving on this woman right now.

I flip the sundress up and knead her ass. She rocks in my lap, her wetness soaking through my pants as she rubs her sweet pussy along my aching cock.

Lightning floods every nerve as she bends down and nips my neck, dusting kisses up toward my jaw. Teeth close around my pounding pulse, so light it razes me to the ground. Her tenderness. Her tender heart, putting mine back together.

"Stay right here," Evie breathes against my ear. "Stay with me, here."

"Not going anywhere, baby girl."

Her hands wander until the button on my pants pops and she is desperately tugging at them. I rise and set her on her feet. When I'm naked as the day I came into this life and she is standing bared before me, I settle back on the crate. She takes a slow, small step toward me. My mouth aches to savor those dusky nipples. Cock so fucking hard it's painful, I wait through each small step she takes.

Drawing it out like she knows it's our last time.

Like a weapon she can wield against me.

Her legs straddle my lap, still standing, and I run my hands over her hips, leaning down and kissing her belly. Her fingers weave through my hair as I dip and swirl my tongue over her clit, digging into my scalp.

Fuck me, Evie.

I was born to love you, woman. I could spend the rest of my days like this.

The taste of her.

The feel of her.

Every tiny fucking sweet sound that slips through those pretty damn lips . . .

The last of the light slips away outside, and I lift one elegant, long leg to drape it over my shoulder.

"Cal," she breathes. One hand moves to my other shoulder as she steadies herself. I dive in, desperate to devour her. To suck, to devastate her pussy. I want to have her on my tongue. A permanent imprint of her taste I can't wash off.

I tug at her sweet little nub with my teeth and then suckle the burn I created.

She shakes, balancing on one foot.

"Heavens, how do—" Her words dissolve into the sweetest little mewl.

I trace a finger around her entrance. I want to be deep inside this pussy. I want her to watch me slide into her, slow and deep. I suckle her clit, sliding one finger inside. Her hips wriggle in protest of the lack of digits. But I plan on fucking her so thoroughly, she won't get the memory of us out of her head. Ever.

Her grip on my shoulder wavers, and I slip her leg down and pull her onto my lap. Breathless, she moves for my mouth.

I lean back a little. "Watch, baby."

She swallows, and her gaze drops.

I lift her hips, and she lines my cock to her entrance. Her fine fingers wrapped around my aching shaft is almost too much. Once I'm notched at her entrance, I groan. "Down, baby girl. Slow. Look at us."

The slow, agonizing stroke it takes to get me deep inside her rips the last shred of control from me.

"Christ," I growl.

"I love that," she rasps. "Do it again."

On the edge of blowing my load on the second thrust, I distract myself with her addictive flesh. I suck a nipple into my mouth as she rises, and my cock pulses. Threatening to betray me in the worst way possible. No way is this going to be over in a few minutes. If this is our last time, we're going to take all damn night.

My cock slips from her pussy, and I groan. Fuck that. Not being inside this incredible woman is a place I don't want to be.

"Baby, that ain't gonna work for me. I can't do without you."

I'm fucking *desperate*.

The cool ocean breeze winds through the slatted, round enclosure. The stars outside blanket the dark sky before I realize the lamp is about to beam to life.

Fuck.

I can't move.

I don't want to.

The whir and click of the automated lamp system starts up.

"What the?" Evie turns her head toward the light, and I catch her face in my hands just in time. Like a moth to a flame. I can't remember a person who's been up here and been able to resist a glance. It's like telling someone not to look at the sun.

Light blasts room, oscillating on its axis.

"Oh! Oh my god, that's amazing."

"Keep your eyes on me, baby girl. Don't look at it." I chuckle, dipping my head to hide from the light as it comes around. With Evie's back to the light, I can hide from its beam in her shadow.

Analyze that one, McCreary.

"The stars disappear every time it comes around," she says, fascinated.

"That's not the most amazing thing about this old lantern room, baby."

She huffs a breathy laugh as if remembering what we were doing before the lamp came on.

Lowering herself slower than I can handle, she whispers, "Where were we?"

"You trying to kill me with a slow, sweet death."

"Ditto, grumpy old lighthouse keeper."

I chuckle and slap her ass, hard.

She jerks over my lap with the impact. "Ah!"

I raise an eyebrow. She liked that.

Fuck, I did, too. The way she jolted on my cock when my hand connected with her ass.

"Do it again," she begs.

I slap her ass hard. A whimper spills from her lips as she rocks forward.

Fuck me, it takes everything I have to not come.

"Baby, as much as I love this for us, the lantern room isn't where we want to be right now."

"Where will you take me, Mr. McCreary?"

I huff a sound. "Now, I sound old."

The cheekiest smile grows on her face, but when she wriggles those damn hips, the insult fades. My needy cock throbs inside her, threatening to send me over the edge at any second.

"We're going downstairs," I grumble.

Pushing to my feet, I hold her on my waist. Leaving our clothes behind, I tread the winding stairs until I make the ground level. A handful of heartbeats later, I deposit Evie on the kitchen table.

And fuck, if this angle isn't the best view I've ever seen.

Still inside her, I tug her to the edge of the table. The old wooden piece groans and wobbles. Now her gaze drops to where mine is stuck. The place where we are joined. Her perfect glistening pussy, my engorged cock sunk deep, like it fucking belongs there.

"God, we are beautiful," she pants, a fine hand exploring the sensitive skin where she's wrapped around my cock. She runs a finger over one side of her entrance, and a moan slips out. Her fingers travel, sliding under my balls.

I grind out a growl. "Baby girl . . ."

"You like that?"

"Turn a man feral . . ."

She huffs a low sound.

"I wan—I need to see you slamming into me."

I haul her up toward me and crash my mouth over hers as I push in deep. Letting her settle around my girth. Breaking away, I press her down to the wooden surface, one hand on her chest. I slam into her, hard. Fast. She breaks under the heel of my hand, her cries tumbling from her mouth as her pussy clenches down.

Back arching, she comes, milking me in waves. I lift her up. "See me fill this perfect pussy, Evie baby."

"Cal . . ."

I thunder into her. Harder than I should. The table scrapes along the floor, and she grips the edges as she tightens around me again. I drop my head, plucking her nipple between my teeth. I'll make this woman come as many times as I can. Fuck, the way she tightens for me every damn time.

Fucking bliss.

One thumb circling her clit, I suck her peak hard. She bucks on the table, crying out as she clamps down in a vice grip.

"Fu-uck!" I roar, spilling. Hot ropes shoot deep into her, claiming this lithe, beautiful body as mine.

Owning her.

Never before was a man so delusional.

Thirty

EVIE

Sherry stares at me like I'm the one who has her wires crossed.

"You said the carton of books arrived before the festival?" I ask.

"Yes, from the publishing house, I assumed, although there was no sender details. I thought it was some kind of promo you arranged."

"I didn't, no. And I haven't heard from Livvy, my editor, for weeks."

"Oh, well. I guess no harm, no foul. They all sold. One young man bought ten copies. Nice young chap, around your age."

I look around the library like he could still be here.

"Was he a local?" I ask.

"No, just here for his sabbatical. A few months, I think he said. Not sure if he's still here."

"Okay."

Dammit.

None of this feels right. The fact that someone set up a signing that wasn't approved by the publishing house, that Livvy didn't know about, puts me on edge.

"Will you tell me if he comes back?" I ask.

"You'll want to sign all those copies he bought, I suppose," Sherry chirps.

Yeah, something like that.

Shit.

"Thanks for your help with the research last month, it was really helpful." I wander toward the loans desk as Sherry slips behind it.

"That's wonderful. But what were the Gaelic reference books for? Is your novel set in a fantasy version of Scotland? Oh, that would be something!"

"No, not exactly. But they were helpful. I'll make sure to return them next week before I go."

"You're leaving already? Gosh, we will miss having a writer in residence in our little library. Make sure you come back to visit sometime, okay?"

I huff out a chuckle. "Sure thing, Sherry."

She shoots me a smile and turns to a patron with an armload full of books to check out. My phone buzzes, and I dig through my bag. Finding paper, I pull it out. And almost drop it when I realize what it is.

The letter Iris gave me on the night of the festival.

I'd been so busy with the signing and with trying to soak up every little experience with Cal before my days here are over that I completely forgot about it. I wander outside to the bench seats in the garden, the colorful blooms hedging the town center's water fountain and grass area we sat on at the festival popping from behind the seat.

Flipping the envelope in my hands, I brace for the contents. The emotions that follow opening one of these letters. A prickle of fear washes down my spine as the wind changes. Something like cedar carries on the wind. I slide a finger under the envelope flap.

It sticks and I rip it, wanting this over and done with.

The envelope tears in half. The burned ash of a tiny insect body and tattered wings, now greyed and singed, flutter from the paper tomb.

"Oh!" I slap a hand over my mouth. A torn-up monarch is one thing. The message clear. One burned with cinders for a bed, trapped in an ivory paper crypt, sends a whole other type of message.

I swipe the remnants of insect from my jeans, and the envelope flutters to the ground, the letter inside slipping out.

Reaching down, I clutch it with a shaking hand.

Breath firmly held, I unfold the page.

I close my eyes, not wanting the words to reach my

vision. I can't take another loss. Another traumatic event that sets my life back years.

No, Evie, that is not main character thinking. Not how the heroine would react. She would take the bull by the horns. The page by the edges, her gaze burning so hard it would surely ignite. Setting the ivory pulp into flames.

With that thought, I open my eyes and scan first, lips pursed, frown dipped so low my face hurts.

You see, this is how things will go, Butterfly.
Me and you, on that little island of his.
Without outside interference, I know you
will come to love me.
And one day you will understand the depth of
my love for you.
It is eternal.
A love to trump all else.
Nothing, no one, will stand in our way of being
together, Butterfly.
I know you will understand when you see how
much I love you.
I have done some things, I know, but
everything was to free you to be with me. That
can't be wrong, can it?
We are so close to having it all.
So close, Butterfly.
Only a matter of days until our life starts.
Really starts.
T xx

Bile rises in my throat, burning its way through the air caught on the sob wanting out. I crumple the paper in my hand. Fire floods my veins.

Nothing, no one, *will stand in our way of being together.*

He means Cal?

He means Cal.

Oh my god.

I jolt from the seat and shove the letter into my bag. This was written—or sent, at least—around the time of the festival.

A matter of days.

Shit!

I sprint back to the marina, fear close on my tail as I desperately search for Cal. For Firefly.

When I reach our slip and the boat floats in its place undisturbed, emotion rushes my senses. I board, tripping over the side. "Cal!?"

The cabin is empty.

He had errands to run.

I press a hand over my chest, trying to calm my bounding, terrified heart.

He's fine. He will be fine.

Footsteps thunder toward Firefly. I spin back, half expecting some strange face I don't know to corner me on the boat, then move in and end this nightmare.

Just end it already.

I slam my eyes shut as a man rushes the boat.

Firefly rocks as he boards. I suck in a lungful, bracing.

A whimper slips from me as a hand touches my shoulder.

"Miss Evie?"

Emmett?

Emmett!

I sob, flying into his chest. The fear from the last ten minutes pours out in ugly, soul-racking cries.

"Holy shit, what happened? Where's Cal?" he says, running a hand over my head in a soothing motion.

I soak his shirt, letting the last six years of heartbreaking torture tumble free.

"Hell, Evie."

His broad hand rubs circles over my back. I try and fail to compose myself. I can imagine what people are thinking, the tall, handsome, and somewhat taken Coast Guard officer consoling the woman living with his best friend. God.

Ugh. Stupid small towns.

I push out of his hold.

His grip keeps me at arm's length. "Evie, you okay?"

Nodding, I sniff back the tears. "Fine. Sorry, just had a moment."

His head tilts. "Didn't look like a moment."

I shudder through a breath and set my shoulders back. "I'm leaving soon. It's a lot, that's all."

His face softens, then morphs to a frown. "You don't have to go. Staying is always an option."

I shake my head.

No.

No, it's not.

It's really not.

"I can't." The words choke out.

"Okay, well, if you change your mind, you're always welcome. And, hell." He plucks his cap from his head, running a hand through his hair. "I know Cal wants you to stay."

I frown. "What? No, he doesn't."

Em raises an eyebrow. "That so?"

"He doesn't what?" Cal's voice cuts into our conversation.

I sag with relief.

Thank god.

"Nothing, forget it." I adjust my bag over my shoulder and snag Em's gaze. He forces a smile and turns back to his friend. When he disembarks Firefly, he gives me a kind smile and tips his cap. So old school, that Emmett. It's sweet. I feel terrible for unloading my baggage on his chest. But I'm thankful Cal wasn't here. I don't think I could explain that one away.

Thankfully, Emmett looks like he's good at keeping things to himself.

"Get your errands done?" I ask, hoping my voice doesn't betray me.

Cal steps onto the boat and then into my space. "Yup." His eyes study my face as if what I'm not saying is printed in Times New Roman all over it.

I feel like it is.

Now, with the last letter and its impending—and very

real—threat to Cal, I have to leave. Whether or not Emmett's offer has any truth to it, I can't stay.

I made a promise to leave.

And I make a new one to myself right here and now—when I go back to the city, I am going to the police. I won't make the mistake of keeping this to myself again.

I can't let anything happen to Cal.

I won't.

Settling into the cabin, I send my gaze around the marina. Cal starts the engine, and we glide from the slip. We clear the last row in the marina, and I glance back toward the Coast Guard building. The oversized windows reflect the day's sunlight. I swear I make out a figure under the overhanging watch room. The figure holds something to their face.

My gut sinks, churning like I imagine a gazelle's does when they get their first sniff of lion.

Shit.

Has he been here all this time?

The festival.

The signing.

The week we came to Iris's for Em's birthday dinner?

Oh my lord.

Fear shrouds me for the second time today and I grip my bag tight, setting my eyes on the horizon.

The boats that were tampered with . . . Were they a warning?

Surely, he wouldn't venture out to the island.

But what if he does?

If he is keeping tabs on me, the only way to keep Cal safe is to leave.

Teeth gritted, I breathe through a curled lip as anger flings through my veins like wildfire.

Fine. He wants me, he's going to have to come and damn well get me.

In the heart of the city.

When I'm ready.

Surrounded by people.

With the trap baited and set.

I may be just a nerdy author, but my research is extensive. My FMCs have been through much, much worse.

Game on, T.

Cal won't look at me. He's been that way since the marina.

"Spill it, McCreary."

"Nope."

"Urgh, will you just tell me what's eating you?"

Now, here in the greenhouse, I stab the soil in the bed for tomatoes with the trowel.

He continues to shovel fertilizer into the new bed he's

prepping for the last half of summer. He's tense and far too quiet. Already a man of few words, he's now down to single syllables. Short of seducing it out of him, which would be a gross abuse of power on my part, I am left with begging for an explanation.

"Come on, talk about it before it starts taking chunks out of that handsome heart of yours."

He raises an eyebrow at me.

Okay, not my best word choice. But seeing him upset does something visceral to me.

I abandon the tomato bushes and close in on him, tugging my gardening gloves off. "Please, talk to me."

He slams the tip of the shovel into the pile of fertilizer. Good lord, it reeks. If it wasn't so amazing at growing the most delicious food, I wouldn't support this stinky endeavor.

"You're not telling me something," he snaps.

I reel back, jerking my head like he slapped me.

It's not because I disagree. It's because by hiding this from him, I feel like I'm lying. Maybe I am. Did not telling Joshua contribute to his death? I guess I will never truly know.

But . . .

"That's not true," I hear myself say.

The same go-to answer every time. Avoidance. I'm great at it.

He's in my space a heartbeat later. "Don't fucking lie to me, Evie."

I almost crumble under his scrutiny. But I don't. The last thing I need is Callum hunting this guy down and getting hurt, or worse. God, I can't even think about that without panicking.

"I am not. Is this really how you want to spend our last few days together?"

That takes him down a peg. His shoulders drop and he turns back to the shovel at his side.

"No, it isn't. But . . ."

His throat works.

I touch his arm, desperate to eliminate the distance between us. "What? What is it?"

"Forget it," he breathes.

Forget it. Just like that.

I guess he's got a point. No argument we could have holds now. I'm leaving. Everything we could ever fight about is a moot point.

So I turn back to my beautiful crop of tomatoes, admiring all I have done here in nine months.

A yellow butterfly lands on a branch by my hand. Somehow, I have become fond of these pretty little yellow flutterbys.

A tiny, ever so minuscule ray of hope stings my senses.

Maybe one day I will come back.

If my heart can stand it.

firefly

Thirty-One

CALLUM

It seems we are both putting distance between us. Evie's been holed up in the bedroom, working on the last pages of her novel, I assume. She rarely talks about it lately. And I don't know the first thing about writing fiction to even ask. With the clipboard in one hand, I hold the old-school weather station's slatted door open. I scan the gauges and take down the recordings. The summer sun, high in the sky, sears into my skin.

Wiping the sweat from my brow, I return my cap, pulling it down. The button-down work shirt I picked this morning sticks to my back, damp from only the smallest task. The days are getting hotter by the second. Another humid coastal summer to mark another year.

Gravel crunches behind me. I glance over my shoulder, hoping it's her. Maybe she decided the distance is too much.

I have, but I'll be damned if I'm going to make it harder for her to leave. I force my focus back to the contents of the old-school instruments. One glance at the sky tells me storms are on their way. Like clockwork when the air heats up. Summer on Fire Island swings between heaven and hell.

Sometimes without warning.

Always settling in for days over my tiny slice of peace and quiet.

"Cal?"

I close my eyes and pretend that one syllable from her lips doesn't do the things it does to me. Sliding the clipboard into the side of the weather station, I shut the door and latch it.

"Yeah?"

When I turn to face her, she's hugging her arms around herself with flushed cheeks and her hair piled onto the top of her head. She steps forward. The tank top and tiny shorts she wears highlight her perfect curves. I shutter the thoughts wanting to bloom at the sliver of skin showing around her elegant waist. She drops her gaze to the ground and shifts on her feet, and I set my shoulders back and cross my arms, imitating her position.

"Did you need something?" I ask.

"I—ah, is it okay if you take me to the hut, one last time? I have a building in my book, same kind of build . . . and I wanted to make sure I have the details right. If that's okay?"

I wasn't expecting that.

"Like for a couple of hours, or?"

"An hour should do it. I can go by myself if you're busy, but I thought I should ask first."

Nothing about this is okay.

Evie feeling the need to ask my fucking permission to do things. Wrapping things up . . . to leave.

Fuck me.

"You want company? In case the weather rolls in?" I ask, not able to let this go. The feeling she's slipping away. Of course she is. It's what I asked her to do.

"Oh sure, if you're not busy."

"Give me thirty. I'll just finish the day's inspections."

She rocks on her heels, eyes looking anywhere but at me. "Great. I'll grab my stuff."

I force a smile.

It's incredible how fast we went from full throttle, heart in and soul deep, to this awkward shuffle four feet apart.

If anything was ever a shitty deal, a bad hand of fate, the universe screwing a man over, this is it.

I wander to the dock, running an eye over the boat, double-checking it's full of fuel, the life jackets are functional and stored properly. Like it ever fucking changes.

Running a hand over the two life preservers secured at the stern, I find nothing of note. Still in good condition. Unlike this heart of mine . . .

One last trip to the hut is going to be a tough gig. I turn the key to ALT and check the radio, reporting the weather to the watch house before shutting it down. Firefly's served this island and the mariners of the waters to the east for years. She's earned her keep, that's for sure.

I make it back to the house to change into my boots and grab up a water bottle and the handheld radio, just in case.

Evie bounds down the stairs, her gait slowing when she sees me.

It's like just being in a room with me pulls the oxygen from her. I don't know how to do this awkward bullshit. "Ready?"

"Yep, need to grab my phone. Is it okay if I take pictures?"

"Sure thing."

She offers a meek smile and gathers her things. We secure the lighthouse before leaving for the forest tree line. When we breach the cooler, shaded space, I can't take it any longer. "This can't be how we leave things."

She doesn't respond, pushing through the underbrush.

I stalk at her back, every step ratcheting up the tension between us. The fire in my core flares to life.

"Hey." The word snaps out much harsher than I intend it to.

She stops, so still. Looking ahead. Not turning back.

"Evie, look at me."

She doesn't move.

I round her position and close in until we are so close our breath mingles. "What is this?"

"It's what it has to be," she utters.

"Bullshit. Stop with the meek people-pleasing crap."

Her brows draw down and those deep browns lace with fire.

There she is.

"I'm not *with* anything. This is me leaving you, like you asked me to."

"One last trip to the hut? Do you actually even need photos of some busted old shack, or is this you procrastinating? We both know you're great at that."

The slap that connects with my cheek burns.

Her chin wobbles.

Struggling to hold back a sob, she spins on her heels and all but sprints through the trees.

Christ, I'm the world's biggest asshole.

This is hurting us both. We both knew this was going to end with our hearts in tatters. Now I'm rubbing it in her face.

All she wanted was to spend a few more hours with me.

My gut churns as I take off in her direction. It doesn't take long to find her standing at the edge of the waterhole we never got to swim in. We never made that particular memory, even though I promised her we would. If anyone is breaking promises, it's me.

"Evie, I'm sorry. Baby girl, I was outta line."

When she finally looks at me, tears streak her face.

Fuck.

She stills her wobbling mouth with the flattest smile I've ever seen on her pretty face. I step closer. Not holding her when she's hurting is tearing me to shreds. "Come here."

She shakes her head, and I move a little closer.

"Now, baby girl."

I fold her into my arms and drop my face into her neck. "I wish things were different. I wish we . . ." The breathy words fade.

Sucking in a ragged breath, she pushes from my arms. "This is how things have to be. I have to go home. You need to stay here, safe on your island. It has to be this way." She forces a smile.

I know this.

I made her promise to do just that.

Go home.

Leave me.

Safe? From what?

The last thing I want is for her to leave. I want to beg her to stay. For the first time in my life, being alone is terrifying. It's something I can no longer comprehend.

The radio in my back pocket squawks. The static is inaudible.

We both pause.

When nothing comes after, I turn her toward the south. "Let's get to the hut before the weather finds us."

We make the hut in good time, and I have no doubt the

need to ignore each other and go about the business of making the trip as quick as possible spurs Evie forward.

A woman on a mission, she paces in front of the old rustic shack, taking in the warped front door, the knives moving on their hooks in the ocean breeze finding its way through the trees to the little secluded place.

Talking to herself, she touches the opaque glass windows at the front. Removing the knives from the hooks, she disappears inside, mumbling something about aesthetics. She comes back out and stands by my side, snapping images.

Now I realize this place that's served as my sanctuary, my last piece of my father, I have handed over to her without a second thought. I know she isn't hurting it. She's not tearing it down. But I let her in so easily. Never before has a woman—or anyone, for that matter—had access to the fishing hut.

I think Em has been here a total of twice. With me both times, and only for a short stop on the way to the south end of the island where we hunt through the craggy treasure-filled rocks.

". . . should be enough." Evie purses her lips, returning her phone to her back pocket, her journal tucked in one arm.

"Huh?" I startle, remembering what we were doing.

"I'm done here."

More painful words have never been spoken. I nod, not bothering to hide the regret eating at me now.

"Sure, we should head back before the weather folds in." I make for north, not checking if she follows. Picking my way through the soft undergrowth, I sink back into my weighty thoughts.

Torture is being trapped on an island with the one woman you can't—no, shouldn't—have.

A soft hand lands on my shoulder. "Wait up, will you?"

I slow, but not by much.

I can't.

I thought I could do this.

Let her go.

But I feel each chip of my heart as it cracks and falls away. Each more painful than the last.

"Callum, slow down!"

Harried footsteps rush behind me. Short pants snap through the air around us as the debris under our feet crunches.

"Gotta head back."

I glance at the sky through the small gap the canopy overhead affords. The sky, once dotted with fluffy white clouds, has turned. It must be around three by now. We didn't take that long, surely. I track the bright sunlight poking through the leafy ceiling. Sure enough, it's descending to the west.

Fuck.

"We have to get home," I call back to Evie. I have paper-work to sort out for a meeting in Rockland tomorrow, where they will decide my fate. Well, the lighthouse's fate. The publishing house money from Evie's stay has boosted the accounts, but we are still short. A bunch of stuffy old farts will decide whether I keep my house. No, my home.

Home.

A novel concept.

My home. No longer hers.

God, misery's really stuck her talons in deep. And so soon.

We finally break through the tree line at the north end, and I stalk across the grassy area, hell bent on getting inside, up to the lantern room before I do something I'll regret.

Something she doesn't deserve.

I take the internal stairs two at a time. Smashing a hand to the door of the top room, I stumble inside and round the oversized light, dropping to my seat at its base, hands crawling through my hair as my palms press into my face.

I let loose a raw groan. "Fuck!"

When nobody enters my coveted space, I lie on the floor, flat on my back, staring at nothing. A million thoughts plunder my mind. None make any of this easier. None offer a solution to the heartbreak I know is coming. The telltale rumble of it is rushing toward me. The vibrations of the freight train aimed right at my heart reverberate through my body. Inch by painful fucking inch.

The house is quiet when I finally sit up.

The stars pop in the lavender sky to the east.

The lamp whirs to life, reminding me of its own impending doom, if the Restoration Society gets its way. I need to get the paperwork in order.

Dammit.

Running both hands through my hair, I haul in a fortifying breath. It's our last night here. Together.

I should be civil.

I should leave things on a good note.

Make the last memory she has here something special.

I should . . .

I climb back down the spiral stairs and pass the bedroom. Evie's sitting on the bed, looking out the window, her packed suitcase by her side.

Hell.

I leave her to her thoughts and make a start on dinner. Last one. Gotta make sure it's good.

Tugging the refrigerator open, I lean down. A tray of her tomatoes sits on the top shelf. Some shredded chicken left over from yesterday. I pull them out and hunt for pasta in the pantry.

Twenty minutes later, I have the makings of a chicken and tomato pasta topped with basil, fresh from the garden, that smells divine.

I set the food on the table. Gathering up cutlery and the old bottle of red wine, I add it to our last meal.

God, that's morbid.

Fuck me, Cal.

Satisfied with the table I've laid out for her, I call Evie down.

A moment later, beautiful, red-rimmed brown eyes meet mine, and I'm rooted to the spot.

You're breaking my heart, mo ghràdh.

Thirty-Two

EVIE

Why does it feel like one of us is dying?

Cal's hands are tight on the boat's wheel.

He hasn't said a word since dinner last night. It's like I can see his heart breaking all over his face. I hate it.

I hate this.

I had to force myself to reread every letter from T this morning. To make myself get out of bed. To make myself get dressed and get off the island. Fire Island will always be the place where I found myself. Where my heart bloomed. Where my soul cracked wide open.

I loved every moment of it.

And I will do everything in my power to make certain Cal stays undisturbed, safe on his island. The way he wants.

So, why does the thought of him there alone—more accurately, without me—feel so damn wrong?

I once heard a saying. It went something along the lines of *love will always take sacrifice.*

And this feels like the ultimate sacrifice.

Leave the man.

Leave him safe.

Break my heart to save his.

A fair and noble price to pay in light of all that's been lost to my cowardice in this situation thus far. In theory, I'm a brave woman scorned. I hope when the reality manifests I still hold that bravery.

God, I hope so.

I swallow around the stone wedged in my airway.

The marina comes into view, and my heart starts to race.

This is it. The last minutes of being part of Callum McCreary's life. My grip on my bag tightens. Air, short and swift, burns my lungs.

I knew it would.

It's better than I deserve.

He throttles down and we glide into Firefly's slip. I move to the side, rolling the bumpers over the side as the boat closes in on the gangway. Look at me, doing sailorly things like I belong on this old tub. My first mate status, coming a little too late.

When the engine splutters out, I can't look at Cal.

Emmett jogs toward us, and I shake my head and suck in a breath.

"Hell, Miss Evie, how are nine months up already?" He holds a hand out to me, and I disembark.

"Thanks." I land safely on the jetty. "Time flies when you're . . ."

I can't even finish the sentence.

"You taking Evie to the bus stop, Cal?"

Cal is busy tying off as he says, "Can't. Gotta get Iris and head over to Rockland for the restoration meeting. You take her, Em."

"I'm right here," I breathe.

But he doesn't look up, doesn't look at me.

No, that's fine.

Totally fine. I get it.

He's making space.

Making it easier. Emmett grabs my bag as Cal hands it up. For a moment I can't believe I lived through the last nine months with so few possessions. One bag was all it took for my life to be uprooted and turned around. It looks too insignificant. My time on Fire Island, the place that changed my life, reduced to one small piece of luggage.

I can't decide if that's freeing or depressing.

"Come on, Miss Eve, let's get you back to the city." Em's smile is sad. I turn back, desperate to say goodbye to Cal, but he's ducked back inside the cabin.

Like he doesn't do goodbyes.

Figures.

May the ending emulate the beginning.

The man of few words.

The sound of tiny plastic wheels rolling over jetty boards drowns out my thoughts, and I turn to follow Emmett toward the marina parking lot.

"I bet you're ready for civilization again, hey?"

I tug my sunglasses from my bag and slide them on. "Maybe."

"Maybe?"

"Yeah, maybe." I give him a sad smile.

He shakes his head, blowing out a breath. "You can always come home. We'll always be here."

"Thank you," I say quickly, before the burn nailing the back of my eyes can choke me.

He tugs me into his side and rubs a hand over my hair, playfully mussing it. Big brother move of the century.

That's all it takes for my heart to crack.

These people took me in so easily.

"Can I say goodbye to Iris before I go?" I ask, steeling against my misery.

"Sure," he says, and it never fails to make my heart glow the way just the mention of Iris lights up his face.

We swing a left and head for the café. It's busy, but Iris rounds the counter with arms open when I push through the door and the bell jingles. Em hangs back, and I take my bag from him. Hands in the pockets of his Coast Guard uniform, he really is handsome. Iris oughta get onto that. I chuckle at my casual ship of these two.

Tight arms hug me, and I return the gesture.

"You take care of yourself, you hear?" Iris whispers. I swear her voice wobbles.

I push from her hold and nod. My bag bumps against my side, reminding me of its contents.

Pulling out her blue ombré scarf, I hand it to her, opening my palm as it hangs draped over. "Sorry it took me so long to return it. It's just so pretty."

She closes my hand over it. "Keep it. I have a suspicion blue is your favorite color." She smiles at me.

Something buzzes on the counter.

Her phone.

"You really should put your phone behind the counter. Someone is going to swipe it and run one of these days," I say.

She scrunches her face. "Nah, small town. Where would they run to?"

I laugh, and she presses her jaw to my cheek. "Thank you for keeping my brother company. He needed it more than he knows."

I can't breathe.

Now tears flood my eyes, welling for all to see.

She pulls me into her arms instantly. "We are dead serious when we say this place is your home, Evie. Make sure you don't forget that."

I shake my head furiously.

When both of us are blubbering like babies, we part.

"We better keep moving if you're going to catch the last bus, Miss Evie." Em shoots Iris a look, something like a tangle of sadness and gratitude.

"Of course." I give Iris one last look.

She tilts her head as she watches us go. On the sidewalk, I blow out a low, wobbly breath.

God, this is so hard.

Ten minutes later, Em pulls into the bus terminal. He kills the engine on his truck and jumps out, grabbing my bag. "You want me to walk with you?"

"No, I'm okay. Thank you for everything."

He gives me one last tight hug and nods. Pulling his cap down, he climbs back up into his truck and drives away.

I wander through the terminal and find my bus number before scouting out a spot to sit. Only three minutes until call. I pull out my phone and shoot Allie a text.

> Coming back today, you want to eat at Murphy's?

My phone buzzes.

> OMG! Yes! It's been at least twenty years, girl.

I chuckle. It kind of feels like I lived a lifetime on that little island. Or maybe it's all that happened. It's weighted heavier because it mattered, it meant so much more than anything else I've ever lived through.

The speaker overhead crackles with a static-laced call for the city. I stand, pulling the handle of my rolling bag up, and head for my ticket away from Bay Shore. Away from Fire Island. Away from Callum McCreary.

Toward my life . . .

My career.

The author life I have worked years for. The only thing I have wanted since I was young.

So why do I feel so damn hollow?

Livvy glances from the last page of the manuscript up to me. I'm a bundle of nerves, knowing all too well that the work she has in her hands is not what she wanted to see. Not what I was contracted to write.

Gripping the armrests of the chair I sit restlessly on, I hold my breath, worrying my bottom lip through my teeth.

Finally placing the pages down, she takes her time straightening them. She clears her throat, leaning back in her chair before her hands land in her lap.

"Well, *that*"—she nods to the manuscript—"is not what I was expecting."

"I know. I'm sorry, it felt like the story is more impactful, more authentic being a duology. The character arcs come to completion just so easily . . ."

Livvy sucks in a breath.

"It's not that I don't love the writing or the story as is." She leans forward now. "Evie, it's a breach of contract. That's what worries me most."

"I-I . . ." Heat consumes my chest as I flail through hopeless thought after hopeless thought. "I can't write what I don't feel. Not anymore. I'm sorry."

Livvy raises a hand. "Don't apologize. But Evie, you have made a career in the fantasy romance genre. What story would feel right for you?"

I huff out a breathy laugh. This is the part where I stand up for what I want. For my dreams.

And I can just hear Cal calling me out on my bullshit.

Emotion flares, sending my last breath out with a choke.

Fuck it.

God, I really have spent far too long on that beautiful island. Even my inner monologue sounds like him.

"So, I want to write contemporary romance. The meet-cutes that imitate real-life happily-ever-afters that are relatable, reachable." My chin quivers when my words contradict my own love life.

The sentiment burns, and I can't stand to be in my own skin right now. I push from the chair and wander to the wall of shelves to the left.

Livvy sighs.

"Do you have anything to submit?"

I reach the shelves and run a hand over the leather-bound books.

"No. But I would love the chance to." I study her shelves, not game to turn back and see the look of disapproval on her face. The office chair creaks and soft footfalls close in. I turn back to plead my case. The sunlight streaming through her wide windows catches a gilded frame. Livvy comes to stand beside me.

I pluck up the frame.

"Recognize the place, hey?" Livvy says with a smile.

I turn to her. A little confused, I stare at the photo in the frame. Two people stand on a beach, and is that . . . a lighthouse in the background? Cal's lighthouse.

My lighthouse.

Cal and Iris stand with the biggest smiles on their faces, although Cal's face is half hidden. But I would recognize that man anywhere.

"Livvy?"

She chuckles and takes the frame from my hand. "That was a great day."

"I know I saw this last time I was here, but I didn't know them then. Why do you have this?"

"Oh, those are my cousins. If it wasn't for Iris, I wouldn't have been brave enough to come to New York. They're good people." She gives me a sad smile. "You needed good people, Evie."

Tears well in my eyes as everything comes together. She sent me to Cal, knowing what he'd been through, losing Ava. She knew Iris would take me in like a sister, and her fire for life would rub off on me.

I slap a hand to my mouth.

"Oh, hon. You were so lost. It broke my heart watching you try to piece things back together after the accident. And you shut yourself off from everyone. Cal maybe a tough nut to crack, but he is one of the few people I knew might have had a chance to pull you out of the place you'd fallen into. Did he?"

Did Cal drag me kicking and screaming from my grief?

Maybe.

Did Cal show me what life is supposed to feel like?

Raw, messy, stunning, and incredible . . .

Absolutely.

And I just . . . *left him behind*. There wasn't one grieving person on that floating rock, as he calls it. There were two.

I gained the most from our arranged forced proximity. Guilt and sadness sink heavy in my belly. I never should have left him. I should have fought for what we had instead of making that ridiculous promise to leave.

"Evie?"

"Yes," I breathe, "he—"

Tears stream down my face, and Livvy is folding me into a hug a second later.

"I just want you to be okay. To look forward to the life that's yours if you want it," she says softly.

"Even if I'm not writing fantasy?" I choke out.

She huffs a laugh. "Even then."

Good people.

Livvy, Em, Iris, and Cal. Good people.

Somewhere, my bag vibrates. Livvy releases me and I move to the chair, tugging the bag from the floor where it sits. I fumble for my phone and pull it out.

The screen is lit up with a text from Iris.

Odd. Even though I've had her cell from day one, she's only ever texted me once—on the night of the festival, when I was lured into the library for the late-night signing.

> He went out on a call out and didn't come back. I need you here.

He?

Cal?

What on earth?

I have been watching the weather on Google Earth since last night—I guess new habits die hard—and nothing significant has rolled in near Fire Island.

I tap the phone and call her.

It rings out. I try again.

No answer.

Something's not right.

firefly

Thirty-Three

CALLUM

"**M**ayday. *Mayday. Mayday.*"

The radio squawks, echoing up the stairs and through my open bedroom door. I crack one eye open. It's still pitch-black outside.

Dammit.

With a groan, I roll out of bed and shove the heels of my palms into my eyes, like that will make them work better. In only my underwear, I stagger to the cupboard and pull on jeans and a shirt.

"Mayday! Can anyone hear me?" The desperate voice crackles through the old system.

"I'm coming!" I yell at the VHF. As if it can relay an untranscribed message.

Fumbling with the radio, I turn the dial to reduce the sound and reverberation.

"Fire Island Lighthouse, we hear you loud and clear. What's your position?"

"East, I think. I can see the lighthouse, but we are taking on water. On the port side. Was heading north." The breathless reply rapid fires through the speaker.

"Turn all your lights on, buddy. Make sure you have a life jacket. Stay on the radio, I might need more information. Grab your EPIRB, tie it to your person. I'll be out as soon as I can."

"Copy. Out."

I pluck my cap from the too-empty hooks by the door and shove my feet into my boots. Running for the jetty, I realize I didn't bring my own phone, only the handheld radio for backup if the boat's radio fails. No time to backtrack.

Tossing the lines off the jetty, I board Firefly and fire her up. East of the lighthouse means I have to round the northern end before I can gain ground, so to speak, on the vessel in distress. I push the old girl as fast as she can go, praying the man on the boat—and any other passengers, for that matter—have life vests and he did as I asked and grabbed his EPIRB.

"Watch house this is Firefly, come in?"

"Watch house to Firefly," Errol's voice slurs.

Great. Just fucking great.

"Heading for a vessel in distress northeast of the lighthouse, requesting Coast Guard assistance."

"Negative, Firefly. The boat is out on another call."

Fuck.

It's standard protocol to radio in for backup. This old tub isn't built for speed, unlike Emmett's big shiny boat.

"Errol, I swear to god, man."

"Radio back if you need assistance when you get there," he says reluctantly. "I'll divert the cruiser."

"Copy. Out."

I send Firefly faster. The gauges flicker as the engine whines under protest.

"Firefly to vessel east of the lighthouse, do you copy?"

Static echoes back at me.

Double fuck.

We round the northern tip, and I send her into open waters. It's choppy, and the low, foggy clouds have reduced visibility to around fifty feet. Fucking perfect. My luck, I won't see them until I'm almost on top of them.

I try the distressed boat on the radio one last time.

Nothing comes back.

Hands gripping the wheel with white knuckles, I peer through the fog, desperate to see them floating. Drifting.

Best case scenario, they are still topside.

Worse case is a capsize.

The fog swirls around Firefly, encapsulating her in its dense shroud. The cabin windscreen fogs up, and I wipe a patch clear with my hand. The moist air leaves droplets over the glass.

Christ, how am I meant to find anybody in this goddamn soup?

I throttle back.

Drifting among the eerie whiteout around me, I make another radio call.

Nothing comes back, and the pit of my stomach turns like a mossy boulder, disturbed.

I switch the handheld over to the megaphone that was installed when Firefly went from fishing boat to lighthouse first response vessel.

"This is Firefly. Can you hear me?"

The loud sound echoes through the fog.

Shivers rack my spine, slipping along my rib cage and through my bones.

"This is Firefly. Vessel east of the lighthouse, can you hear me?"

"Over here!" The faint reply comes from the south.

I turn toward it, slowly making my way to its position. "Firefly to Coast Guard. I have located the stranded vessel. Three miles due east of the northern end of the island. Over."

Static screeches back at me before Errol says, "Copy Firefly. Over and out."

When I finally see the small boat, its port side is almost level with the water.

Jesus Christ.

I can't make out anyone on board. I search the water

around the boat quickly. But there is nobody bobbing in the choppy waves. No hands waving at me to save them.

Fuck. I'm going to have to step aboard this disaster.

I idle Firefly, sliding her in beside the smaller boat. Nobody appears, so I tie off to the small vessel on its port side so we don't drift apart in the manic sea.

"Coming aboard!" I call out.

I need to find whoever is out here. This little tub is going to roll over any second.

Carefully, I make my way along the slippery, tilted deck to the companionway. Leaning down, I peer inside, bracing with both hands. "Hello?"

My only answer is the choppy waves hitting the starboard side and the creak of the boat as she takes on more water. With tentative, slow steps, I descend halfway into the living quarters. It's half flooded with items, food, and papers scattered everywhere. Most floating in the water.

Nobody's down here.

Thirty-Four

EVIE

Iris isn't answering. Still.

I stalk my way down the sidewalk of Bay Shore. Having taken the night bus, I rolled in with the sun. The walk from the bus felt like an eternity. But I don't have time to waste trying to hail a cab in this one-seagull town.

Horrified by the lamest pun the world's ever bared witness to, I huff a strained noise.

I close in on the café. The place is lit up and bustling, even at six in the morning. Iris weaves and rushes behind the counter. I hesitate before pushing through the door. The happy, routine chatter that's she's deep into sends another stone to my gut. If something happened to Cal, why is she here?

The doorbell chimes as the door slips closed behind me.

Iris looks up, green eyes widening with joy.

Is this some kind of cruel joke?

Did she not realize what was between Cal and me?

My face breaks around a sob, and she is in my space a heartbeat later.

"Hey, Evie. What?" She holds me at arm's length, her expression now reflecting mine. "What's going on?"

"You—you sent me a message . . ." The words peter out. "About Cal."

She's shaking her head, her brows lowering more and more by the second.

"No, I lost my phone yesterday afternoon."

"You *lost* it?"

"Well, I had it on the counter by the register, like always. I went to call Em, and it wasn't there. Hold on. Why are you here? Why," she starts, her face lightening, hope filling it like flood gates opening. "Why did you come back?"

Her grip on my arms tightens, and she nods gently, as if that will coax an answer from my seized-up throat.

"The message . . . Cal's in trouble."

If Iris didn't send it, then—

God, fuck.

I sink onto the seat behind me. Gripping my hair in my hands, I keen through a low, raw noise.

It's Joshua all over again.

Iris squats in front of me, her green eyes imploring. "I'm sure Cal's fine. Did someone hurt you?"

I shake my head furiously. "Not me. Never me."

Tears swell and spill over in rapid succession.

"Cal?" she says, straining, her head tilting.

"Maybe. I don't know."

I need Emmett.

I bolt from the chair and fly out of the café, sprinting to the watch house. The large building hanging over the water is easy to navigate. Searching each section, I find Errol in the watch room, feet on the large desk where they monitor all things marina and the surrounding seas.

He's asleep, head leaning over the top of the office chair, his feet crossed and propped up on the desk to the left of the large radar screen.

"Errol!"

He bolts up, coffee sloshing from the cup on his desk.

"What the hell?"

"Where is he?"

"Where is he, who?" He turns to face me.

"Emmett! I need Emmett."

"He's out on a call, up north."

"I need to go back to the island. Now!"

"Tame your petticoats, lassie, I'm almost off shift. Wait for day shift."

"No! I can *not* wait. You either take me, or I'll find my own way."

"You mean steal some poor unsuspecting sod's boat?"

"If I have to."

He groans, running a hand through his messy grey hair.

"Fine, but I ain't hanging around to wait for whatever this drama is. I'll take you over, you find your way back."

"Fine, let's go."

Errol gets to his feet, shaking his head. He grabs a cap from a hook, his Coast Guard uniform wrinkled and bulging at the waist. Nothing like how it looks on Emmett.

We march for the secondary rig. Errol unties her before we board, and he fires her up.

I take a seat in the cabin, and he throws me a dirty look.

Apparently, his dislike for Cal extends to me now. It never used to.

Whatever, old man.

"You got any idea what you're gettin' yourself into, missy?"

Missy. It tracks. I roll my eyes before meeting his gaze.

"What is it with you people? Holding a grudge your favorite sport?"

He chuckles, but there's no humor in it. "Every choice has consequences. You just remember that."

"Sure." I give him the most saccharine smile I can force.

Twenty minutes later, Fire Island comes into view, its rocky western shoreline shrouded in fog. The pit of my stomach rolls. It's impossible to sit still. I fidget like my skin's on fire.

Errol gives me a sideways look before throttling back and gliding the cruiser in beside the jetty.

firefly

Thirty-Five

CALLUM

Something moves at the back of the boat. A narrow door snaps shut.

"Hello? Buddy, time to leave!"

Fuck my luck. I'm going to have to carry him out.

Why do people come out on the water if everything about it terrifies them?

Edging around the flooded portion of the living quarters, I make my way to the door. "We need to get out of this boat before she tips over, bud. Now would be good."

I pull the door open. A gangly thirty-something guy stands with a snarl on his face.

A fucking snarl. That's what I get for coming out to save his skinny hide. He's almost as tall as me, messy brown hair, and somewhat familiar.

I've seen him bef—

The book signing.

I grab his arm. "Let's go. This tub is about to flip on us."

He tugs his arm from mine. "You don't touch me," he hisses.

Holding my hands up in surrender, I grind out, "Whatever floats your boat."

Should have stayed in bed and let him sink.

I start for the stairs, hoping if I leave he'll follow. A few seconds later, frantic footsteps catch up to me.

"Right, ladies first," I say, waving a hand toward the stairs as I glance back.

Something hard smacks into the back of my head. I stagger, grappling for purchase on the tilted innards of the living area. Fingers finding an open cupboard, I steady myself.

"The fuck," I rasp, hand pressing against my throbbing skull. My fingers come away, blood covering my palm and running down my wrist. "The hell did you do?"

The gangly man closes in, his face twisted with hate. "She is *mine*, and I have waited for six fucking years. You will not touch her *ever again*."

"She—"

Evie.

"No," I breathe.

Rushing him, I grab for his throat. Over my dead body is this deluded piece of shit going anywhere near Evie.

He dodges my advance. I slip on the watery floor, my head pounding.

"You lay a finger on her, get within a hundred yards of her, and I will fucking kill you," I growl, but the last few words slur as my vision wobbles.

"No, you won't." He darts to the side.

A bat swings at my head, and I jolt sideways to avoid it. My feet lose purchase of the floor. My ass hits the water. The boat rocks to the side even further.

Fuck.

The guy rushes up the stairs, slamming the companionway door shut. A lock clunks on the other side.

I stagger to my feet, tripping up the stairs. I slam my fists into the door.

It doesn't budge.

I roar, releasing every bit of grief I've ever accumulated in one agonizing sound.

Stars invade my vision as blood runs down my face and neck.

I pull on the door. Slam my shoulder into it.

Firefly roars from the idle I left her in beside the small boat.

She's tied to this vessel.

"No, stop!" I holler at the pasty little fucker.

Smashing my fists against the door, I scream. Firefly's engine growls louder. The whoosh and purr of her blades through the water below us sends a sick sensation right through my gut.

Panic settles to serene nothingness. Bile rises and burns.

Stilling, I dwell on the memories of Evie that flood in. The irony of it all is not lost on me.

Her beautiful face.

Her soft little ways, always full of life.

That is, once she got that part of herself back.

Her fiery streak that came out when I denied her.

I slide down the small kitchen built-ins. The engine outside grows louder.

The slack in the line snaps outside. The tilted floor under my seat jerks upward.

I close my eyes.

Free-falling, I go limp.

My back hits the ceiling with a painful crack. My head whips backward.

Water rolls over me.

Air leaves my lungs.

Eyes open, I watch helplessly as the contents of the little boat sink into the water from above. Something heavy and dark plummets toward me. I can't move fast enough.

It cracks against my temple.

Darkness swallows me whole.

Thirty-Six

EVIE

I fly from the cruiser's cabin, not looking back as I take the gap between the jetty and the boat's starboard side at a wobbly leap. I run up the jetty and to the house, my lungs burning. Errol yells something I can't make out. The Coast Guard boat drifts from the jetty and turns back before the engines power up, shooting the boat back out to the water.

The lighthouse front door gives way under the heel of my hand.

"Cal!"

I spin around inside, looking at everything at once.

"Callum!"

Only the rasping breaths leaving my lungs and silence reply.

Whimpering, I try desperately to stave off the sobs piling up behind the stone choking me.

Flashes of the crumpled car and my dead, limp husband hunched over the steering wheel flood in.

"No . . ."

I spin back to the door and run for the greenhouse, sliding the oversized door open. Moist, warm air greets me, and I jog through the aisles. "Cal! Please, Callum!?"

The gravel sprays from every footfall as my strides turn sloppy, and my desperation takes hold.

I close the greenhouse door, protecting Cal's crops and hard work, and I sprint for the forest. Maybe he's at the fishing hut. He told me he goes there when he needs to think . . .

I move in on the tree line, and the wind changes, whipping around me. My hair slaps my face from the east. The drone of an engine drifts in.

Gasping, I slam to a halt. Firefly is coasting toward the beach. From the east.

What on earth?

Cal never leaves her on that side. It's too exposed.

I take a tentative step toward the fishing boat that's crossing the water, heading straight for the sand. Maybe he's hurt? Maybe he can't wait long enough to sail around the northern tip and dock at the jetty.

"Oh no." The words are no more than a whisper.

I take off, heading for the beach, and slip on the tufty grass where the dune meets grassy land. Stumbling, I falter to steady myself and push forward. Firefly slows, turning before drifting to a halt in the shallow water, and I stand rooted in the sand.

The engine dies.

He moves in the cabin. I see his dark figure . . .

The sun's early light blurs everything in a gold hue. I squint, raising a hand to protect my eyes and see better.

He jumps from the boat and wades through the water.

Wha—

He makes the beach, slowing in the wet sand.

His clothes are—

Fear slips into my veins, sickly and hot.

No.

I gasp for air, my hands trembling by my sides.

"No," I choke.

He has Cal's boat.

The distance between us seems to shrink at a rapid rate.

How did he get Firefly?

Does that mean . . .

The distance between us evaporates, the aroma of cedar shrouding me where I stand.

"No! Please, ju—sto—" I scream, crumpling as I step back, holding a hand up, palm out.

Icy blue eyes burn into me. His messy pale-brown hair is

oily and slicked down. His mouth kicks up in a half smile as he reaches for me.

"Hello, Butterfly."

Get Cal & Evie's final instalment here - https://books2read.com/u/3JMeoX

FIRE ISLAND SERIES

Book 2

ALEXANDRA BANKS

firefly

Scot's Gaelic

AS USED BY CAL (AND SOMETIMES EVIE)

Just in case you need it . . .

mo ghràdh ~ my love

mo nighean ~ my girl

nighean bhrèagha ~ beautiful girl

fear milis ~ sweet man

cailín luachmhor ~ precious girl

Beannachd leat, a nighean milis ~ goodbye, sweet girl

Acknowledgments

Evie & Cal (and Iris & Emmett) have been with me for a long time. So when it was time to write their story, I was so stinking excited!! I hope that I have done it well enough that they shine. Grump and people pleasing aside, these two are incredible. And I hope you think so too.

As always, *thanks to my editors, Lindsey and Zainab.* Your input and guidance is always wanted and appreciated.

To every **ARC reader** who volunteered to read this book, thank you!!

And lastly, but most certainly not least, my family for putting up with the endless playlists that I made them endure during the writing process to get into the zone. Sorry... ;)

Alex xx

About the Author

Alexandra Banks is a romantic at heart, and an optimist down to her very bones. Her love for everything romance sees her writing HEAs all day long.

But don't be fooled, there will be angst along the way, possibly heartbreak. But her fierce heroines can handle just about anything!

For more heartwarming reads, follow her on socials and join the mailing list so you never miss another heart throb!